Dancing to the Flute

WITHDRAWN
FROM THE RODMAN PUBLIC LIBRARY

Dancing
to the Flute

A NOVEL

MANISHA JOLIE AMIN

ATRIA PAPERBACK

New York   London   Toronto   Sydney   New Delhi

RODMAN PUBLIC LIBRARY

ATRIA PAPERBACK
A Division of Simon & Schuster, Inc.
1230 Avenue of the Americas
New York, NY 10020

This book is a work of fiction. Names, characters, places, and incidents either are products of the author's imagination or are used fictitiously. Any resemblance to actual events or locales or persons, living or dead, is entirely coincidental.

Copyright © 2012 by Manisha Jolie Amin

Originally published in 2012 in Australia by Allen & Unwin.

All rights reserved, including the right to reproduce this book or portions thereof in any form whatsoever. For information, address Atria Paperback Subsidiary Rights Department, 1230 Avenue of the Americas, New York, NY 10020.

First Atria Paperback edition February 2013

ATRIA PAPERBACK and colophon are trademarks of Simon & Schuster, Inc.

For information about special discounts for bulk purchases, please contact Simon & Schuster Special Sales at 1-866-506-1949 or business@simonandschuster.com.

The Simon & Schuster Speakers Bureau can bring authors to your live event. For more information or to book an event, contact the Simon & Schuster Speakers Bureau at 1-866-248-3049 or visit our website at www.simonspeakers.com.

Designed by Kyoko Watanabe

Manufactured in the United States of America

10 9 8 7 6 5 4 3 2 1

Library of Congress Cataloging-in-Publication Data

Amin, Manisha.
Dancing to the flute : a novel / Manisha Amin.
—First Atria paperback edition.
pp. cm.
"Originally published in 2012 in Australia by Allen & Unwin"
—Title page verso.
Includes glossary.
1. Boys—Fiction. 2. Street children—Fiction. 3. Friendship—Fiction.
4. Music—Fiction. 5. Healers—Fiction. 6. India—Fiction. I. Title.
PR9619.4.A485D36 2013
823'.92—dc23
        2012002009
ISBN 978-1-4516-7204-6
ISBN 978-1-4516-7205-3 (ebook)

38212005779274

Main Adult Fiction

Amin, M

Amin, Manisha

Dancing to the flute

This book is for my "babies"
Shekha, Shivali, and Tara
and my son
Sohum

Note to Reader

This novel uses the Indian raag as a theme. Each part of the novel mimics a part of the raag, starting slowly and gathering momentum as the novel progresses. While there are many forms and ways to describe a raag, I've used the one that worked best for the story.

Many words in this novel are not English words. I have tried to use spellings that the reader would intuitively understand. There is a glossary at the back of the novel for those wishing to make use of it. You can find links to the music at my website www.manishajolieamin.com.

Part 1

AALAAP

The aalaap and jor should be a slow and meditative exploration of the raag. There is no rhythm in the aalaap. You must slowly and with precision introduce the listener to the various notes of the raag, showing their relationships in ascent and descent. The jor, which flows on from the aalaap, introduces a rhythm gently, with no accompaniment. The purpose is to explore the mood and characteristics of the raag.

Performed well, the aalaap enfolds the performer and listener in a common devotion to the spirit of the raag and the Divine.

—GURUJI

1

KALU STOOD STILL, staring up into the banyan tree, oblivious to the sounds around him or to the man resting against one of the tree's many trunks. Finally, spotting the perfect leaf, the boy began to climb.

Kalu's right foot clung to root and branch while his left brushed the tree, toes skimming the surface like a blind man's cane, making sure the path was clear. The banyan seemed to help, its rough, scored bark and twisted limbs providing support, until he reached the branch holding his leaf. It was fresh and green, the color of a ripe lime. It was the size of his hand, and just as supple.

He steadied himself in the branches, plucked the chosen leaf, and rolled it into a pipe. He softened one end in his mouth, pressed down with his teeth to flatten the tube, and blew. The sound, sweet and clear, rode the wind, snaking through the tree and down into the village. It cut between the movie songs blaring out from the village shops and the triple horns of lorries competing for airspace. It slipped around the ringing of bicycle bells, weaving through the village and down to the rocks, where it met the river.

The women washing clothes on the rocks stopped for a

moment, lifting their heads to the sound, before continuing to beat the cloth, this time in rhythm with the music. Kalu settled into the arms of the tree and kept playing.

The man sitting at the base of the tree relaxed his shoulders, his head dropping back to rest against the shadowed bark. He had stopped on impulse at the foot of the banyan that day, and regretted it as soon as he saw the boy. The child was reed thin. He looked no more than ten. His face had the withered look of a ripe sapota, dusty and creased as if the skin were made for a bigger fruit.

The man sat still, not wanting to be disturbed, and had been pleased when the boy decided to climb the tree rather than walk around it. The view in front of the man was expansive, over the cliffs to the River Narmada on one side and the village on the other. His spot under the tree was quiet. When it came, the music carried him away from the heat of the day, back to the crispness of the morning.

The child he had seen seemed too small to make the sound coming from the tree, a sound that was neither worn nor common.

Kalu stayed sheltered in the cool leaves of the banyan, away from the midday sun, for a few more minutes. His belly growled at the thought of food and he knew if he wanted to eat, he'd have to go down and beg. It had been a long time between meals. The last time he ate his fill was just before he hurt his foot.

It had been a moonless night. The kind of night Kalu liked least. The type that carried nightmares if he wasn't careful. He would wake with a shock, his body shaking, unable to recall anything but an ache that clung to his lean frame and the fear that made him want to vomit. That particular night he'd crept to his favorite sleeping place, in the shadows behind the paan-biddi shop. Close enough to people for company and hidden away from harm.

He listened to the film songs played through the loud-speakers at the front of the shop, accompanied by the drone of the generator and the loud, tangled arguments of the men smoking beedis or cigarettes or chewing paan. They spoke of politics, films, and women, but never religion.

The noise often kept the rats away. They traveled up from the river, as big as bandicoots and with teeth strong enough to cut through wire; Kalu worried that they would attack his fingers or toes while he slept. But he was safe here.

The area outside the shop was a mess of broken concrete, splattered red from the betel juice. When she saw the place in the morning, Jaya-shree Ben, the paan-waala's wife, would screech like a bright green parrot at her husband, Ravi. It was comforting, part of the pattern of each day for Kalu. If he was lucky, Jaya-shree Ben would pay him to clean the area for her. He could do that before running errands. It all depended on her mood in the morning.

Kalu never slept deeply, but that night he was tired. He'd worked hard during the day, delivering goods for the ration store near the bazaar. It had been hot work, especially when the deliveries were for the rich folk on the hill. He wrapped his hand around the small, sharp stone he always kept by him in the night, and closed his eyes.

Later, in the coolness of the early morning, he'd felt something slice into his foot like a red-hot knife. He leaped up at the pain, dropping the stone, then collapsed again as his foot buckled under his weight. There was no one nearby, not a human, snake, or scorpion. The light from the paan-biddi shop and the graying sky illuminated a reddish lump and a line of blood near his ankle. By midday, the area around his heel was covered with small sores and the joint was stiff, as if the bones had fused.

Until then Kalu had earned what money he could by helping in the fields or running errands. Now, his not being able to run fast or even walk without limping had reduced him to begging. Nothing, not constant washing or even the paste he'd borrowed from the paan-waala, had helped to heal his foot.

He still tried to work whenever the opportunity arose, but his damaged heel and ankle made it difficult to walk, let alone run. The sores soon began to fester. After the first few days, Kalu became immune to the sweet, overripe smell that lingered around him like cheap cologne; others didn't. People had once smiled when they saw Kalu's jaunty stride or heard him whistle as he ran from job to job. Now they turned away, holding handkerchiefs to their noses while shooing him off the pavement.

The smell eventually led Jaya-shree Ben to Kalu's makeshift home behind her shop. "Kalu, out! You're driving away our customers, dirty boy. Wash yourself. Don't you have any respect?" She held one hand firmly on her hip while waving him away with the other.

"Go to the community doctor, Kalu," scolded Ganga Ba, an elderly, healthy woman with sharp eyes and a sharper tongue.

Kalu had delivered letters for Ganga Ba since the day he first arrived in Hastinapore, two years earlier. He'd been confused and disorientated after walking for what had seemed like miles. His throat had hurt, and he'd asked her for milk. She'd given him milk in return for delivering a letter to the post office. He couldn't remember anything from his past, not even his name, so Ganga Ba called him Kalu, because of his black hair and sun-scorched skin. She said that calling out "boy" was demeaning and that everyone deserved at least a name. Besides, how would he know which boy she meant?

While Kalu accepted a name and work from Ganga Ba, he had refused to go to the community doctor for his ankle. He'd seen what the daacter had done to other patients. Jasumati, the wife of the sweets merchant, took her mother-in-law to the clinic when the family noticed the old lady's toes had blackened. Instead of fixing her toes, the daacter cut off her foot! Besides, everyone knew the daacter spent more time drinking than practicing medicine. Kalu had seen the effects of alcohol. Some people became so funny that it was better than a film show. Others you just had to avoid for fear of a beating. There was no way he was going to trust a drunken daacter to fix his foot.

He had come to the banyan tree instead, knowing that he could sit and play for a while without disturbance. Although his seat in the tree hid the village from his view, he could see parts of the River Narmada far below. The cliffs were lined with trees and farmland, punctuated with white, domed temples, each with its own colored flag. Kalu had heard that there was a temple every mile along this part of the river. If you looked closely, you could see the paths and man-made stairs in the cliff face. Each provided a way down to the river, which wound in sweeping curves. Kalu could see his friend Bal taking the buffaloes down for a drink at one spot. Farther away still were workers in the fields, like brown specks of dust weaving between rows of green.

As the women walked back toward the village with baskets of wet, clean clothes, wrung and roped together and balanced on their heads, Kalu thought about leaving the tree. He came down reluctantly, moving slowly, wincing at the roughness of the curved branches and the folded trunk. Soon, even climbing the banyan would be impossible.

The man resting in the roots opened his eyes and spoke just as Kalu reached the ground. "Do you only play into the sky for the gods, or can you play down on earth as well?"

Surprised, Kalu gripped the trunk so as not to fall over. The man sitting on the cotton towel looked tall. He wore a traditional kurta rather than a smart shirt and pants, and his sandals were strong and new, even though the case beside him was battered. If he was lucky, Kalu would earn enough for a meal right here.

"If you liked it, sir, please spare some paise. . . . I'm hungry."

The man's expression hardened. "Begging?"

"My foot." Kalu waved his foot around, hoping the smell would make the man pay him quickly. "I can't work anymore, sir . . . some paise?"

The man looked at the foot. It was clearly infected. Sores covered most of the heel and part of the ankle, and it was obvious that the problem had been in existence for some time. The boy stood straight, balancing like a paper kite on the wind, his toes holding him steady. The man focused on the boy's eyes; just as Kalu decided to speak, the man smiled and said, "Come, beta, how about I treat you instead of giving you paise?"

Kalu took a step back. "I don't need treating."

"Your foot does."

"How can you fix it when no one else can?" He wrapped his good foot around the bad, taking care not to touch the sores.

"I'm a vaid, a healer. It's my job to help. Now, I can't promise anything. I'll need to get closer to do a proper inspection. Then much depends on your following my instructions—all of them. Sickness can take many forms. The outward manifestation is often the least complicated part."

As the words flowed around him. Kalu had heard about vaids from Malti, Ganga Ba's servant and his friend. Apparently, a vaid healed Ganga Ba's sister when she had cancer. And she didn't even know she had cancer at the time. Malti said that Ganga Ba had told her friends a vaid often understood things most people in India had forgotten. And they didn't open you up or cut your bones. This man didn't smell of alcohol like the daacter, either. There was something about his face that Kalu, who was normally wary of strangers, automatically trusted. He wondered if he had seen the vaid before.

Kalu moved to rest his back against the trunk of the banyan, positioning himself so the stench from his foot blew away from the vaid. "I have no money. I can't pay." Kalu's voice was clear and sweet when he wasn't begging. "I used to work, but no one wants me now."

"And your parents?"

"I don't have any."

"What about other relations, or are you completely alone here, boy?"

"I just woke up one day by the roadside. I walked to the village and I've been here since." Kalu didn't mention the dizziness he'd felt that day or the dreams that had followed him. "But I'm never alone," said Kalu, cautious of the man's interest. He counted on his fingers. "There are my friends near where I sleep; and Malti, who works for Ganga Ba; and Ganga Ba herself, who gave me my name, Kalu; and Bal, who looks after buffaloes and smells more than I do." The boy's sudden laughter made him sound more like the child he should have been. "Even without this stupid foot—and, oh, lots of others."

"Kalu, is it? Krishna's name and a flute player, too."

Kalu sat next to the vaid, forgetting that the smell and

sight of his foot drove most people away. He liked this man. No one he remembered had ever called him beta, their child.

"All I do is play leaves from trees. That's not a flute. I can't even work now, with my foot."

The vaid smiled. He'd seen a mix of determination, strength, and laughter in the child's eyes. The strength and suppleness of bamboo before it was burned. It was the same look he used to see in his brother's eyes, all those years ago.

"Don't worry about the payment; I have no doubt you'll be able to pay. The kind of payment I want doesn't involve money." The vaid dragged his bag through the dirt beneath the tree to a clear space. "First let me see how far the rot has gone."

As Kalu moved his foot toward the vaid he heard a shout. "Oy! You, boy, get away! What do you think you're doing harassing Masterji? Get away, filth!"

Kalu scrambled behind the vaid, gasping as he grazed his heel on an upraised root in an effort to get away from the angry man.

"Calm down, bhai, this boy is my patient. Just as your wife is."

Kalu stayed behind the vaid's back, watching and waiting, ready to escape if need be. The man wore shiny lace-up shoes that looked hot and tight, together with socks that should have been white but were now gray and brown, stained by a mix of shoe polish and dirt.

"But, Masterji, he's nothing but a worthless beggar. And the baby's coming. To be wasting your precious time on the likes of him!" The man never looked at Kalu, choosing to focus only on the vaid.

"Time is never precious if you don't use it wisely. Kalu needs my help more than many others. He should be treated no differently than anyone else."

Kalu's shoulders relaxed as he listened. While he knew that other people had better lives, he'd never thought of himself as worthless. Not in the sense this man did. While he did not live in a house, he was a good runner. At least, he had been until his foot was damaged. Maybe the vaid could fix it. Why, even the angry man seemed to respect the vaid.

"Please, Masterji, my wife. The baby. We need you."

The vaid turned and refastened his case, and the man seemed to deflate just a little.

"Beta," the vaid said, turning to Kalu as he rose, "unfortunately, babies cannot wait as long as little boys. But tonight, just after sunset, go to Ganga Ba's house. Knock on the door and ask for me. I'll tell her to expect you. Don't forget. I'll need some extra herbs for your foot in any case. And here." He pressed ten rupees into the boy's hand.

"But I'll . . ."

"No, son, this is for the music I enjoyed so much. Fair is fair. And, remember, you have given your word."

"I'll come."

"I'm depending on you." The vaid smiled before leaving with the man. Kalu watched the vaid move with slow deliberate steps, while the other strode, waving his hands as if fighting a swarm of mosquitoes as he urged the vaid on.

Kalu rubbed his thumb against the soft edge of the note. It was more money than he'd ever had. He'd be able to buy so much: that flute he'd seen at the paan-waala's and maybe some sweet barfi for Ganga Ba and Malti.

Malti washed clothes in the morning, cleaned during the day, and often called Kalu to pick up messages and make deliveries for Ganga Ba in between. She was at least four years older and a full head taller than Kalu. Malti was old enough to give advice with authority, if not strict accuracy, and young enough to understand Kalu's point of view.

She had described her first taste of barfi to Kalu one warm, lazy afternoon. They'd been sitting in this exact spot, under the tree. Most people slept through the midday sun. The heat rose from the ground, the shops closed, and the streets were left empty. Once the dishes were washed, the tables wiped and the floors cleaned, Malti, along with everyone else who worked for Ganga Ba, normally rested on a saadadi, the crisscross of straw or plastic mats laid out each afternoon on the green granite floor of the dining room. It was the coolest place during the summer heat. When the temperature dropped, however, Malti and the other servants often moved to the living room, still on the floor but with the television switched on. Ganga Ba didn't mind what they watched as long as it didn't disturb her nap or her comfort in any way.

That particular day had been a little too warm. Tempers flared in both the kitchen and the dining room. As the youngest in the household, Malti was often the easiest target. She was small for her age, and even though she'd grown in the past two years, the other servants continued to remind her of her junior status.

On still, humid days when even the lizards stayed under their rocks rather than bask in the sun, she felt the taunts more than usual. So that day she'd escaped from the house and walked the long path down from the good houses to the banyan tree, in search of at least a small breeze cooled by the water below.

Kalu was resting high in the arms of the banyan, hidden from the view of the villagers, being entertained by the squirrels that ran up and down the tree chasing their own tails as well as one another's. He watched as Malti settled in the roots, her skirt covering her legs, her back relaxing into the wide trunk, before he swung down in front of her.

"Hey, yaar." Kalu laughed as Malti jumped.

"Don't—just don't ever scare me again." She punched him lightly on the arm before settling again. The river before them was restless that day, flowing quickly on her way through towns down to the coast, to join her sister, the sea.

"Sometimes I wish I could float away on the river," said Malti. "I'd travel far, far away. Then I wouldn't have to listen to Bhraamanji grumbling. 'Malti, do this. Malti, do that . . .' It's always the same. I'd find a place where no one knows me. Where I could eat barfi all day."

"Barfi?" asked Kalu, his stomach growling at the thought of the sweet. Though he'd seen barfi in the sweetshop, he'd never had enough money to buy any. "What does it taste like? When did you try it?"

"Ganga Ba bought some when her daughter came from America. Bhraamanji said that he could easily have made it . . . and nicer, too. Ha! He's lucky Ganga Ba keeps him. But I ate a little of a broken piece. It was lovely. Sweet and powdery."

"Like mango?"

"Since when is mango powdery? It was nicer, much nicer. If we have it again, I'll see if I can get you a little. Unless of course Bhraamanji makes a fuss." Malti bit her lip and stared down at the river. "Sometimes I wish I wasn't here."

"If you went, where would you go? Would you leave soon?" asked Kalu.

Malti looked down at Kalu and nudged his shoulder. His problems were far greater than her own. "Don't worry, big eyes, I'm just angry and tired and hot. I'm not going anywhere. Nowhere far, anyway. I earn a good wage here, enough to send money home. And it's a good town. I've heard stories about the city." The shadows beneath her eyes became more pronounced. "A friend of mine went to the city when I came here. They offered her more money than she would get in a village. There were more people, too. You even had to queue to go to the mandir to pray. She could go to the cinema, even the ocean. Can you imagine? The ocean! Then one day we stopped hearing from her. No one has heard from her since."

Now, sitting alone beneath the tree, Kalu remembered the sadness in Malti's eyes the day she told him that story. He laughed now as he thought of how pleased and surprised she'd be when she saw the barfi he would buy her. He wrapped the money between a couple of large leaves, so that no one would see it, and then tied the whole bundle in the corner of his shirt before limping toward the shops.

If he was careful with his choice, there would even be enough money to buy a few sweets for Bal. He knew that Bal, like him, had never eaten anything as fine as barfi. After Bal's mother died, his father had sold him to a farmer as a bonded servant. His job was to look after the buffaloes from dawn until the evening, finishing work when the buffaloes were housed.

Most people ignored Bal, making room around him and the animal smell that lingered no matter how much he scrubbed. Bal, in turn, barely spoke to anyone, except his buffaloes. Kalu was his only real friend. The two of them had first met one evening after Kalu was given a little rice by one of the villagers. As Kalu sat by the river to eat it, he saw the other boy, half hidden in the shadows. Kalu offered him some food. Not because he had eaten too much but because the older boy had seemed insubstantial, ghost thin. Bal said no to the food but slowly moved from the shadows to sit by Kalu. After that, the two of them met most days, sometimes for only a few minutes, other times for an hour or two. Neither could rely on a family but they each had the other. While Bal was thinner and quieter than Kalu, he was street-smart, and the younger boy knew he could count on him. Both boys had been abandoned, but, unlike Kalu, Bal could remember his parents.

Bal was one of the few people who still welcomed Kalu unconditionally, even after Kalu's foot was injured, and he would be just as excited as Malti to have the barfi. Kalu decided to buy the flute first, and then make his way to the sweetshop for the barfi.

The flute wasn't normal stock at the paan-waala's shop; however, Ravi had gone to the big town to buy one for his son. Kalu had heard Ravi explain to Jaya-shree Ben that it was much cheaper to buy three than one, and they could easily sell the other two in the shop. Jaya-shree Ben had not been amused. A paan-waala's shop attracted men and often servants; it didn't attract children or doting parents looking for gifts.

The flutes were small and plastic, just big enough that your fingers didn't overlap when you closed the holes. They were green on one side and yellow on the other. It was more a toy than a real flute, but much better than nothing. Ravi's son had broken his flute after four days, and stepped on the other after six. Jaya-shree Ben had then taken the last one and placed it firmly beside the cash register.

Kalu knew that if he asked just so and promised free labor in return, Jaya-shree Ben would give him a good discount on the flute. She loved a bargain, and so did he.

2

BY THE TIME Kalu arrived at Ganga Ba's house, he'd eaten four pieces of barfi. He rearranged the rest before retying the thin gold ribbon around the red box.

The house was dark save the two small candles, or divas, in little enclosures on either side of the entrance. The red, rusted fence and the garden that Kalu knew well in the daytime were hidden under an unlit sky.

As he walked up the path toward the building, Kalu noticed a thread of light in the recess leading to the front door. He ignored it and made his way more by memory than sight to the kitchen entrance at the side of the house.

Malti, washing the last of the dishes under the tap outside, straightened the sari that she had tucked up out of the water and took Kalu into the living room. He followed her, stepping out of the kitchen, then stopping short. This was the first time he'd entered Ganga Ba's house without being asked in to complete a task. The place looked different. Unfamiliar.

He took a deep breath and remembered how he'd felt up in the banyan tree as he played that morning. He started to hum softly, under his breath. He'd been to the house many times. He loved taking messages for Ganga Ba. He got paid more for this job than any other, and he could take his time completing it. Ganga Ba never beat him, but she did have a sharp tongue. She'd scold him if he returned too late and blame Malti for any mishap. And Malti often kept some food for him, so the money he received lasted longer.

Kalu stepped into the room and, seeing it empty, called out, "Ganga Maasi, hey, Maasi!"

Ganga Ba had stayed upstairs in her room as long as she could, muttering to herself, picking up objects and replacing them—annoyed that there was no television up there or anything else to keep her occupied. Just because the vaid was well known, it didn't give him the right to force her to use her house as a hospital. She had thought to have him work on the boy outside, so as not to dirty her house, but realized that it wouldn't be comfortable at all for her to sit outside. Ganga Ba leaned against the rail as she came downstairs, her eyes moving to the red box that Kalu held in dirt-crusted hands.

"For you, Maasi, and Malti, too," said Kalu, wiping his hands against his torn shorts before holding out the box of sweets. "You can even keep the ribbon."

She smiled. He was the only person who still called her "maasi" rather than "ba," and her mind, if not her bones, was far better suited to "auntie" than "grandmother." The term "maasi" reminded her of her own aunts. They were strong, active women, considered quite dangerous by the men in the family. The word "ba" always made her feel old and brittle in comparison. She straightened.

"What are you wasting money on us for? You should be saving your money, rascal." Ganga Ba scowled as she loosened the ribbon and opened the box. It was a long time since anyone had given Ganga Ba anything. Normally it was the other way around: most people wanted something from her. When it was family it was even worse.

"Malti, take those sweets into the kitchen. Put them in a steel container. I don't want the rats to get them. And bring a towel for the boy to sit on before you light some agarbati. Use those legs, girl, we don't have all night."

Ganga Ba collapsed on the green divan, ignoring Malti's raised eyebrows before continuing, "You are traveling in fine company now, Kalu. The vaid, no less, came and told me that you would be arriving and should be treated as his guest in my house. And what is that smell? Malti, agarbati, please." She harrumphed, reminding Kalu of the black-spotted cow in the village, who made a similar sound when she wanted to scare away boys trying to steal her milk.

"I'm sorry," he said, responding to Ganga Ba's tone rather than her words. He hadn't really been listening, focusing more on what was to come. He'd been checking the exits as Ganga Ba spoke so he knew which way to go if the vaid mentioned removing his foot. There was no way he would allow that to happen. Without his foot he would never be able to earn a living.

Kalu wasn't sure where to sit, or what more to say. So he stood next to the table until Malti returned with an old, torn cloth for him to sit on. He placed his hand directly on the granite floor, feeling its clean, hard coolness, so different from the warm earth. Kalu turned his ankle so that his foot, resting softly in the folds of the material, pointed away from Ganga Ba.

"Hey Bhagwaan," Ganga Ba said. "I don't know what the world is coming to—beggar boys and a famous vaid in the same room. You're very lucky. Though why he wanted to come here of all places I don't know. Malti! Water! Kalu, you don't know how lucky you are."

Kalu didn't feel lucky. He just felt tiny. The smell of incense only highlighted the stink of his foot. He'd been so caught up in buying and then tasting those rich sugary sweets that he hadn't thought much about the vaid or his promise. Kalu's stomach churned.

Malti returned with a silver tray and metal cups containing cold water. She grinned at Kalu as he shook his head. "Don't look so worried, big eyes," she whispered.

Kalu heard the sound of the gate opening. Malti held his shoulder as Ganga Ba rose and, moving faster than Kalu had ever seen her go, went to meet the vaid as he reached the door. Short words followed a long pause. Kalu was sure that Ganga Ba would throw the man out and his foot would never be looked at.

He shrugged off Malti's hand and stood up so that he could leave with the vaid if need be, when he heard Ganga Ba laugh. The two entered, the vaid gently supporting Ganga Ba under her arm. He sat her on the sofa, complimenting her on her health.

"Don't you try to sweet-talk me, young man. I know exactly how long these bones have been around and what sort of mischief they get up to. . . . Now see to the boy. We all know you didn't come here to see me."

The vaid finally turned to face Kalu. He looked the same as he had that morning. White hair, clean clothes, and kind eyes. Only Ganga Ba could have called him young. He asked Kalu to sit, and knelt beside him, claiming it was the best place to work from.

"Are you ready, Kalu?"

"Of course he is!" replied Ganga Ba.

The vaid looked deep into Kalu's wide eyes. "Are you willing, Kalu? This is your decision. I'm not promising you a cure, and it won't always be comfortable. It will take time to heal both the original wound and the infection that has grown from it."

Kalu nodded and brought his foot forward. He looked straight at the vaid, almost mesmerized. He did not notice Malti leave and then return with boiling water. Kalu's world contracted to the space between the vaid's eyes and hands. The vaid's strong, clean fingers left no mark as they pressed around the wound, testing the skin, just a lingering trace of warmth.

The vaid cleaned Kalu's foot with hot water, removing dirt and pus before rinsing the area with a sharp, tingling pale green mixture. The smell of earth, turmeric, and mint slowly replaced the stench of decay. He opened a worn glass jar containing a premade paste and applied it with his index finger on and around the wound, before adding a layer of dried herbs and then a strong crepe bandage.

"Leave it like this. Don't touch the bandage or wet the area until I get back. Then we'll see."

Kalu looked down at his foot. It was the first time he'd seen anything so white. The soft, stretchy material of the bandage was completely foreign. Its very tightness and whiteness made him feel secure.

The vaid wiped his hands with a warm, moist towel. "Keep him here if you can, Ganga Ba. I know it's an added responsibility. But if you aren't up to it . . ."

After Ganga Ba informed the vaid there was "no one more up to looking after this rascal," he left, refusing all food and drink, having barely spoken at all.

The open door let in pieces of night: the distant ringing of bicycle bells and the smell of jasmine mixed with camphor. As the door closed, Kalu realized the vaid had left before he could thank him or even offer payment.

Malti placed a hand on the boy's shoulder, calming him as he struggled to rise and follow the vaid. "He'll be back, Kalu. Let's just wait and see if it works first."

"Of course it'll work. You'll sleep in the yard tonight, Kalu.

And every night until the vaid returns." Ganga Ba flicked her fingers as if swiping a mosquito. "I'll not have it said that Vaidji's remedy didn't work because of anything I did or that you would have been better off elsewhere. No arguing, now, and out with you! I'm going to watch my television in peace."

Kalu spent the next few months sleeping in Ganga Ba's courtyard. She wanted to keep him close until the vaid returned to remove the bandage. "No one can say I didn't do my duty," she said.

He left each morning to work, beg, and roam before returning at midday for a meal. He checked his old place by the paan-waala's every afternoon and made sure that Jayashree Ben hadn't let anyone else into the area. He even swept the pathway for her for free, just to make sure no one stole his spot.

In the evenings he returned to Ganga Ba's house, full of stories and music for the household servants. Ganga Ba, hearing the laughter outside, would often call him in. Then he would sit on the floor by her feet and entertain her.

He was a funny boy, thought Malti. Happy one day, quiet the next. Since the injury to his foot, his movements had become measured. They remained so now that the ankle was strapped. The bandage wrapped around it had changed color, from white to the rich brown of jaggery, lighter in some parts and darker in others. When Ganga Ba refused to let Malti remove the bandage to clean it, she gave Kalu a large, old sock to cover it. The sock was brown, so it always looked dirty—even after Malti had just washed it.

The story of Kalu's injury had grown in the telling, with most people agreeing that his foot had been barely hanging on by a sinew before the vaid arrived. Others were sure that Kalu had a new form of elephantiasis. While some gave Kalu extra money on his rounds, others avoided him, expressing surprise and disapproval that Ganga Ba would even allow him onto her property.

Then, finally, the vaid returned.

Ganga Ba made the most of the occasion and filled her house for the great unbandaging. If she was going to have Kalu sheltering in her yard, she wanted everyone, especially the ladies' group, to know of this occasion. Malti smiled, remembering the fuss Ganga Ba made when the vaid first came to ask if he could treat Kalu at her house. Now it seemed that the whole idea had been hers in the first place.

Malti was kept busy throughout the night, serving water, collecting empty glasses, and trying to make sure she was actually in the room when the vaid undid the bandages.

This time, Kalu sat on a dining room chair, not the floor. The vaid lifted the foot, and slowly unraveled the cloth. It turned from brown to cream as the outer layer was removed, and then changed back to brown as the stains from the paste were revealed.

Malti held a bowl of warm water, so the vaid could clean the foot once the bandage had been completely removed. He started near the heel, moving upward to the ankle.

Kalu sat completely still, scared that any movement would change the result. His wound was pink, the skin creased like thin netting, scores of lines intersecting one another. The vaid rotated the ankle, pressed the flesh around the tender section, then lowered the heel to the floor with the very tips of his fingers. Seeing him nod, Kalu rose. Slowly, focusing only on his feet, he balanced on the ball of one foot, then the other, before standing, his weight evenly distributed.

"Try to walk, beta," said the vaid.

"I . . ."

"One foot at a time. If you fall, I'll catch you, beta."

Kalu inched the injured foot forward, resting his hand on the table as he moved. Malti held on to the bowl tightly, to stop from reaching out to help him.

Slowly Kalu placed his full weight on the injured foot. Around him the crowd started to cheer and clap.

The vaid turned to face the room. "Ganga Ba, may I use one of your other rooms? I'd like to discuss Kalu's payment in private."

Payment. Kalu's foot trembled a little. Malti knew that this was the moment he'd been dreading. The reason he had kept working as best he could during the past month. She just hoped he had saved enough.

Ganga Ba waved toward the small guest room to the right of the living room. As Kalu and the vaid left, the sound in the living room rose like a wave, a pent-up breath exploding in sound and energy. Ladies squawking like parrots, men wiping their foreheads with handkerchiefs, Ganga Ba loudly ordering chai for the guests, pleased at the reaction her miracle had caused. Ha! Now look at all the fools who said that Kalu belonged in the leper colony.

No one knew what the vaid said to Kalu. If anyone had listened to what was happening in the guest room, they would have heard the sound of a plastic flute being blown. First an ascending scale. Then descending. They would have heard phrases being played. A few minutes later, the vaid simply left through the kitchen, telling Bhraamanji, the cook, that he would be back soon. Kalu, pale-faced and clutching his plastic flute, slipped out with him. Malti thought he was saying good-bye to the vaid, only he didn't return, either.

Malti scrubbed the pots in the covered courtyard, under the shade of the frangipani tree. Jif powder for the pots and pans; a small, cracked bar of soap, made from a composite of pieces too small for Ganga Ba, to use on anything more delicate.

She automatically scraped the excess food from the pans into a broken but clean plastic container for Kalu, then shook her head, remembering he was no longer there. It had been five long weeks.

She had become so used to having Kalu around that his absence was like an itch. She could ignore it for a while, but just when she thought it was gone, something would trigger it, and she'd remember that he had disappeared. Kalu would think it a grand joke to be thought of as an itch.

As her lips curved, Malti's hands continued working by habit. The froth from the soap gathered in mounds and rivulets over her hands, forming new lines on her palms.

Malti had heard by the river that the vaid would be returning soon, and she hoped Kalu would be with him. Ganga Ba had taken Kalu's departure badly, first blaming Kalu for his disloyalty, and then later the vaid for taking the boy. She was vocal in her denouncement when questioned by friends over tea, all the while insisting that it really didn't matter to her anyway—that her part in the drama was long over. Malti knew better.

Although Malti and Ganga Ba never spoke to each other about Kalu's absence, it hung between them. Every time the gates opened, or the wind presented them with a half-heard tune, Malti's movements would falter and Ganga Ba's head would turn slightly. Just in case.

Maybe today was the day he'd return, Malti thought, as she had every day since he walked out the kitchen door.

She carried the clean utensils back into the kitchen.

3

He walked down the dark path, stumbling in the shadows. He could hear the temple priests chanting over the sound of the wind.

Mano buddhya-hankara chittaani naaham.
I am not the intellect, the ego, nor the consciousness.

The chant drove him toward the mighty river, continuing in his mind, even when the priests' voices could be heard only in snatches over the wind. Water pounded against the high cliffs, thunder adding to the sound of rocks sliding and crashing as yet another piece of the stone succumbed to the water below.

Na cha shrotra jihve, na cha ghraana netre.
Nor am I that which is related to sound, sight, or
  smell.

Tonight he'd cleanse himself in this water, just as the River Ganga did when she became too polluted. They said she came to the Narmada in the form of a black cow to wash herself in the holy waters. Maybe the Narmada would wash away the smell of smoke and the dirt that coated his skin. He had failed his family and failed his god.

Na cha vyoma bhumirna tejo na vaayuhu.
I am not the sky, earth, light, or the wind.

He hadn't realized that the smell of spirits could be so seductive. One drink was all he'd intended. Why, even Lord Shiva took in the poisons of the world. Then as the night wore on, he realized that one had turned into two, into three. And the cards, which had at first seemed so good, failed him.

His young wife waited for him. Before he'd left, full of hope, she'd made an offering to Lord Shiva and told her husband that she knew he would find work that would support the family. She had faith in him. He never thought he'd let her down. The cards had been his last resort and he'd lost his land along with his reason.

He stood at the very edge of the river, watching the wild currents drag the water this way, then that. The Narmada was born of Shiva, the river he made by meditating so hard that his sweat formed the start of it.

Now he would give his life to Shiva. *I'm sorry, my lord. For the pain I've caused.*

Chidaananda rupah shivoham shivoham.
In the form of eternal bliss I am the essence of Shiva
the Supreme.

The chant calmed him, as he took one step, then another, into the water. He'd never learned to swim. This was now a blessing, not a curse. The water took him in its arms. He closed his eyes and waited for peace. The sound of Shiva's name on his lips.

Shivoham shivoham.
I am Shiva, I am Shiva.

They found him wedged between rock and stone. One man hit his back until he threw up the water filling his lungs. He wondered if he'd arrived in hell. Then, as his eyes cleared, he realized that he was still alive. The tide had ebbed, and somehow during the night he'd found and clung to a shiv-ling, stuck fast between two rocks. The stone of Lord Shiva was ebony in color, smooth and long. By rights his hands should have slipped off it, but the stone had somehow stopped him from drowning.

The priests called it a miracle. They had never seen such a large or smooth ling before. Most shiv-lings were made by sculptors, but this one had been born of the river itself. They said the ling was obviously a message of good fortune.

But he knew it was a message from Lord Shiva, for him. He gave the stone to the village, knowing that it would be cherished in the temple, and made his slow way back home.

~

The moon was high and full the night Kalu left Ganga Ba's house. The vaid had given him a task, and Kalu, fueled by a new hunger, walked away from the village, passing the houses on the ridge before heading away from the river and the banyan tree, toward the moonlit fields edged by dark jungle. Hours later, he slowly stepped from the road onto a small, winding path so insignificant that only someone Kalu's size would have even recognized it as a trail. He walked partly by memory, partly by moonlight, until the path ended at the base of a large tree.

Kalu bent briefly to touch the ground. He always did this when he came here. His earliest memories were of this spot.

That first day. Waking up with an imprint of earth on his face and the heat of the sun baking his skin, at just this spot, where the path met the tree. It had felt like he'd emerged from a long, deep sleep. The day was silent. His head spun if he moved too fast. Even the leaves were still, the birds quiet. He had crawled toward the tree, out of the sun. As he parted the undergrowth, he noticed a small, dark hole. There in the roots of the tree he'd found an opening, a fissure that led to an underground temple.

The small room was blessedly cool. Kalu placed his hand on one wall. Shafts of light entered through the gaps created between brick, soil, and root, creating patterns of light across the room. If he stretched out his other hand, his fingertips barely reached the shoulder-height shiv-ling in the middle of the chamber. The curved black stone rose from the ground. Shadows moved on its smooth surface. The shiv-ling was the only object in the space, and Kalu wondered where it had come from.

That first day, Kalu had rested there against the stone, out of the sun, until the sounds from his stomach became too loud and he knew that if he didn't find food, he would surely die of hunger and the pain in his head.

He had finally climbed out and followed the path as it widened to meet the road. The sun neared the horizon before he came to Hastinapore, and that town was where he stayed. By the end of that first day, Ganga Ba had given him a name and a way to earn a living. She had also supplied him with milk and scraps of food in return for a trip to the ration store to collect some items she'd forgotten.

He couldn't remember anything before that day. Not a smell or sound. Nothing. There was no link to his family, if he had had one, or to his past life. Even the clothes he had been wearing had long since been exchanged or simply worn through. The only things that remained were the nightmares, and he didn't know if they were old or new.

He never questioned his lack of a family, the way he spoke, fast and fluent, or his mannerisms. Neither did anyone else. People on the street never asked too many questions. Especially about where people had come from or where they were heading. These were personal things. People who lived in houses, however, often asked questions, but rarely about his past, as if fearful of the responsibility the answers would demand of them.

Each day evolved into part work, part game, and always a quest for food and shelter, though every now and then Kalu would return to this tree with its hidden room.

He hadn't been here since his injury, however, telling himself that he was far too busy to visit the secluded temple. Now that he could walk again, he finally acknowledged the truth: he had been frightened that his heel would collapse altogether, leaving him alone, far away from all help. He flexed his foot. The walk had been long, but Vaidji had said that while his ankle would remain stiff for a time, he could bear weight on it and that he needed a quiet place, away from people, to practice. Kalu had known that if he took care and walked slowly, he would make it to the temple safely.

It was dark inside. No matter how fierce the sun was outside, it was only able to enter here through small cracks and fissures. He didn't know if the tree had grown over the underground room or if the room had been built under the tree. Either way, it offered him shelter and solitude as could no other place he knew. A gentle breeze kept the air clean. It danced through the space as if to keep Kalu company. As the golden light of the sun turned silver, a sweet scent from the raat-ni-raani flower snaked through the rays. The flower, queen of the night, lived by moonlight.

Here he'd wrap himself around the long black stone shivling, like a creeper around a tree. Gaining strength from the cool, smooth, polished surface. Here he would sleep a deep, dreamless sleep. Here he could concentrate on his promise to the vaid.

Kalu played the notes he'd been taught, ascending and descending scales. Raag Bhairav, the vaid had called it. Much better than those film songs. Harder too. The vaid had told him it was the first raag, the first that students learned, and the first that was ever played. It came from Lord Shiva himself. The raag had a sweet, heavy sound. Kalu played every day. All day.

Early each morning, as the sun rose, he'd leave the shelter of the temple for an hour. He'd bathe in a stream by rice fields, before stealing some fruit. This used to be one of his favorite games, and outwitting the field hands made the fruit taste twice as sweet. Now it was simply sustenance; the juice from a mango meant another wash in the stream, as he couldn't play with sticky fingers. As soon as he was able, he'd return to his underground space and play. The one raag. Only that raag.

The vaid had told him to keep playing until he felt he was ready to return. Slowly, all thoughts of his promise to the vaid receded and the music became more important than anything else. Often he forgot to eat. He no longer had to think of how to play, of what each note should sound like, or how they fitted together. Hours turned into days as Kalu played.

Until one night when the ripe moon rose, casting cool, blue shadows on the ground. He closed his eyes and played, recalling the river as it made its way down to the sea. Imagining the fish swimming through the currents like streamers in the wind. Then he played the wind itself, fading into a rustle between leaves before lifting to the sky once again.

Kalu, immersed in the sound, didn't hear the snake coiling around the base of the shiv-ling. He didn't see its raised hood, swaying to his music, its body thick and long like the roots of the banyan. The air took on the scent of musk, first curling through the perfumed mogra flowers, then overpowering them, as the snake wound through the room, making a circuit before returning to the base of the ling, hood raised toward the boy.

The snake moved with Kalu's fingers, its body mesmerized by the vibrations in the music played by the boy, who sat, eyes closed, immersed in his craft. The sound around Kalu took on a different quality, pushing against him and echoing from other parts of the room, unable to move with quite the same freedom. He opened his eyes and blinked. He was unsure if what he saw in front of him was real or simply a dream. Still caught in the net of his music, as entranced by the snake as it was by him, Kalu kept playing, swaying with the animal, not noticing that his lips had cracked or that his fingers had swollen. When the pale, golden rays of dawn filtered through the temple, the music softened, until each note seemed distinct from those around it.

The snake shivered before sinking to the ground and gliding out—leaving large welts in the soil on the floor from its slow dance—moving in a fluid motion through a space in the wall, before finally disappearing. Kalu's eyes widened. Snakes that size were unheard of around Hastinapore.

He dropped his plastic flute beside him and placed his hand in the tracks left in the earth by the snake. He bent down, nose to ground, smelling the musky odor before tracing the path with his body, absorbing the smell and heat that soaked the ground, until, exhausted, he fell asleep, cradled in the ridges left by the cobra.

Kalu awoke with a start. Sunlight shone in his eyes. It was

closer to midday now than dawn. He looked down, trying to remember his dream. He smiled as he saw the ropelike marks leading out of the temple. There had been a snake, and at least it had valued his tin-whistle music. He traced the trail with his eyes, back to where he sat, looking down at the soft soil in which he had slept.

Just by his hand was a hard ridge a couple of fingers wide, uncovered by the movement on the floor. Kalu started to dig, first carefully, then faster, ignoring the soil flying around him and across the room. Then slowly again, for he saw there, hidden in the ground, a long flute. Kalu lifted it up, holding it fast in both hands, feeling the smoothness of the wood, polished by its years in the soil. It was a side flute. A man's flute. Kalu placed his fingers over the dirt-filled holes. He could hear the music. See the people applauding. The vaid would be in the front row, smiling. Kalu's fingers stopped and the music died. It was time to return to the village.

4

"GANGA MAASI! MALTI! Where are you?" shouted Kalu. A lizard trail of dirt followed him into the house.

"Aré, Kalu—where have you been, boy?" the servants called over one another as they gathered in the front room, cooking and cleaning forgotten in their haste to see Kalu and hear his news.

Ganga Ba had been resting upstairs and took a little longer to rise. She later told her friends that Kalu's clear voice was the only thing that could have woken her from sleep. "These women who don't have enough to do sleep like birds. Asleep one minute, awake the next. In my day, either you slept or you worked. No gaanda-giri, either. We never fooled about. Any other sound and I know I would have slept through it." The other women agreed with Ganga Ba. Life was much easier that way.

Malti ran in and hugged him. Hard. "Idiot. Where did you go?" She felt his bones with her fingertips, first his collarbone, then his wrists, shocked at how little was left of the boy. She shook him as she spoke, then stopped, afraid he'd snap. During the weeks he'd spent at Ganga Ba's while waiting for his foot to heal, he'd fleshed out. Bhraamanji's scraps and a regular supply of milk had rounded the hollows beneath his cheekbones and given his skin a healthy sheen. Now his skin reminded Malti of a wizened old apple.

Malti had told herself that Kalu was safe with the vaid somewhere. But there were times, just as she closed her eyes to sleep, when a voice from within, between her hip and ribs, whispered stories of child kidnapping and pain. Although Ganga Ba knew the vaid, Malti never forgot her friend from the village who disappeared in Bombay.

"Aré, leave that ungracious boy alone, Malti. Look at the mess he's left on the floor for you to clean! You look like you haven't eaten for a month. Couldn't Vaidji feed you? And where is that scoundrel, taking you with him without a word? Not that we were worried." Ganga Ba paused midway down the stairs, using the rail to support her as she drew breath. "Well, Malti was upset, at any rate. Went off her food and work with worry. Malti, get him some water first and stop fussing over him. Take a breath, Kalu, and some food. You're filthy, boy. Have you been rolling in the dirt?" Ganga Ba poked Kalu's shoulder gently before heaving herself onto the divan. "Turn on the hot water switch, Malti. Hey Bhagwaan, come here, boy. Bhraamanji, bring a cloth for him to sit on before he floods us with dirt. Now, sit here beside me—but not until you take that dirty stick outside."

"But, Ganga Maasi, look. It's not a dirty stick, it's a flute! I found it."

"Flute? How did you get that flute? No, don't answer yet, eat, sit. Malti! Malti! Come and hear what your boy has been up to!"

Kalu sat on a towel with Ganga Ba to his right, her plait swinging low rather than contained in the usual bun, wayward strands making patterns on her neck and back.

Malti stood by the stairs, her skirt tucked up as it always

was when she cleaned the floor. The other servants gathered, too. No one made any pretense of doing anything but listening.

"The vaid showed me a raag on my plastic flute," started Kalu. He told them about how he practiced each day and about the snake that led him to the real flute. He didn't tell them how the music made him feel, but his emotions played on his face, and no one interrupted him. Not once.

"A miracle from the gods," said Bhraamanji as Kalu finished.

"No, a gift for his hard work," said Malti, putting a plate of fruit in Kalu's hands. "What will you do now that you have the flute?"

Kalu paused, unsure of how to answer Malti's question. He knew that, above all things, he wanted to play more music in the way he'd played at the temple. He knew that if he could learn more, he could play, all day, every day. In those weeks away, he had stopped thinking about survival and had found both peace and joy. But he wasn't sure of what he still owed the vaid.

"Never mind that for today, enough time to discuss flutes and whatnot tomorrow," said Ganga Ba, filling the brief silence. "Kalu, you need to clean yourself. Now, outside, and no arguments. And, Malti, get him something to wear after you've taken out the water. Those clothes are as worn-out as he is."

Kalu stood up slowly. The run back to the village had tired him, causing a dull ache in his foot. And he still had to find the vaid.

Ganga Ba placed his still-dirty flute on a cloth and laid it in her mandir. The little house temple seemed the most appropriate place for it. Knowing that his flute was safe made it easier for Kalu to go outside to wash.

This was the first time Kalu had used hot water for a wash. Even when he last stayed at Ganga Ba's, the river had been his washroom. Malti brought the bucket of water out to the little area near the tap and helped him to pin up the cloth that the servants used for privacy. The concrete was warm, toasted by the sun. He watched the water as it cascaded down his body, scattering on the concrete before the rivulets ran through the cracks to soak the ground. Kalu scrubbed the musk of the snake and the layers of weariness away with an old yellow piece of soap, savoring the feel of warm water followed by a dash of cold, both poured from a cup onto his skin. The heat seemed to make cleaning that much easier. He squatted on the concrete floor and took his time, letting the water wash over him until it rinsed clear.

Kalu took his flute and an old toothbrush, normally used to clean utensils, down to the river just before sunset. Malti walked with him in silent companionship. It was good to have him back. The path, used every morning when Malti went to wash the clothes, was narrow but well worn. Today, however, her feet were tentative as she trod over ground that should have been familiar. Everything felt a little different. From the time that Kalu had reentered the house she had been unusually conscious of his movements. She found herself following him with her eyes or listening for his footsteps as she worked. Now, as they walked single file down the narrow trail, she noticed the rocks studded across the path and overhanging branches that swung by as if bowing as Kalu walked.

Usually Malti's thoughts were on the task ahead and the stories her friends down by the washing rocks were sure to tell as they scrubbed cotton clothes and beat them on the rocks.

Now each pebble, every bird call, even the tune Kalu whistled in time to their pace, was noted and stored. Just in case.

The intensity of her happiness and relief on Kalu's return took Malti by surprise. She was embarrassed that she had hugged Kalu when he arrived. It was rare for Malti to touch anyone. The last person she could remember hugging was her mother, just before Malti left home to come and work for Ganga Ba.

At night, Malti would often try to recall her mother's scent. A nutty smell, like whole roasting peanuts, that was uniquely hers. She remembered the heat of her mother's heavy calloused hands rubbing a homemade concoction of coconut oil and spices into Malti's hair, massaging her scalp and kneading her shoulders in the warmth of a sun filtered through trees. As a child, Malti could sit on her long, curly locks. Her mother, whose hair was now as thin as an old jute mat, took pride in her daughter's asset. "Look after it, Malti. Oil it after every wash. That's the way to keep your hair good."

Malti had loved this time with her mother. They spent it talking about things that only women discussed. Small matters: the best way to stop the coriander from wilting; the new market man whose eggplant seemed cheaper and fresher than the others'. As she grew older, Malti knew that soon she'd be leaving the house to work for someone else. She would ask her mother to rub slower, complaining that going faster hurt her scalp, only to extend the time they spent together.

The day Shami Ben, her mother's friend, informed her of a suitable situation in Ganga Ba's house, Malti knew that there would be no more massages. Ganga Ba had agreed to take on Malti, despite her young age, but she lived six hours away by bus. Shami Ben's daughter had worked for Ganga Ba, and she assured Malti's parents that Ganga Ba was firm but fair. So Malti had left.

She couldn't complain. Ganga Ba was better than some, and the family needed the money to support her brother's education. But it was hard being alone. She didn't like it when things changed. While changes seemed to make life better for others, they always seemed to make things harder for her.

"Are you glad to be home, Kalu?" she asked as they walked.

"Hmmm. I suppose. I missed you and some of the others. But I was very busy. Did you miss me?"

"Yes, I did. I missed you just as much as I miss Raja."

Kalu knew all about Malti's older brother, Raja. He was the reason that Malti worked for Ganga Ba. "Besides, there's no work on the farm," she'd told him. No one in their family had ever stayed on at school before, but both her mother and father were determined that Raja would study and get a decent job. Malti had explained to Kalu how important this was for the family, despite the taunts from richer children, the ignorance of some of the teachers, and the cost of schoolbooks. Kalu had wanted to know why Raja stayed, why he didn't run away or hit the boys with sticks. Malti explained that her parents had always wanted him to succeed, to have a better life than they did. Ever since he and Malti were children, Raja had known that he would have to study. He needed to get the marks for a good government job, if he was lucky. Malti would work to help earn the money for his tuition and books, until she got married. That way the whole family would be settled.

Kalu had initially thought that it seemed silly for Raja to study when he could have come to Hastinapore to be with Malti. But he slowly understood the difference between Malti's position and that of someone like Ganga Ba or even Jaya-shree Ben. No one told them what to do. Maybe that's what Malti's parents wanted for Raja. Kalu had offered to help; Malti had laughed and shook her head. She'd told him to wait until he was rich before making such generous offers.

"Has Raja finished school yet?" asked Kalu now.

"He has a while to go, Kalu. But he'll finish soon enough."

Despite his and Raja's age difference, Kalu often reminded Malti of her brother. Kalu had grown in the past few weeks, too, like a long water shoot on a bougainvillea: tall and green and pointing straight at the sun. Almost aching to be the tallest and strongest shoot on the vine. Kalu was now nearly as long as she was, and Malti was tall for a girl. Raja used to call her a snake bean, claiming no one would want such a tall bride. As Kalu grew, he'd certainly be taller than she was, taller even than Raja.

"Anyway, don't worry about Raja. What about you?" she asked. "What do you want to do, besides cleaning that flute?"

They had reached the riverbank, around the bend from the spot where the women cleaned clothes each morning. There was no one here now, as the women were at home, cooking or cleaning. Most of the men would be out, telling stories or playing cards around the banyan tree. Even the birds had left the water. The sun would soon set.

Malti and Kalu squatted on the dry sand near the river. Kalu slowly started to remove the dirt from the flute. First he brushed away the loose dirt, then gently rubbed it with the old toothbrush, dislodging the soft, brown dirt from the wood.

"You know, Kalu, that flute could take you anywhere you wanted. Not many people could live away from everyone and play for days, let alone charm snakes. You wouldn't have found the flute if there wasn't some purpose. You need to make the most of it."

"If it was mine to play." He frowned. "What would you do, Malti? Where would you go if you had the flute?"

"I wouldn't go anywhere. I wouldn't be able to play it, stupid. Why, I'd probably have given it to you!"

Kalu lifted his head and smiled. "That's true. Forget playing, your singing would scare buffaloes!" He ducked as Malti went to cuff him, overbalancing slightly in the process. "Hey, don't hit me, yaar—the flute!" He took his time steadying himself before he spoke again. "But if you could play, what would you do?"

Malti sat back against a stone. "Honestly, I don't know. Maybe just wait and see."

"That's what I'll do, wait and see. Besides, I still need to speak to the vaid."

The flute was almost clean and Kalu made his way to the river, dipped a corner of his shirt in the water, and proceeded to wipe the last remnants of dirt from the flute. The wood reminded Malti of henna. A deep, rich brown with just a hint of red, a touch of fire beneath the calm. It shone as if polished with the richest of oils, and the air slid over and around it like the softest of silks.

"It's beautiful, Kalu. My mother would love to hear you play it." Malti's eyes moved from the flute to his small, brown fingers holding it. She realized that there was no one to tell him to keep them clean. "Do you ever feel alone, Kalu? Sometimes I do. I miss my mother."

"No, I never had anyone to miss. And I don't know how you can feel alone, with all of us here to keep you company. This is where I belong, and you do, too. And I can play for your mother one day if you like! Will that make you feel better?"

"You know how far away she is?" Malti rubbed her forearm. "Never mind. Enough of this nonsense. It's good to have you back, Kalu. Besides, now there's someone else around for Ganga Ba to scold! Hai, we will get a scolding if we aren't quick, the sun's setting. It's almost time for dinner and Bhraamanji will get angry if I'm not there to help."

The two of them scrambled to their feet and hurried back the way they'd come, this time with a gleaming rosewood flute.

The night lights had been turned on by the time Malti and Kalu returned to the house. Malti ran into the kitchen.

Kalu stroked the flute once with his index finger before placing it on the yellow cloth in the mandir. The flute was smooth, colored like liquid amber, textured like molten honey. It amazed him that a tree, rough bark and dry flesh, could, when sanded and varnished, offer up such beauty. He turned and walked back out to the garden. It was peaceful there in the dark, under the shelter of the shrubs. He had forgotten how noisy it was in the village. Sounds that were once comforting now tired him. His ears longed for silence or music. Strong single notes. Quiet music. Kalu closed his eyes, willing himself to return to that place within him. The place the music came from. But here, even in the garden, the task seemed too great.

"Kalu! Kalu! Food . . ."

Kalu jumped up, alert at the sound of his name, forgetting for an instant that it was unlikely anyone was summoning him for work. It was Bhraamanji calling.

"So you think you're a star now, do you?" Bhraamanji frowned as Kalu entered the kitchen, motioning the boy to sit.

Kalu was used to Bhraamanji. He had never seen the man smile in all the time he had known him. Bhraamanji cooked for the whole house. While the servants, and now Kalu, ate variations of Ganga Ba's food, minus the delicacies, Bhraamanji cooked all his meals in separate vessels, stirred with a special spoon. Kalu had asked him about this and Bhraamanji had explained that as a Brahmin he ate food and used a plate untouched by the other castes. Kalu had thought this entirely wasteful and rather foolish.

"What happens when someone gives you food? Why, I'd starve if I followed your rules." Kalu grinned as Bhraamanji's frown deepened.

"You will never have that problem, Kalu. People living on the street have a different set of rules."

"Just as long as you don't mind feeding me, Bhraamanji," replied Kalu. Even before Kalu came to sleep at Ganga Ba's, the Brahmin had kept scraps for him every now and then. He'd give them to Malti to give to Kalu, scolding her at the same time. It had been war from the time those two met. But as Kalu told Malti, despite the gruff tone, Bhraamanji was really a nice man. Today Kalu saw that his plate included a small sweet.

He'd almost forgotten what good dhal tasted like, the mix of salt and sugar—Gujarati dhal was always a little sweet. He poured the dhal over his rice and wrapped his fingers around the wet bundles before twisting his fingers and catching the food in his mouth, smiling as Malti berated Bhraamanji for his sarcastic comments. It felt good to be back. He wiped the plate clean with the side of his hand, catching any stray liquid with his fingers. Then he double-checked the plate, in case any spare grain had been left behind, before drinking some water and finally stepping out to wash his hands and rinse his plate and glass.

Malti came out a few minutes later. "Kalu, I'll do those. You can help tomorrow. Go in and sit with Ganga Ba for a while today. She's missed having your big eyes and monkey face around, even if she won't admit it."

Ganga Ba sat on the divan watching her favorite serial on the television. "Come here, Kalu, sit and watch. You can learn so much from these shows, maybe even more than you did from that vaid. Television has opened up India." Kalu sat where he had that first night, on the floor by the table. Had Ganga Ba offered him the divan, he would have refused, preferring to sit on the floor, closer to the ground, where Ganga Ba's voice could wash over him.

"See this girl? Her mother-in-law is so cruel to her and her father used to beat her. Now she wants to run away but she loves her husband. What to do. Silly girl. Should stop wasting her time and start acting like a good wife." Her focus on the television didn't waver as she changed tack. "And Vaidji—he's coming to visit tomorrow. He returned to the town last night apparently. My friend Sukenya Ben met him. I told her to tell him to come in the morning, so no running off."

Kalu watched first the television and then Ganga Ba in amazement. How could she have so much to say about so many things and still watch the television?

"Aré, look now, did you see what that man did? So weak, these men. I don't know what she's thinking." It was good that Vaid Dada was coming tomorrow. It would save Kalu going to look for him. Still, in one way he would have preferred a little more time. Just some time alone with his flute.

A little while later, Ganga Ba looked down and saw that the boy had fallen asleep, one leg curled around the leg of the table, the other straight out underneath.

She rose and called to Malti, asking her to collect a pillow and blanket. Ganga Ba bent, a little stiffly, placing the pillow under his head and the blanket over his frail body. None of the children in her circle ever looked this fragile, yet Kalu was stronger than the lot of them. He'd had to be to survive on his own. Ganga Ba brushed his hair away from his eyes with a gentle touch before turning out the living room light. That night Kalu stayed where he was, under the table in the middle of the room.

• • •

The next morning the whole household waited for the vaid. Malti asked Kalu to try his new flute, or at least play his plastic flute, to break the building tension, but he refused to touch either instrument. Instead he sat under the frangipani tree in the back garden. From there he could hear the creaking of the front gate as people entered.

He sat still, cross-legged, humming quietly to himself as he waited for the vaid. Only his hands moved, clenching and relaxing, stroking the latticed scars on his ankle before clenching once more. He heard the gate open again and close.

Kalu stayed where he was until the sound of his name cut through the air. "Kaaallluuu! Come, Kalu." Kalu rose and entered the house with the dignity and gait of an old man.

The vaid sat straight and tall on the divan. He rose as Kalu entered, and smiled, as if seeing an old and valued friend. "Kalu, come here, beta. I hear you have news for me. Did you play the raag? How did you feel?"

Kalu walked close but didn't touch the vaid. He sat on the floor, near Ganga Ba, and retold his story, this time with Ganga Ba and the others interrupting to add this detail or that.

The vaid asked few questions but watched Kalu's face as he spoke, seeing how the boy's love for music, awe of the snake, and reserve when speaking of the buried flute played out in his expressions.

"May I see this flute?" the vaid asked as Kalu's voice thinned.

Kalu went to the mandir and collected the instrument. He stood in front of the vaid, his hands shaking as he held them out, offering the flute. "Here, it's your payment; it's the only thing I have. Here, take it."

The vaid took the flute from Kalu. "I cleaned it," said

Kalu, his body unconsciously swaying toward the vaid like a reed caught in a gentle breeze.

The vaid looked up. "And you want to give me the flute? Why is that?"

"You said I had to pay. That there was a price. Please . . . just take it and go."

The man stroked the satin finish on the flute. He checked the length of the instrument, then looked for cracks in the wood. There were none. The flute looked fresh and new.

"It's only fair," continued Kalu. "You fixed my foot. It's the payment. Please, it's all I have," he repeated.

"Have you played it?"

Kalu shook his head.

"No? Well, I want you to play it for me."

"Please . . ." The word held a mixture of fear and longing. It was as if the boy knew that to play the flute would automatically increase the price he paid.

Malti started to speak but stopped at the feel of Ganga Ba's hand on her arm.

"You must play music for this bargain to take place, Kalu." The vaid held the flute out just as Kalu had a few moments before.

"Please . . ."

"I want to hear the raag, Kalu. I want to see what you've learned," said the vaid, his voice softening. "Now play."

Kalu brought out his plastic flute. Already, it felt insubstantial. When compared to the rosewood flute, its green front and yellow back looked cheap and incomplete. A little like Kalu felt when it came to playing in front of the vaid. "I'll play my own flute if I have to play," he said.

Kalu's chest heaved. He sat on the floor, crossed his legs, and closed his eyes. There was silence for a few minutes until he started, a long, soft note, so gentle that Ganga Ba wasn't sure when the silence ended and the sound began. The one note merged into two, then three, until the listeners were drawn in completely by the music.

Ganga Ba remembered the feel of her child suckling for the first time. Malti remembered the security of sleeping in the shelter of her mother's arms. The vaid sat still, amazed at the sound the boy wrought from the little plastic toy. The tune lasted only a few minutes. Kalu stopped abruptly and flung the plastic flute away. It slid across the floor. Malti grabbed it before it hit the leg of the table.

"That's enough," said Kalu. "I can't play more. Not now. Not ever."

"Kalu, hush." The vaid leaned forward, grasping the boy's hands in his. "Never be scared to play. This sound, this music, is a part of you, just like the tears on your face. You cannot throw it away. It will not let you."

He knelt beside the trembling boy. "Beta, I need to tell you a story. About two brothers. When they were young, they were very close. But one was always more interested in people, the other in music. The younger would sit for hours trying to read medical journals and listen to healers. The older wanted to do nothing but play music. They both worked hard until they had the means to fulfill their dreams. But when you reach for one thing, something else often gives way.

"The younger brother traveled far and wide, helping people when he could. As time passed the man grew older, still working, still traveling. Until one day, he looked up and realized that there was no one place he called home.

"He was sad about this, but understood the cost of his decision. He had made the choice himself, you see—to follow his calling. And he could always visit his brother, the one who played music. He loved his brother dearly. There was no one who could make music speak the same way. And his music took him around the globe. Everyone thought the one who played music was great. And he was. A pundit. People loved to hear his music. He traveled everywhere, coming back to India for breaks and to get away from the applause. Until the day when the applause and adulation became more important than the people who loved him and the music itself. And he forgot that he needed to give as well as receive, taking the things most precious to him for granted.

"That day the music dried up. Completely. He said he had become tired of hotels and wanted to return home to rest. In reality we knew it was the only way that he could continue to play at all. Far away from distraction and destruction. And like you, he had no choice. He had to play. Only, the cost of fame had been great.

"My brother still lives in the hills. People visit him from around the world, but he never leaves his house."

The vaid placed the rosewood flute in Kalu's hand and closed his fingers tightly around it, binding them to the instrument.

"The flute is yours, Kalu. I never expected you to give it to me. The music was the payment. I wanted to see what you could do. Whether you would rise to the challenge. Your music reminds me of my brother's when we were children. Now I want you to do something else altogether. I want you to come and live with my brother. He could make you one of the greatest players in India."

"But, Dada, I'm no student. I need to earn my living."

The vaid smiled when Kalu called him Dada. He'd never thought of himself as someone's grandfather before. He tightened his grip on Kalu's shoulder. "When someone has a talent like yours, it's important that it's looked after, Kalu. And you will be good for my brother. He needs someone like you in his life. Let me help you. Let me help you both."

"Hey Bhagwaan," exclaimed Ganga Ba. She'd been quiet for long enough. "What an opportunity. Aré, Kalu, you'll be famous! Who would have thought when I first gave you a job all that time ago that you would be sitting here now? When will you be leaving? We have to prepare."

"No!" Malti's response was deep and instinctual. Everyone, including the still-silent Kalu, turned toward her.

"Malti!" said Ganga Ba. "It's not your decision to make. This is for Kalu to decide. Think of the opportunity."

"No!" Malti focused her gaze on Ganga Ba. "We don't really know the vaid and we don't know his brother. What if he's some goonda from the mountains?"

"Malti!"

"But, Ganga Ba, the vaid has already taken Kalu away from us once. Why build Kalu's hopes like this? You know he's from the street—what pundit would accept him? And what about money? I don't know who this man is to do this to him or to us. I won't let it happen. Kalu is my friend. How do I know he'll be safe? How do we know it's not all a lie? If Kalu goes, what will be the price?"

5

FROM THE MOMENT Vaid Dada made the offer to take him to a real teacher, Kalu stopped listening. He didn't hear Malti or Ganga Ba argue. He didn't hear the vaid's response or his suggestion of regular phone calls. Now that his foot was fixed, Kalu could work anywhere, but the promise of music was more than he ever expected—to spend his days and his nights playing. Playing the flute was like coming home.

"Does he know more music than you do?" Kalu finally asked just as the vaid was leaving. "What will it cost?" Nothing came without payment of some sort.

The vaid repeated that the issue would not be money but commitment. As was the tradition, at first Kalu would pay the teacher by working around the house; he would pay in money once he started earning. In return he would be taught, fed, and housed. The apprenticeship would last as long as the teacher felt it necessary. All of this was, of course, conditional on the musician accepting Kalu as a pupil.

Ganga Ba checked and double-checked the vaid's information. She spoke to her friends about his brother the musician and came back with glowing reports, which she related to both Kalu and Malti. She even obtained a cassette record-ing of the musician in concert in America, from the daughter of a friend who she disparagingly referred to as a nonresident Indian. "I don't know why, but as soon as these NRIs return to India, they think we know nothing of our own culture. Fancy bringing a tape of an Indian musician all the way from America! As if Indian music was only discovered in the West. You don't know how much trouble I went to to get this, either—you know he stopped playing professionally just after this concert, some twenty years ago."

Malti always made sure to be in the room when Ganga Ba had news. If Kalu was going, she wanted to be sure that she knew exactly where and how. That way he could never be lost the way her friend was.

Malti and Kalu sat on the concrete under the frangipani tree, away from night insects living in the grass. Kalu would be leaving in a few days and they both knew this was one of the last times they would have together. Ganga Ba was busy watching the latest family drama on the television, and the other servants sat in the covered space outside, gossiping and playing cards. Malti and Kalu leaned back against the wall and looked up at the sky rather than at each other.

"I wonder how we got so many stars in the sky, Malti."

"I don't know, but I do know which is my favorite—Dhruv-taara." Malti pointed to the sky, following the line of the frangipani tree and then moving her hand up higher still, to a small, bright star.

"Dhruv-taara?"

"You don't know the story? When I was little, my father would sometimes tell my brother and me stories to help us go to sleep. This was one of my favorites."

"Well, tell me, then, yaar."

Malti moved her gaze to Kalu. "A long, long time ago, there was a small boy just about your age called Dhruv. His father, Uttaanpaad, was a great and famous king."

"I wonder if my father was a king." Kalu imagined a man's face, his skin the same color as Kalu's own, with a warm smile, a sparkling gold crown, and a thick mustache.

"Could have been, would have been. It's no use guessing. You're here now, and that's what counts. Now . . ." Malti's voice became deep, like the Narmada in winter, when the river was full and heavy. "The king had two wives and two sons. In those days men were allowed to marry more than one woman. Suneeti was Dhruv's mother, and Suruchi was Uttam's mother. Luckily for Uttam, his mother was the king's favorite, and so he got far more attention than his brother did."

"Why was she the favorite?"

"Well, I'm not sure, but I think it was because she was so beautiful. She had big, brown eyes and a graceful mouth. I'm sure she made the king relax and forget all the business he had to deal with." Malti laughed, adding, "When my father told us this story, he would say that Suruchi had wavy hair, just like my mother's. Ma would get so angry with him. Once she even threw the rolling pin at him. It missed my father but made such a dent in the wall. He refused to fix the hole, just to remind her of her temper.

"Anyway, Suruchi wanted her son to be king, even though Dhruv was the elder. So in spite of being the favorite, she wasn't a very nice person. Suneeti shielded her son from Suruchi's pettiness whenever she could, but sometimes it was impossible.

"One day, when Dhruv was seven, just maybe a little younger than you, he was playing in the gardens. There he saw King Uttaanpaad sitting in a bower, admiring the flowers. The king had Dhruv's brother, Uttam, on his knee and was bouncing him up and down. Uttam laughed and laughed. Dhruv, thinking this looked like lots of fun, ran up to the king, calling, 'Father, me too, please. Father, me too!' The king picked him up and placed him on his other knee.

"Suruchi was furious when she saw Dhruv on the king's knee. 'You dirty boy, what on earth are you doing?' She snatched Dhruv and tore him from the king's lap. 'Get off there, there isn't enough room for the two of you. Out of here, and don't disturb the king again.'

"Dhruv looked at his father, but the king was too busy soothing his wife to have time for Dhruv. Maybe he would have turned to Dhruv later, after he had calmed Suruchi down, and maybe not. At any rate, it was too late. Poor Dhruv ran out of the garden and back to his mother.

"He cried as he told her what had happened. Suneeti held her son tight. She was just as angry and upset but didn't want Dhruv to know. Dhruv finally stopped crying. 'Do you think that Suruchi Ma will ever let me sit on my father's knee, Ma?' he asked.

"His mother replied very quietly, 'No, son, I don't think she will ever be happy seeing you on your father's knee.' She stroked Dhruv's hair, just like I'm stroking yours, and said, 'If you want something badly, all you need to do is ask Naaraayan Bhagwaan. He is far more powerful than Suruchi. Far more powerful than the king.'

"'So how do I find him?' Dhruv asked.

"'Go deep into the forest, with my blessings, son, and pray. You will find Naaraayan Bhagwaan.'

"Now, my father told me that when you leave home with blessings, you're sure to find someone to help you, and Dhruv found Naaradji, who taught the boy how to meditate and pray for Naaraayan Bhagwaan—Lord Vishnu. Only Dhruv didn't pray to sit on the king's lap, he prayed to sit on the lap of the most powerful person of all. Dhruv prayed and prayed with all his heart.

"Finally Vishnu appeared before Dhruv. 'You have prayed so long and hard, Dhruv, what is it that you desire?'

"But now Dhruv, seeing God, could only smile with joy. In the presence of his power, Dhruv couldn't even speak. He'd forgotten everything in his love for God. Luckily, Vishnu knew what Dhruv desired. 'From now on, Dhruv, you can sit on my lap. I am more powerful than the king. And no one will ever be able to remove you.'

"And that's how Dhruv ended up in the sky. My father used to finish the story by telling us that God was every-where, especially around those who prayed, and Dhruv was transformed into that little blue star that never moves and can never be removed. I think that's why it's my favorite. I know that Dhruv will always be there, even longer than we'll both be here," Malti finished.

"Will I always be able to find Dhruv-taara in the sky?"

"Yes—anywhere in India. Maybe even beyond. Even in America, I think. I guess Dhruv made a good wish, then, to be high in the sky, where no one could touch him but where he could see all of us."

Kalu disagreed. "I'd rather be near people. And I don't need a father's lap to sit on, the ground's fine for me."

Malti laughed. "I will miss you, rascal! But when I look at Dhruv-taara, instead of remembering my home, I'll remem-ber you and your ground!"

As news of Kalu's impending departure spread, most of Hasti-napore, both Ganga Ba's friends and Kalu's, visited the house to congratulate him on his good luck, each providing advice or a warning. Even Jaya-shree Ben arrived at the gate with some betelnut leaves for him.

As people said good-bye, Kalu realized the place he'd made for himself in the village, all on his own. No one ordered him around. He wasn't dependent on anyone. His friend Bal, the buffalo boy, was in a far worse position.

He saw Bal the day before he left. Kalu waited for him near the river, knowing that Bal would have to bring the buffaloes past. His friend looked tired and as dirty as the legs of the buffaloes he tended.

Bal rubbed his face hard with his hand. Unsaid words about the future crowded both boys, and they knew that whatever happened, things would never be quite the same. Kalu hugged Bal, who held him tight and whispered in his ear, "Go learn to play, bhai, but always keep your independence. Don't become like me."

The two boys stood cheek to cheek, each receiving the warmth of the other through clothes thin with wear. Kalu refused to let go. "I'll be back, Bal. I'll find a way for you, too. I'll be back."

Bal finally pushed Kalu away. "You don't worry about me, bhai. Just look after yourself."

Bal started to cross the river before turning to wave to Kalu. "And play for me sometime."

Kalu promised himself that he would return someday for Bal. Saying good-bye was difficult, but the decision to go with the vaid was easy. Even as his foot healed, Kalu knew that there was only so much a person could do on the street. While he could keep running errands, he would never have a house like Ganga Ba's. Never be able to concentrate on anything more than getting enough money for food. Now Kalu had a new need. To have the space and time to play music.

As his foot healed, the need to play had become as important as his need to walk.

Kalu and the vaid left early in the morning, before the sun rose. The air was cool, as was the ground, in the stillness before daybreak. It was so quiet he was sure everyone could hear his heart beating loud and fast as he walked down the steps and to the gate, where a car was waiting to take them to the railway station.

Kalu looked very different from the boy the vaid had first seen. He stood straight, although the new clothes that Ganga Ba and the villagers had given him made him look awkward, as though he were walking in someone else's skin. He carried a faded pink zip-up bag with clothes from Ganga Ba in one hand. The bag was a leftover from one of Ganga Ba's daughter's trips home from America. Kalu loved the feel of the nylon fabric, along with the faded print of the blond-haired, pink-skinned woman on the outside pocket. In his other hand he carried a smaller cotton bag covered in red and green advertising from local shops, containing water and food from Bhraamanji. His plastic flute sat in his shirt pocket, like a pen.

Malti had handed him the flute in the garden the night before he left. "Here. Take this with you. You may need it yet. And don't forget to telephone. They can afford it if they can afford you!" She walked away.

Kalu knew by the straightness of her back and the absence of a swing in her hips that she was upset. Whether it was with him or the vaid, Kalu wasn't sure. "Hey, Malti, I'll play for you when I return."

She paused and nodded, unsmiling as she stepped into the shadows.

Kalu and Vaid Dada arrived at the station. Kalu had never seen so many people in one place. The station smelled like hot metal, of diesel and oil, and the tracks went on forever. The carriages, like the station itself, were full of people. Kalu followed the vaid to the second-class, air-conditioned carriage. It should have been cool except that every window was wide open, letting in fumes, dirt, and heat. Kalu sat cushioned between the vaid and a plump lady who spoke nonstop and even shared some of her pakoras with him. They were lukewarm and a little squashed, but Kalu never rejected food.

The vaid closed his eyes. Kalu rested back against the blue vinyl and, copying the vaid, closed his eyes, too, only to open them again. He was too nervous to sleep. The train trip was going to be a long one, followed by a night in a hotel before traveling on by car. Kalu had never traveled by anything but foot, and the occasional rickshaw when the drivers felt sorry for him. The smell of fumes and the sway of the carriage made him feel a little queasy. He swallowed. Maybe eating those pakoras hadn't been the best idea.

He shook his head and took a shallow breath through his mouth. One step at a time, he decided. No use worrying about the future, when the present was new enough. He looked out the window, focusing on the change in scenery rather than the smell, while the lady beside him gave a running commentary on the towns they passed.

Vaid Dada awoke after a couple of hours and told Kalu to get ready—they were getting off at the next stop. Kalu said good-bye to the lady and made his way out of the carriage. This station was even more crowded than the one in Hastinapore, and he held tightly on to the end of Vaid Dada's shirt, not wanting to be pulled away by the tide of people trying to get on and off the trains.

. . .

Kalu lay awake in the hotel room. It was the first time he'd slept in a bedroom. The mattress beneath him was unfamiliar and Vaid Dada's heavy breath filled the silence between the muted hooting of horns and ringing of bells outside. It seemed that no one slept in this town, except maybe the vaid.

Kalu squeezed his eyes shut to stop the mattress from swaying like the train and clutched his plastic flute as he turned, trying to sleep. He held it tighter, as if the feel of the flute would take him back to the village and the fresh air. However, he knew that he was here, in this room, because he wanted to be. No one had forced him. And tomorrow he would meet the vaid's brother for the first time.

He started to weave a melody in his mind. Using the vaid's breathing as a rhythm and the sounds outside as accompaniment, he replayed the last few days. He played his friends— each came in as a different strand: Ganga Ba, loud and a little strident; Bal, solemn; and Malti, sometimes lively, sometimes sad. He wove each strand together tight. Small happiness and large uncertainty all bound together in harmony, until slowly, finally, he fell asleep.

⁓

Kalu and the vaid traveled by Jeep for the final part of their journey, stopping for breakfast as the day slowly warmed.

Drinking chai from thick, chipped glasses, the man and boy sat silently at the edge of the road, where the trees provided the most shade. To Kalu, the people around them looked foreign, as if the mountain air had molded higher cheekbones and creases around eyes.

On the first day, Kalu had looked around him, trying to

take in the villages, trees, and plantations they passed in the train. Today his mind was on the end of the journey. His stomach ached as if he had eaten either too much food or not enough.

The vaid, who was used to Kalu humming or talking, squeezed the boy's shoulder. "Don't worry too much, beta. You'll like my brother's place, although you may find it a little quiet at first. There will only be the three of you. My brother lives alone, except of course for Ashwin, who looks after the house." The vaid held his cup high, angling it so the liquid fell straight into his mouth without the glass ever touching his lips. Kalu followed suit, although not as neatly. Vaid Dada handed him a large, white handkerchief. It took Kalu a moment to work out what it was for.

"Ashwin? Is he another student?" Kalu twisted the damp cotton square around in his hands.

"No, child, Ashwin has been with us a long time. Maybe twenty years. From when he was a boy, a little older than you. When my brother chose to stop performing and to move away into the mountains, Ashwin chose to go with him. He keeps house for us." The vaid paused before continuing with a smile, "I'd love to see my brother's face if he was asked to teach Ashwin!" He laughed and rubbed Kalu's head before striding to the chai stall with both glasses.

The sun was high in the sky. The Jeep lurched over rocks on the winding road, which seemed to lead nowhere. Dust and grime rose in clouds around them only to settle as the car slowed. They stopped by a lone house on the side of a hill, dwarfed by the mountains that touched the sky. It had to be the musician's.

A tall, lime-washed wall surrounded the building and grounds. The original white could be seen only where the rising damp hadn't yet touched it; the remaining areas were the orange and brown of a mottled alley cat, one color fading into the other.

From the car, the place looked quiet, peaceful, and a little run-down. The driver jumped out to open the tall iron gates, which were crowned with barbed wire and tipped with broken glass. As they drove in, Kalu saw a long, single-story bungalow surrounded by a veranda that was supported by ornately carved wooden posts. The garden was filled with plants and the occasional stone statue. Blood-colored bougainvillea tangled with coral plants, and Kalu had never seen so many shades of green. The scent of jasmine and incense floated like the lightest of melodies over the path. Large trees sheltered plants still heavy with dew. The grass below was thick and green, and the garden was alive with the whisper of leaves and the call of birds.

This musician had to be richer than even Ganga Ba. Kalu rested one hand in the vaid's, careful not to betray his feelings by holding it too tight. In the other he grasped his bags.

The vaid released Kalu's hand at the door. He gave a large, bronze bell a tug before removing his champal, setting them down beside the doorway, and beckoning Kalu into the house. Kalu wiped his bare feet on the mat and his hands on his shorts before following him in.

The granite floor was cool after the warmth of the day. It was dark inside the house, making it hard at first to see anything or anyone. He followed Vaidji's silhouette down a short corridor until he turned into a room on the right.

This room was almost dazzling in its brightness. Kalu stayed by the entrance, placing his two bags carefully on the floor and leaning lightly on the door frame. Kalu heard a voice while his eyes adjusted to the light.

"Bhai, welcome, I'm sorry I didn't greet you at the door. I was so absorbed that the sound of the car didn't register." The man removed his glasses and rose from a desk covered with books. He looked taller than the vaid, but Kalu realized when they embraced that they were really the same height. The man stood straight. His long, white hair, calm and ordered, framed his face. He wore a plain cream kurta and a cotton dhoti, together with socks and a pale blue scarf.

"So this is Kalu." Kalu straightened as the man turned to face him. The musician's eyes were clear and sharp.

"I've heard a lot about you, boy. Don't just stand there, enter." He invited Kalu in with a fluid movement. His hands were large, the calluses on the pads of his fingertips marked with small, hard, circular indentations from years of practice on the flute and perhaps other instruments. Kalu rubbed his own hands, feeling their rough edges, the dents and cuts of labor.

The musician turned to an earthenware urn on a small table and ladled water into glasses as the vaid moved toward the divan, describing his travels since the brothers last met. Three cane-backed chairs framed the divan, one on the side close to the table and the door, the other two directly opposite. The chairs were frayed around the edges and the cushions faded. Kalu's first thought had been to sit on the floor next to the vaid, but instead he chose the edge of the chair nearest the door. The seat was high. Kalu kept the toes of one foot on the ground, while the other foot swung in midair.

The musician, holding two glasses of water, turned toward Kalu, lifting an eyebrow in his direction. The boy shook his head violently at the offer. The musician paused, looking straight into Kalu's face and then down to his feet, before keeping one glass as his own and passing the other to his brother.

"So, was the journey restful?" asked the musician with a twist of his lips.

The vaid accepted the glass. "Restful? Given that you selected this place specifically so you were difficult to reach, I don't know why you bother asking me about my journey every time I return. Does it please you to talk about my aches and pains?"

"Well, you are the vaid—heal thyself."

The two men sat side by side on the divan and turned slightly to face each other. The vaid relaxed back into the seat, while his brother sat straight and tall, one foot tucked up. The tone of their voices, the phrases they used, and their comfort in each other's company marked the two men as brothers, but their faces were as different as the moon and the sun. While the vaid's eyes were clear and calm, the lines on his face were creased and curved, just like the roads he traveled. His brother's skin was lighter and his face more mobile. His eyes were as keen as a hawk's; dangerous, Kalu thought.

Kalu began to look around him as the brothers talked, keeping as still as possible so they wouldn't notice. He wished he could sit on the floor rather than the chair. Large windows started a foot up from the floor and seemed more like doors, opening out onto the veranda and the garden. The place felt as if it had grown in the same wild way as the plants outside— each object jostling the next for room.

The walls were covered in shelves full of books. Kalu couldn't imagine anyone having the time or patience to read them all. Ganga Ba only ever read magazines, and she often complained about the fact that there was no time to read any- thing longer. He could hear her now: "All those newfangled books. They are all rubbish. Full of hera-feri and God knows what."

He was brought back to the present as Vaid Dada men- tioned his name.

"Well, you know that when you take Kalu as a student,

you'll have to really work on that road. There'll be nothing left of him if he travels up and down too much. I don't know how Ashwin copes. And what about me? There will obviously be more time spent here now that I'll be seeing both teacher and student."

The man frowned and his hands stilled. "I told you on the telephone. You know I'm not interested in full-time students."

"I know what you are interested in and not interested in, bhai, but as I explained, you have no choice. Kalu owes me a debt, and this is how I want him to pay it off. Would I have dragged him all this way if I didn't think you two would be good for each other?"

"I'm not interested in what's good for me or for anyone else. You know that as well. It takes more to teach than you know or understand. An all-consuming journey for both teacher and student. And you bring me a street urchin. I don't take even competent people, and I'd have to teach him to read and talk before we could start on the music. Take him to a normal teacher at one of the charity schools."

Although the man didn't raise his voice, Kalu felt the force of the words hit his body, and he stood.

"See," continued the man, "the boy is obviously as keen to go as I am to see him go. I take it he isn't deaf, just mute."

"Enough." The vaid raised a hand as he spoke. "Have you been practicing this little speech since you learned I'd be bringing Kalu? I take it that's also why Ashwin is not here to welcome me?"

To Kalu's surprise, the musician's face changed again until he looked like a sulky child. "Ashwin will return soon. He needed to collect rations from the village and has obviously been delayed; otherwise he'd have been outside waiting for you. It has nothing to do with whether or not the boy should stay here."

"Just listen to him. Listen to him play."

Kalu turned to Vaid Dada. "I will not stay where I'm not wanted." It was the first thing he had said since he left the car. His voice sounded small.

"See, brother—I knew I'd made the right decision. A boy who gets offended just because he's not wanted will never make it as a musician. He doesn't have it in him."

Kalu faced the man. "You don't know what I have or haven't got. Because . . . because you are just a silly goat. You don't know anything about me. I could have been anything and you wouldn't have liked me . . . and I do want to play— but with someone good, who will teach me." Kalu stopped, horrified, and spun to leave, landing badly on his weak ankle as the room tilted around him. Vaid Dada caught him just before he hit the ground.

"He's right, you know." Vaid Dada spoke to his brother as he held the boy tight. Kalu knew that he'd lost his chance but he was too tired, too drained to care.

"And what makes you think he has it in him?" The man's voice was measured now. Slow and textured like Vaid Dada's. It upset Kalu that this man could sound like his dada. He buried his head in the folds of the vaid's sleeve.

"Can he play?" continued the musician. "Really play? Playing takes more than talent. It takes hard work and strength."

"Hear for yourself, bhai," the vaid interjected. "Just listen to him. With an open mind. Kalu, play for my brother, please."

Kalu shook his head, but the vaid drew him up and held him straight, letting him know that this wasn't a request. Kalu rubbed his tender ankle with the toes of his other foot and took a shaky breath.

"The flute?" he asked.

The vaid paused. He had stored the rosewood flute in his

medicine bag so it would not be damaged during the journey. "Actually, I think you were right when you chose to play your other flute at Ganga Ba's house, beta. It's the one you're comfortable with."

"But it's not a real flute."

"I'm not interested in the instrument, boy," the musician leaned forward, "I'm interested in you. So play for me. Anything at all, on anything at all. Just play."

Kalu hesitated, then pulled the plastic flute out of his bag. He turned, took a quick breath, and moved the whistle to his lips.

"Stop!"

Kalu stopped, facing the man for the first time since his outburst, trying to let go of his resentment.

The musician's expression was severe. "At least take the time to breathe. I don't want to hear a school band. Sit on the floor. Close your eyes and for goodness' sake, breathe before you play."

Kalu slipped down to the floor. He was more comfortable there. He closed his eyes and imagined himself back in the temple, in the early hours of the morning. The sun was pale and the air just a little dry as the earth awoke from a deep, deep sleep. He lifted the flute to his lips and began to play. The melody started slow and small before spreading through the room like sunlight.

Afterward, he could never remember what or for how long he played. All he would remember was finally returning to the room, smelling the faintest scent of cinnamon, and opening his eyes to the sight of the vaid with tears running down his cheeks. The vaid's brother wasn't crying, but his eyes shone and his hands grasped the divan as if to anchor himself against a storm. The whites of his knuckles slowly returned to brown as he faced his brother.

"So." His voice sounded cracked, fragile. "If that's what he can do on a plastic . . . He has no technique and needs much training. It was good you didn't try to teach him yourself, bhai. Bhairav is a powerful raag, its simplicity makes it so; however, anyone who has the gift needs to be careful. Any raag played properly has the power to sever as well as heal."

Kalu clutched his plastic flute. All of a sudden, the effort of playing and the tension in the room seemed too great. The vaid placed his warm hands under Kalu's arms and lifted him up off the floor to sit by him as the musician asked, "You have his flute, the one that you spoke of?"

The vaid squeezed Kalu with one arm before collecting the flute from his bag. "Thank you, beta. You reminded me of my mother and the sweets she made for my birthday when I was your age." He passed the flute to his brother.

"Interesting," the musician responded, inspecting the instrument. Kalu didn't know if he was talking about the music, the flute, or Vaidji's comment. "Hmm," he continued. "It's rosewood, too. Heavier than bamboo."

Kalu felt a hot storm rising from the pit of his stomach, at odds with the heaviness of his limbs. His flute was better than any bamboo flute.

"Still," the man went on, "it will do. It will do very well. And . . ." He pinned Kalu with a sharp look. "I may be able to teach you. If you are willing to learn."

Kalu fought to keep his temper in check. "Maybe I should try elsewhere."

"Kalu," the vaid spoke, "my brother may sound abrupt and say things you disagree with, but he is the best teacher for you. There aren't many people who will take a boy off the street in any shape or form, regardless of how well you play. He will either make or break you. Are you willing to take that chance?"

"If you want me to be your teacher, your guru, then you'll have to put up with me, and I'll have to put up with you. But . . ." The musician's voice rose. "You will obey me, in all things. Is that clear? This isn't just about music. I can transform you from a scrubby street urchin into a musician."

"This is not *Pygmalion,* brother."

"Maybe not—but you brought him here. You knew the risks. It'll be under my terms or not at all."

Kalu thought about his life back in the village. He looked down at his ankle, with its intertwining scars, the only reminder of the wound that had almost rendered him useless, then back up to Vaidji, who had healed him and then showed him how to play. "And is this the price you want me to pay?" he asked the vaid. At the vaid's nod, Kalu took a deep breath and turned to the vaid's brother. "Will you teach me how to play the flute?"

"Yes."

"Really well?"

"Yes," barked the musician. He sounded angrier than he looked.

"Then I'll listen." Kalu held out his hand. The musician covered Kalu's hand with his. The boy's handshake was firm and strong despite the fact that he was more skin and bone than muscle.

"From now on, you can call me Guruji, your teacher. I'll take you as my shishya, my student. You have a gift, one that not many can work with. Luckily, I'm one of those who can. I will teach you, but you will do whatever I ask. And you will work hard. Sometimes you will think it's useless. But if you persist, we'll make progress. You'll learn. You'll live here with Ashwin and me and we will work through the day and into the night."

Kalu stood absolutely still, focused on Guruji's words.

"You should be comfortable enough here. Breakfast is at six. You'll help Ashwin and myself as required. I hold with the old system, so I'll see to your food and clothing."

Kalu leaned forward, taking a breath as if in protest. He'd always looked after himself.

Guruji raised his hand. "You'll even get some money once a month for extras but I will be paid back. You'll only play in public if I say so, and all your earnings will come to me until you cease being my student. And . . ." Guruji linked his fingers so the tips touched. "And we'll have a trial period. One year and one month. If at the end of that time either one of us still has doubts, you will leave. Is that understood?"

Kalu concentrated on the hard, calloused hand that had recently held his. He looked directly into the face of the musician in a way that Kalu-of-the-streets never would have. "That's understood. If you teach me well, I'll stay and learn; otherwise I'll go."

"That's all I ask." Guruji smiled at the small, solemn face looking up at him. "Enough of this. Sit, boy, sit. You bounce up and down like a jack-in-the-box."

As Kalu sat, a man entered the room carrying a tray with a plate of biscuits and four teacups. His arms, visible beneath the sleeves of a worn red T-shirt, were muscular, and the hands that carried the tray looked capable and strong, hard and smooth. By contrast, his legs were gnarled and dark, like limbs of the banyan tree, and as wayward as the River Narmada. They gave him the appearance of a child still unsteady on his feet, but the hint of stubble on his chin and the dusting of silver in his hair betrayed his age.

"Ah, Ashwin, good timing. Meet Kalu, our new resident. He has deigned to honor us with his company for a while."

Ashwin surprised Kalu by hurriedly putting his tray on the nearest table, touching Vaid Dada's feet, then hugging him. The vaid didn't seem at all startled by this behavior and hugged the man back, stooping a little to meet Ashwin halfway.

"Aré, you again. He's missed you, you know," Ashwin said. Guruji's lips twitched and Vaid Dada laughed as he released the man. "I rely on you, Ashwin, for the truth." He turned Ashwin around to face Kalu.

Kalu had never seen a servant behave quite like Ashwin and wasn't sure how to greet him. He pressed his palms together and bowed.

"Quite the little sir, aren't you?" said Ashwin, bowing back. "Now, let me get some food into you. I'll have you nice and round in no time." Ashwin poured the tea, turning and speaking to Kalu while he handed a cup to Guruji. "You'll need to watch your tongue around him, but you're safe with me."

"Nonsense!" said Guruji. "As long as he listens and practices diligently, there will be no problems."

"Ha, you'll see, Kalu!"

Ashwin's smile reminded Kalu of Malti. Wide and open, as if to include the whole world. Kalu returned to his seat, cup and saucer in hand. He watched the three men talk about people they knew as they drank tea and balanced both saucer and cup with ease. Kalu sighed. He couldn't manage sitting on a chair, balancing a cup and holding a saucer. He took another small sip before placing both the cup and saucer on the floor for safety.

Even the tea here tasted different, stronger, as if the masala was fresher. Back in Hastinapore, he normally drank at a roadside shop, like the place they'd stopped at this morning. Tea was served in a thick glass, often chipped at the lip, rather than in a delicate teacup. On most mornings he'd run tea rounds for the roadside chai-waala.

The place was always busy early mornings; the truck drivers would come by for their chai before continuing on their way. The chai-waala couldn't leave the shop, but he didn't want to lose any business in town, so Kalu would take the metal carrier, complete with ten cups of tea, to the various shopkeepers, returning with money and the empty glasses. As payment, the chai-waala would give Kalu a glass of tea along with paise. Kalu would sit on a stone by the trestle table and wooden benches, sipping his drink while listening to the truck drivers. In this way, he learned about the busy roads in Orissa and the new freeway to Bombay. He heard about the riots in Ahmedabad and how the mafia played a part in inciting violence. He listened to the men talk about women they met on their journeys. Although he didn't understand everything the men spoke about, Kalu liked to hear them talk. The men, in turn, forgot the small boy on the stone; he became a part of the background, just like the peeling blue paint and the ageless posters of the latest films that were already clothed in a fine layer of dust.

Now, in Guruji's house, listening to the three men, Kalu was reminded of the truck drivers. The interplay of voices, the way one person started a story and another caught it, expanding it and then passing it on to the next man.

He'd get used to the tea. He'd get used to it all if it meant that he could learn to play.

Ashwin noted the darkness beneath the boy's eyes and the way his hands trembled slightly as he tried to remain upright. "Come, Kalu, later I'll show you the house, but now it's the bath and then rest for you before we sit down for dinner."

Kalu turned to the vaid, who smiled in approval as his brother added, "Off you go, then. Ashwin won't bite you. I'm going to rest, too. It's been a long day for both of us."

"We'll call Ganga Ba this evening, beta," said the vaid. "Rest well."

Kalu took no notice of where Ashwin led him; he was just happy to be out of the room. They turned from the corridor into yet another chamber.

"You know that you have succeeded where so many have failed." Ashwin shook his head. "Hey Ram. I bet it was fireworks at first. Guruji can be rather testing."

"He was terrible. I don't think he wants me here still."

"The trouble he causes with that tongue of his. Don't you worry about that. That man always seems worse than he is. Quick to anger, quick to laugh, that's Guruji." Ashwin turned and bent down so that he was level with Kalu. "Listen, Kalu, you have a gift. Vaid Dada wouldn't have brought you here otherwise. You need to trust that. And Guruji will make a real musician of you, Kalu, despite himself."

Part 2

ANTARA

The sthaayi and antara follow the aalaap. Now we introduce rhythm and melody. At this stage, the percussion instruments may join in, and gradually the tempo increases.

The melodic line also becomes more of a focal point. Two or three different tunes, each in harmony, both with each other and with the whole, sing their own song, crossing and recrossing each other.

—GURUJI

6

IT TOOK THREE days for Kalu to explore the whole house.

On the first day, he followed Vaid Dada at a distance. Dada didn't seem to mind; he'd look across and smile, but left the boy alone to find his own rhythm. Kalu also watched Guruji, who for the most part ignored him. Sitting in the shadows, he realized that he had agreed to be this man's apprentice without even finding out how he taught or hearing him play. He listened to the pitch and lilt of Guruji's voice. Unlike his brother, Guruji never seemed to be completely still; it was as if the energy inside him could not be contained.

On the second day, Kalu waited until everyone was busy talking after breakfast before deciding to explore the house. He took a few steps at a time, ready to retreat to a corner if necessary. However, Guruji and Dada continued their discussions as if Kalu wasn't there. He edged toward the door, and slowly, against the retreating sound of the two men talking and Ashwin's clatter of pans against granite in the kitchen, he started to wander through the house.

There were three bedrooms in the house: Kalu's room, the

one Vaid Dada slept in, and one for Guruji. No one shared a room or sleeping space. Even Ashwin had his own outbuilding at the back, behind the kitchen. All the rooms circled an open space in the center of the house.

The first room Kalu went into was Guruji's. This was the room he was the most curious about, and the open door invited him to enter. He looked around and threw a piece of paper with Ganga Ba's number ahead of him. He had specially collected it from beside the telephone so if anyone asked, he could tell them truthfully that he went in only to retrieve it. Besides, no one had told him he wasn't allowed in this or any other room. Still, he tiptoed, just in case.

He noticed the bed first. Like the bed in his own room, it was modern, with a wooden base and a mattress, rather than the string ones that most of the villagers in Hastinapore had. Ganga Ba would have a similar bed, thought Kalu, only much, much wider.

The walls were bare and lime-washed blue. The small table next to the bed was covered with books and magazines that overflowed into uneven stacks against the wall. The recycling man would have paid good money for all those magazines. Kalu later found out that Guruji never let Ashwin move these old copies of the *Times of India* and the *Illustrated Weekly of India*. "You never know when they'll come in handy, and besides, no one else need be disturbed by them in here," Guruji would say.

Kalu had never known anyone who valued reading or books as much as Guruji. Perhaps that was how the musician got to be so clever. Big words, in all different languages, flowed naturally from his tongue. While Vaid Dada's personality showed through his actions, Guruji's moods could be read by the tone of his voice.

Kalu didn't touch the cupboard or drawers but opened a

few of the books, carefully replacing them in the same order. All the writing was different; Kalu counted five different scripts.

The book room itself had even more books. Kalu returned to this room next. Although it was the room where he had spent the most time, he hadn't really had the opportunity to explore it the day before.

It housed a small television Kalu would later learn was tuned to the BBC World Service when Guruji watched it, but which most often showed Doordarshan programs for Ashwin, who was far more interested in watching television than reading books. Then there was the dining and music area. The flute box, the sarod, the taanpura, and the different drums all sat in one corner, together with a mat, ready for practice time. On the other side of the room was a stereo and a stack of records. Kalu lifted each dust-covered disk. A couple near the bottom had pictures of Guruji on the front. Kalu wiped these down and moved them closer to the top of the pile.

The divan room was more spacious than the book room, and less lived in. It reminded him of the main room at Ganga Ba's house: a room where people could just sit and talk but not do much else.

Kalu hesitated at Vaid Dada's room. He could smell the incense, a mix of pine and sandalwood, that Vaid Dada burned each morning. He turned and walked past, leaving the room alone.

The house was far too big for Ashwin and the guru, even if Vaid Dada also stayed sometimes. They could fit at least twenty more people in the place. Kalu mentally allocated rooms to whole families, people he knew who would appreciate a roof and four solid walls.

· · ·

On the third day, Kalu walked around the garden and toward the outhouse, where Ashwin lived. This building was directly behind the kitchen, and Kalu waited until he knew Ashwin was busy with Guruji before slipping inside. The door was unlocked. The room inside was dark; Kalu waited, blinking, until his eyes adjusted.

The room was very neat, much neater than Guruji's. A row of combs were placed at attention in a straight sturdy line across the tabletop. Each was a different colored plastic. Red, blue, green, orange, a lighter green, and brown. Only the red one still had all its teeth. One wall, the one closest to the door, was covered with film-star pictures collected from magazines. White crease marks from the centerfolds dissected faces from bodies. There were two large cupboards by the wall across from the bed. Later Kalu was to learn that these contained Ashwin's treasures. He hoarded collectibles—items from Guruji and his friends, knickknacks from airports and concert halls, small bags containing bottles of evaporated cologne and still-folded socks provided by airlines for international flights. There was one special shelf just for his albums, containing photos, press clippings, and memorabilia from Guruji's performances, together with scraps of paper, reviews, and dried flowers pressed between the pages. The smell of paper and old memories filled the room.

Kalu chose to explore the garden in the middle of the day, when everyone was asleep, and then in the cool of the night, when the shadows became as interesting as the thick, sweet smell of night flowers. The grounds were at least four times the size of Ganga Ba's and even had an outdoor stone temple. The grass felt rich and soft under his feet.

However, what impressed Kalu most wasn't the thick tangle of flowers or the trees or the tickle of grass beneath his toes but the mountains, rising up as far as he could see, so that this huge house and vast garden still seemed small in the scheme of things.

Outside the compound gates there were no shops, no chai-waala. There were no fields, at least not cultivated ones. In the mornings, there were no hawkers competing with one another, each with his own song, no horns. The closest village was at the bottom of the hill, a twenty-minute walk. The nearest town was a drive or a cycle ride away. At first this had worried him. But now that he knew where the small side gate was, which tree was the easiest to climb, and which spot each door and window opened onto, the walls around him felt solid.

~

Kalu sat under a tall tree, partly shaded from the hot, white summer sun. The sunlight touched parts of his body, warming them, until he moved a fraction so the pattern of radiance and shadow moved again. He could hear Guruji playing in the distance, and his fingers moved to the music. He had been here two weeks, and he still hadn't been allowed to play his flute for the master.

A young, green leaf floated from the tree into his palm. He automatically rolled it into a whistle. Instead of getting the chance to prove to Guruji he was a good student, he had been ordered to run, walk, polish, and eat. He didn't mind the eating, but the other tasks didn't seem to have any meaning.

Vaid Dada had explained that the aim was to give his body a chance to strengthen. "You can't play for hours if your mind and muscles are too tired and weak to absorb anything." Kalu had stayed silent and continued to wipe the books, not noticing Vaid Dada's sharp glance. He did exactly what was asked of him and kept his mouth shut. At first, this wasn't hard. His head hurt as he tried to get used to all the new things he had to learn—when to eat, how to walk in shoes, how to sit, and how to dust. Those books took up too much space and needed to be dusted so often that Kalu was sure it would be easier just to be rid of them.

"So what do you think of our humble abode?" Guruji had asked Kalu while they all sat together for the evening meal at the end of the first week.

Kalu didn't think anything he had seen was humble. "Do you really need all those books?" he asked.

"Books can teach you things, can take you to places you couldn't possibly go otherwise. And they are the great equalizer," said Guruji. "Anyone can learn to read."

Kalu had thought of the books he'd been dusting. There were leather-bound books, ones with gold lettering; others had lost their coverings through age, so he could see the stitches that held them together. He wondered what it would be like to know so much. To own so much. He looked at Vaidji, who smiled back, tilting his head just a little as if waiting for Kalu to speak.

"Yes, but not everyone can read," returned Kalu. "Some of us have to work for a living. And then who can afford to buy books?" Vaid Dada stopped eating as Kalu's voice rose.

Guruji looked up at Kalu. "We all have choices in life and we all make sacrifices." He paused, as if waiting for Kalu to interrupt.

"But—"

"The ability to read gives you the power to make informed choices and stops you from being hoodwinked."

Kalu remembered looking at a ration-shop receipt someone had dropped on the street. The marks on it had meant nothing to him. If he could read, at least he could buy things without the shopkeeper stealing from him or shooing him away.

Guruji continued. "You'll be learning to read soon. I won't have an uneducated child in the house."

"Well, I'd like to read, but . . . I'd like to learn to play the flute even more," Kalu completed in a rush.

"That will come, boy. We're doing things my way. You'll start lessons in the next few days."

Flute lessons or reading, Kalu longed to ask. Instead he gave a small nod before concentrating on his food.

Now, a week later, sitting under the tree, Kalu let the last of the notes from his leaf whistle fade away. His stomach gave a small rumble, as if to remind him of the hours since breakfast. He moved a little to the left, so the heat of the sun baked his ever-hungry stomach. Some things never changed.

He had more energy now but was restless. Ashwin was always interesting, but he had his work to do. The house had started to feel enclosed. Here he had shelter, music, and scenery. He had the promise of a new career as a musician. But the crickets here made more noise throughout the night than did the men at the paan-waala's in Hastinapore, and though the air was fresher, it wasn't as full of life and the living.

Kalu shook his head and brushed the longer locks of his hair away from his face. Malti used to say complaining never helped anyone. Besides, he had other things to think about.

Vaid Dada would be leaving tomorrow. It would be the last time he saw the vaid or anyone from his old life for a long time, and soon he'd start his new life for real. Despite the summer heat, Kalu shivered.

⁓

Kalu lay awake in his room. Lime-washed walls, a single wooden bed, and two small cupboards, both with firm metal grilles on the front to stop the rats. The one on the right housed the clothing that had been given to him by the villagers. The other was to be used for his books. It was still empty, a promise of what was to come. A mosquito net shrouded the bed, and the one large window beside it let in a soft, light breeze carrying the smell of the garden. The net moved gently as Kalu turned over onto his side, and then over again. Finally he climbed out of the bed and stepped through the window and onto the veranda.

The paved concrete was cool. Kalu curled around some chair legs and lay on the floor looking up at the roof above him. He slid to the right and forward a little, until he could see through the gap in the overhang. The stars shone brightly just as they did above the fields surrounding Hastinapore, but those nights sleeping out in the fields seemed a lifetime ago.

He could just see Dhruv-taara, the star Malti had told him about. It was clear and blue in the vastness of the sky. He wondered if the boy Dhruv had ever felt as alone as he did. Maybe. Even so, just knowing that Dhruv was up there and that Malti could see the same star made him feel a little better. The star cradled him in a cool blue light connecting his past to the present. Kalu sighed, closed his eyes, and recalled the night Malti had told him Dhruv's story. Kalu's breathing softened. With Malti's laughter echoing in his mind, he finally fell asleep.

～

A fortnight later, Kalu walked into the kitchen after a long session with Guruji. His legs were stiff after two hours of sitting with them crossed. He had to walk with his knees as bent as bowlegged Ashwin's.

The kitchen smelled of warm, charred chapattis and turmeric, like Bhraamanji's kitchen had; however, it looked very different. Not a chili or bean was out of place. There was no pile of spinach to be washed or container of milk cooling on the tabletop, ready to be made into yogurt. Everything was in its place. This neatness, along with the pictures on the wall, marked the room as particularly Ashwin's.

Three magazine cutouts of film stars with dewy eyes and polished lips smiled over the kitchen from their place on the wall, above the radio, which was kept continuously on the old film-song channel. The film stars, though, would change every time Ashwin saw a new film at the cinema.

Kalu winced as he lowered himself down to sit on the small, red stool that had quickly become his own. Ashwin moved from the Western-style stove alongside the gas cylinders to the pale blue fridge with its large, silver handle. The fridge contained more cool water than Kalu had ever seen, along with delicacies like cheese and Kalu's favorite: cold, cold milk.

Angling his feet toward the fridge, Kalu found himself face-to-face with Lord Krishna as a plump, young child. His big eyes twinkled over round blue cheeks and pink lips as he smiled out from the top of the calendar on the wall. Blue skin contrasted with the gold ornaments on his head and arms. Beside Krishna, Hanuman, the monkey god, strode across last year's calendar. Hanuman carried a mace in one hand and a mountain in the other, his tail waving, its tip bright with flames.

Kalu would much rather be Hanuman than Krishna. Who wanted to be blue and surrounded by girls when you could leap from building to building or fly through the sky instead? But with the current state of his legs, he didn't think he'd ever walk properly again, let alone leap. He'd be like Ashwin, with his rolling gait. The size of Hanuman but without the superhuman strength or magic tail. He slowly moved his bottom around the stool, trying to find a soft spot. He'd never thought about how Ashwin's legs came to be so bent.

"Ashwin, were your legs okay before you came to live with Guruji?"

Ashwin laughed. "No, not at all, little one. I was born like this. You don't get legs like mine from a little bit of sitting practice. Don't worry. You'll be standing straight again in no time."

"Yes, but once I'm straight, I won't be able to bend again, and then Guruji will stare at me from beneath those bushy eyebrows."

"Aré, baba, don't worry so." Ashwin placed a glass of milk mixed with sugar in Kalu's hands. "It will take time, that's all. Time to iron the street out of you. Time for your body to adjust along with your mind. Look, put this towel on the stool, you'll feel much better with something soft under your bottom. And don't forget, after a few months, you won't notice the floor, you'll be too busy playing music and reading those books. You'll be spouting all sorts of ideas, first in Gujarati, then Hindi or English."

Ashwin pulled the corners of his eyes as the next song, "Mera Joota Hai Japani," an old favorite, was announced on the radio. It was about a man with clothing from countries around the world but who remained Indian at heart. "In a few years, I wouldn't be surprised to see you sitting here reading Japanese, let alone wearing Japanese shoes like in the song," Ashwin said as the song continued. Both Kalu and Ashwin sang at the tops of their voices. As Ashwin pranced around the kitchen, Kalu bounced up and down on the stool, all aches and pains forgotten, at least for the moment.

Later that night, Kalu took the cotton mat from beside his bed and spread it on the floor beneath the doorway. Then he placed a stool on the mat and stood on it, grasping the top of the door frame. Kicking the stool out from under him, he hung there, feeling the weight of his body pull downward, until every part of him stretched, until his legs were as long as they could possibly be. Then, as his hands gave way, he dropped with a dull thud to the floor. It paid to take precautions where one's legs were concerned.

It was the quietest time, the hour before the moon finally descended and the sun rose. Kalu heard the sarod being tuned. He turned, smiling at the sound.

Although Kalu had now been in the house for almost three months, this was the first time he had heard Guruji play at this time.

During the day, Guruji's music was measured, calm, and controlled. Now, though, it was a wild, untamed thing, a cry from the heart, a plea that hung in the air, that never found a response. Kalu could taste the bitterness of regret in the notes as they covered him, encasing him in a story that wasn't his. This sound spoke of rage and pain.

His eyes closed, Kalu listened, absorbed in the sound, focused on the notes. Regardless of why Guruji played this way, Kalu knew only a virtuoso could make this sound. The music rose like a wave, only to come crashing down, then slowly softening, as if the process of playing transformed the pain into something quieter, melancholy.

Kalu sat listening until the music finished. This was the music he wanted to make. He lay down and fell back to sleep with the sound of the sarod echoing in his dreams.

At breakfast that morning he waited for either Guruji or Ashwin to comment on the predawn music, but neither did.

Distracted and distant, Guruji seemed to have forgotten Kalu was even in the house.

Once Guruji had left the breakfast table, Ashwin sent Kalu outside. "Go and enjoy yourself, child. Take a break today."

"What about the music? Can I ask him about the music?" asked Kalu.

"There was no music, babu, only memories. And none that we need to talk about."

"But—"

"No buts now, babu. Just go out for the day, it's better that way."

Kalu walked out of the house and into the garden. He turned toward the village, then changed direction to walk up through the rocky paths of the mountains, where he could look down on the house, encased in its lime-washed walls, and ensure everything remained the same.

7

She looked down at the boy, curled like a cat, asleep on the mat. His body was covered with scars, short scratches, crisscrossing one another. Her hands clenched and unclenched as she cleaned the room around him.

He still wouldn't use the toilet. When they first found him, she didn't mind. But as the weeks passed, she wondered when he would change from half wolf back to her child. When they found him, she had praised God. Now she wasn't so sure.

She remembered the child he had been, a small three-year-old. Without a name. No name until he was five, her mother had told her, just in case. At five, he would be old enough to name and old enough, safe enough, to claim as her own. He was her first child. The child of her heart. The one that offered promise for her marriage.

Each night, she'd sung to him:

> *Naana maara haath, té taali paadé saath, éto kevi*
> *ajab jevi vaat chhé*
> *My little hands, see how they clap, is it not a*
> *wonderful thing*

She hadn't minded that it was so much harder to have a second child. That she continually miscarried, her body rejecting the children-to-be. Her husband hadn't minded, either. "Let's enjoy this child," he'd said, happy with their budding family. She remembered her child laughing and clapping his hands as she sang,

Naanu maaru naak, té sunghé ful majaanu, éto kevi
*   ajab jevi vaat chhé*
My tiny nose, it enjoys the flower's fragrance, a
*   wonderful thing*

Then he'd started to walk. Run, she corrected herself. Her boy never did learn to walk, just run. She tried to keep him near her. But as the days turned to months, and her work increased, she let him run farther. Across the fields and through the village. She couldn't keep up with him and the work. And she knew in her heart that he'd be safe. Her only child. Everyone knew him. And though he didn't have a name, if she sang—even just a few words—he'd come running to her from wherever he'd been exploring and wrap his little hands around the hem of her sari.

But one day he didn't come back. The villagers all looked for him; one search party, then the next, then the next again came back without the child. No matter how loud or long she sang, he didn't return. This child of her heart.

And when her husband turned to other women, she understood. Because she blamed herself as much as he did and because she felt as if her heart had been taken by her boy. The child she called Nikhil in her dreams, even though he wasn't yet five. Even though she was tempting fate.

When they brought him back, three years later, found running with a pack of wolves, she hadn't recognized her child at first. He still ran, but now on all fours. He spoke in barks and grunts and looked at her through wild, angry eyes.

The only thing he seemed to recognize was her voice when she sang. That was the only thing that calmed him. That quietened him.

> *Naani maari aankh, té joti kaank kaank, éto kevi ajab jevi vaat chhé.*
> *My little eyes, that spy here and there, is it not a wonderful thing.*

She wondered what his wolf mother had been like. If she had worried for him, if she had nursed him. If she had lost her heart to him, never to have it returned.

She looked at the cord tied to his leg. The only thing that kept him from running. Quietly, so as not to disturb him, she loosened the cord from his foot before leaving the room.

~

Malti placed the pale blue envelope on top of all Ganga Ba's other letters on the table. Although she couldn't read, she was already familiar with Kalu's round and clear handwriting. She liked these few minutes when she was the only one who knew Kalu had written, before his letter became common property.

The first letters had been short and obviously dictated to someone else. The sentences were stilted. As the months passed, the letters became longer and sounded more like Kalu.

Ganga Ba often spoke to her friends about Kalu's writing skills. "You know, it's amazing a child from the street could be so quick. I knew there was something special about him the minute I saw him." She paused. Malti, passing around spiced, milky chai, would smile quietly as Ganga Ba launched into her often repeated story. "Remember, Malti, how I gave him milk? Why, I even named him. I can always tell good stock."

The gathered women would nod politely before changing the subject.

Malti recalled a story she'd heard of a child found in the jungle, supposedly brought up by a pack of wolves. Kalu was just as interesting because he was unusual—his foot, the miracle of its healing, and his promotion to student from beggar boy made him newsworthy. She hoped he was finding the change easier than she imagined the wolf boy did, or than even she would have. Malti liked things to stay the same.

When Kalu's letter was noticed, Ganga Ba would call all the servants, knowing they had as much interest in the boy's progress as she did. They would, in turn, tell their friends about Kalu's progress. The fact that they knew him added to their prestige, and they all wanted to hear how he was doing. Everyone would stop their work and gather in the living room, standing by the wall or sitting on the floor. Ganga Ba would clear her throat a few times before calling for silence. She would then sit, like a queen in front of her audience, and read aloud.

Malti listened carefully, her body held tight. She noted the spaces between the words, the tilt and sway of each sentence, looking for a break in its rhythm that would indicate Kalu was unhappy, a discordant phrase hinting at loneliness or regret. When she heard strength and security in his description of a meal or the village near Guruji's house, she would release her balled-up fists. While others asked Ganga Ba to repeat specific parts of the letter, Malti returned to her work, humming as she went.

⁓

"Now sing after me: *sa*."

Kalu opened his mouth and belted out the loudest and

longest "*sa*" he could, rocking slightly on the straw mat and swinging his body just enough to extend his breath.

Guruji simply sat, waiting for Kalu to regain his breath. "*Sa*," Guruji repeated, slowly counting the sound out, his hand lightly tapping his folded legs.

"*Sa*," Kalu repeated, this time falling silent when Guruji's hand stopped. His throat hurt as if he'd swallowed diesel.

"*Sa* . . ." sang Guruji.

"What has this to do with playing the flute? I don't want to sing, I want to play."

"If you can't sing, you can't play. That is the way our music works. Now watch and listen. *Sa* . . ."

Kalu took a deep breath. He thought about the way Guruji had started. The way his belly and ribs seemed to expand up and out before he sang, yet the note was deep and soft. Kalu watched as Guruji repeated the note, his chest contracting and expanding again, without a waver in his voice.

Kalu knew if he'd closed his eyes, he would have been unable to tell where one breath ended and the next started. For the third time, Kalu sang, "*Sa* . . ."

Guruji clapped his hand on his knee, raising his eyebrows, as Kalu's note faded to a stop. "Good. Now sit straight and concentrate. Try the next note, and this time with the rhythm included. *Ré* . . ."

Kalu didn't notice Guruji's look of surprise or his added focus as Kalu moved just as easily to the next note and then the next.

~

Kalu found Ashwin's fingers on his scalp unnerving. The heat of his hands, the pressure of his fingertips, and the warm, clove-scented oil only added to his discomfort.

"Aré, baba, stop squirming. You're like a worm that's been cut in half. Don't you want your hair to stay long and thick? If your scalp isn't massaged at least once a week, you'll be bald before you know it."

Ashwin kept pulling Kalu up straight whenever he tried to subtly move away, until oil-stained handprints covered the cloth over Kalu's shoulders. "And breathe, baba. This isn't meant to be torture. You should feel honored that I am even touching your little head."

Kalu exhaled, collapsing slightly with the release of air, causing Ashwin to pull him upright again. No one had ever handled Kalu like this before. He had never had someone play with his hair, poke him in the ribs, tickle him, and casually hug him the way Ashwin did—covering him with flour and a particular scent, a blend of turmeric and Brut 33 cologne from America. He didn't know how to respond. So he just stood, ramrod straight, until Ashwin was finished.

Kalu decided to try to find out if other people behaved in the same way, or if Ashwin was just a little mad. He started by looking at images in books, standing on chairs to reach those on the higher shelves. The books weren't much help, and even on the television it was rare to see anyone hugging. The closest was when the villain grabbed the heroine and she slapped him on the face, crying, "You bastard!"

One afternoon, while the household rested, he walked to the village at the bottom of the hill. It was a long walk. Kalu knew it would have been quicker to walk through the shrubs and tall peepal trees until he found a trail, but he chose the path the Jeep had taken. It was safer, and if he kept just to the side of the road instead of walking in the middle, he could still hide if he needed to.

The village at the bottom of the hill was so small it didn't even have a name, and was known simply as "the village after

Manikot, on the way to Tanakpur." When Kalu reached the outskirts of the village, he found a mango tree to climb and sat high above the road, his body blending in with the branches. It was the perfect place. High enough not to be seen, low enough to hear people talk. As he waited for people to walk past, Kalu sat safe in the tree and hummed a tune from the latest film he'd watched.

When you carried a raw, gnawing emptiness in your belly, it was impossible to worry about "why?" and "how?" These days, with his belly full, Kalu had much more time for thinking and for watching. While the music and learning sometimes made his head hurt, he had plenty of time for just sitting. And no one seemed to mind how he spent that extra time.

He noticed two boys, arms slung over each other's shoulders as they ran across the road toward his tree. They reminded him of himself and Bal and he faltered. He missed being with someone his own age, who knew as little as he did. While the two of them never walked in quite the same manner as the pair below, they would laugh and joke as the buffaloes slowly chewed their way through grass or relaxed in the river. Bal would share his meal, no matter how small, with Kalu, who would bring along stolen bananas or sapota, depending on what was in season.

It had been over four months since he had spoken to anyone his own age. Kalu rubbed his left ankle against the bark of the mango, watching the boys tease each other as they ran beneath the tree, arms twisted around each other's waists, red shirt attached to white.

Later that month, when Ashwin traveled on his scooter to Tanakpur, Kalu went along, sitting on the back. He waited by the scooter as Ashwin haggled with shopkeepers, suddenly feeling unsure in the larger town. He watched babies being cradled tightly in their mothers' saris and girls decorating each other's plaits with flowers, brushing any stray strand from the other's face.

Kalu replayed these images in the night when his mind was too full to allow him to sleep. Perhaps Ashwin wasn't mad after all. It was as if he had discovered a secret language communicated by touch rather than words. One Kalu had never learned.

~

Ganga Ba took off her glasses, rubbed her eyes, and pressed the bridge of her nose. When she was young, it had never occurred to her that growing old meant becoming slow, like those white-saried women she and her friends used to laugh at in the street. It seemed unfair now, when she had the money and the freedom to do what she wanted, that her body seemed to want to do far less than it ever had.

She placed the remaining bills in the drawer, along with her tally book. Ganga Ba used to enjoy doing her bank reconciliation. Anything to do with numbers was fun. Her husband, V.P., had called it his double dowry, although never in the hearing of his parents. Being devout Gandhians, her in-laws were proud of the fact that they had accepted her without a dowry. V.P.'s joke—that he had a wife and a home accountant rolled into one—would never have been amusing to them or their relatives. V.P. was rather different, however. He never liked managing money and was pleased his wife could handle it all for him, as long as no one found out.

Ganga Ba couldn't see the need for a calculator—useless newfangled things, she called them. Better to use one's brain; you didn't need batteries for that. Still, these days her eyes ached and everything took so much longer to do. Maybe there was room for battery-operated humans. Hey Bhagwaan, she was becoming batty in her old age; one day soon she would find it difficult to see, and then what would happen?

She sat in silence for a few minutes before filling her lungs. "Malti!" Luckily her voice was still loud. In this place it needed to be for the servants to hear her.

"Yes, Ganga Ba," Malti panted, out of breath from running up the stairs.

"There you are! Now listen well, Malti, I have a real treat for you."

"Yes, Ganga Ba," Malti said. Her idea of a treat was often vastly different from Ganga Ba's.

"Malti, your brother and now Kalu are busy learning to read and write. How to do the accounts and all. Don't you think it's unfair that you don't have the same opportunity?"

"No," replied Malti. "It's not my job to know such things."

"And why not? In this day and age, no girl should have less education than a boy." Ganga Ba warmed to the theme. "Why, I remember in my day, I had to fight to stay at school. It was only because I won a scholarship that my father let me stay on past the age of twelve."

Malti didn't mention that she'd had no choice about whether she worked or went to school. Nor did she feel Ganga Ba would listen if she told her that schooling held no interest for her. Malti's mother had told her that the most important things for a woman to do were to manage the household, have children, and look after one's in-laws and husband. To make sure there was harmony in the home.

"Still, it's better late than never," Ganga Ba stated. "We start classes tomorrow."

"Classes? I don't think there's room enough in my brain for classes."

"Nonsense! From now on you'll be learning to read and

write. Words first, then numbers. Soon I'll be dictating letters like the best of them."

"But my work. If I'm learning to read, who will do my work?" Malti said stiffly.

"I know I keep more servants than I should. The others can do a little more. You'll spend an hour or two learning in the morning, and then you can practice after dinner. And you can read me the paper when you get better, too. You're bright and you'll learn fast. And your parents will thank me, too. An educated girl has many more prospects, and my eyes will get the break from reading that they deserve. Hey Bhagwaan, I don't know why I didn't think of this sooner."

~

Bal lay under the thatched shelter against the side of the buffalo enclosure. He could see the stars through the lattice. Both ends of the shelter were open, allowing what little breeze existed to circulate through the space. He slept on an old piece of matting one of the servants had discarded. His clothes were bundled at one side.

Even the buffaloes had more room and comfort than Bal, but as Master had once said, they were worth far more than he was. When it rained, Bal often moved into their space but on warm, dry nights like this, it was just too hot to sleep with the animals.

He knew it could have been worse. Master was firm but fair. At least Bal got fed something each day and had a shelter to sleep under. This was more than others had. When Kalu was on the street, he'd had even less than this.

Bal winced, remembering the beating he'd received the time he'd sneaked Kalu into the compound to share his sleeping place. They hadn't tried it again.

At least now Kalu had a proper place to stay. Most people thought Kalu was special because of the music he made. Bal knew it went much deeper. Kalu looked past the surface. He followed his heart, regardless of what other people thought. There were many people like Bal in the world, but only one Kalu. Music and laughter followed Kalu like incense followed the priest.

Kalu was the only person, in the whole of Hastinapore, who Bal laughed with. He smiled, remembering the time Kalu told him about the temple monkey who stole the paan-waala's wife's bananas. Kalu didn't just tell the story, he acted it out, dancing like the monkey, screaming like the angry woman, mimicking the paan-waala, who tried to get the bananas back by throwing his champal at the monkey, only to see the creature take that, too. Kalu pranced as he acted out the part of the paan-waala, who was just as frightened by the monkey as his wife, until even the buffaloes seemed to bay in enjoyment.

Bal had laughed until his stomach hurt.

The best thing he had ever done was to encourage Kalu to go. There was nothing for him in Hastinapore, and Kalu was his brother in all but blood. Bal wanted to support him in any way he could. Even if all he could do was simply rejoice in Kalu's good luck.

Bal couldn't remember his real brother at all. There had been five children, two boys and three girls. After his mother died, his father struggled to keep the family together. He owed money for the medicines they had needed for Bal's mother before she died, as well as for the funeral. His father told him that he didn't want to sell Bal but that as the eldest and strongest child he would fetch the highest price. It was Bal's duty to support the family. Bal hoped that since then his brother and sisters had not been forced into a life like his, but there was no way for him to find out. Although he knew the name of the village he came from, he couldn't read or write. Once Master bought him, he lost contact with his family. Kalu was all he had left.

Bal turned toward the small picture of Hanuman, the monkey god, that he kept in his shelter. He'd found the picture on the side of the road. The size of his palm, it was creased and a little faded, but Bal knew it was a gift for him. A special gift from the monkey god himself, so Bal could pray without having to go near a temple. He had no money to give as a proper offering.

Bal loved the monkey god. Hanuman was strong. He did whatever was asked of him in the service of Ram and his brother Laxman. Hanuman was a good god for a servant like him to love.

Bal rubbed the bottom of the picture with his thumb. "Please, Hanuman, keep Kalu safe from harm. Protect him, let him have a good place to sleep and food to eat. Find him friends, keep him happy." Bal fell asleep with the sound of Kalu's flute in his mind, his hand on the photo beside him.

⁓

Kalu held the pen tightly in his hand, his body curving over the paper as he wrote.

Dear Ganga Ba and Malti,

He turned every now and then to check the letters against the poster of the alphabet Ashwin had found in the markets that now hung in the book room.

"Aré, sit straight, Kalu." Ashwin had taken to joining Guruji and Kalu in the book room in the evenings. Tonight he sat cross-legged in a chair, darning socks. A pile of washing and a heavy iron sat next to him.

"Don't disturb him, Ashwin, let him learn in his own way." Guruji spoke without raising his eyes from the book he was reading. The room was quiet except for the chorus of frogs and crickets enjoying themselves in the night garden. The three of them shared companionship within silence.

It was quite different from Ganga Ba's place, thought Kalu, sucking the end of his pen, trying to think of something to write that would interest her. The whole writing business was frustrating. His mind worked far faster than his fingers did, so once he knew what he wanted to say, it was a case of trying to remember everything while checking that the words went together correctly, finding the appropriate character on the poster when he forgot how to write it, and, of course, trying to make sure it all made sense.

At least his letters to Ganga Ba were in Gujarati, so he didn't have to worry about spelling. As the Gujarati alphabet was organized by sound, reading and writing was much easier than in English. You just spelled things the way you said them. English was far worse. Guruji explained, however, that English was essential. "Even if you never leave India, it helps to know English. As you grow, I'll teach you Hindi, Tamil, and Sanskrit—all important to your education as a musician. But for now let's have you speaking the Queen's English."

"What about the king? Doesn't he speak it, too? How do they all talk to each other?" Kalu couldn't understand why Guruji was amused at his questions. He thought about putting it in his letter but didn't think Malti would understand it, either.

Guruji had explained that in English, unlike Gujarati, words don't always sound quite like they were spelled. This made things difficult, but the two of them had made a game of finding inconsistencies or words that just didn't sound like they read. Kalu looked for ones that should have sounded one way but didn't. His favorite pair was p-u-t, "poot," and c-u-t, "cut."

Ashwin would shake his head solemnly. "Aré, these English, still in the middle ages. If Gujarati was basmati rice, English would be khichdi, made from the broken bits of rice at the bottom of the bin. They still haven't learned how to link the letters with the sound. After all their years in India, you'd think they could have learned at least that, rather than ordering everyone around and stealing our diamonds."

Kalu wrote to Ganga Ba at least once a month. His early letters he had dictated to either Ashwin or Guruji and then copied in his own writing, sounding out the words as he wrote. Now, as his skill improved and he could remember the alphabet and the rules on his own, the letters became longer.

This time he decided to describe Guruji's house, with special mention of Ashwin's kitchen and, for Bhraamanji, the make of the oven. He started with his own room, then moved on to the library, the lounge area that they rarely used, and the music and dining area. Guruji had told him his friends were welcome here, and he mentioned that, too, as he did in every letter.

He didn't mention his lessons or his increasing and secret fear that he would not last longer than the year and one month Guruji had promised. When Kalu had accepted this term, he hadn't realized there would be so much to learn or that it would be so terribly difficult. The hours of breathing, singing, the yoga, listening to music, learning to read and write, all so he could follow written notes. Even when he was free to wander near the village at the bottom of the hill, or to go farther up into the mountains, the fear of failing was always close by.

He hadn't even started playing yet. Not really. Guruji had given him a small bamboo flute and told him to play whatever he wanted, as much as he wanted, outside lessons. During lesson time they would concentrate on "building strength and mental stamina" instead. "I can't see what you are made of when you can't even hold your breath long enough to make a decent sound," said Guruji.

Kalu bent his head and started to write again. The promise he had made to do as he was told lay heavy on his shoulders. The longer Kalu stayed, the more he wanted to prove he was good enough to stay.

He looked down at his finished letter. Two pages of writing on crisp white paper ruled with thin blue lines. He could imagine Ganga Ba reading it to everyone—or maybe it would be Malti now. Ganga Ba had told him she was learning to read, too.

He fought a sigh. Sometimes he could almost smell Hastinapore. The acrid bite of diesel from the trucks, the smoke from corn roasting on street corners. The high-pitched chatter of women going to the shop or the temple. The truck drivers at the chai-waala's, even the men arguing outside the paan-biddi shop as he tried to sleep in the passage behind it.

He often went to sleep with a small twist in his stomach that told him he would have to leave within the year. Regardless of the months he spent practicing, the sounds in his head would always be better than the ones that he sang or tried to play. Maybe the ache in his hands from holding the flute, and trying to close the holes with fingers still too small, was a sign that he didn't have what Guruji was looking for.

On such nights, Kalu would retreat to the veranda and stare at the stars, as if Dhruv-taara could banish the ache. He almost wished for his recurring nightmare to return; it would at least force the doubt from his mind with its violence.

He never spoke about these thoughts. As if letting them loose would somehow give them unnecessary power. Besides, when Guruji played for him, everything else thinned to vapor and he knew he needed to stay here as much as he needed to breathe.

~

Ganga Ba opened the letter, pleased as always that her daughter still thought to send them. She squinted in an effort to decode the writing. This way of reading had become such a habit she no longer wondered if the writing had become smaller or her eyes had become worse.

Her daughter always wrote on aerograms. Blue paper, folded to make six sections. Three outside, three inside. The front was marked in strong black print: "To: Mrs. Ganga Ben V. Patel." She always read this section twice, forgetting between each letter she had once been a "Mrs." V.P.'s death and her transition from wife to widow seemed to have taken place in another lifetime. Jyoti's address—41 Rutherglen Road, New Jersey—was on the back.

Jyoti filled two sections with news from America: her latest purchase, her other Indian-American friends, frozen chapattis purchased from the supermarket, and, of course, how well the children were doing at school. The children wrote in the last two sections of each letter. Both used large letters and colored ink, purple for Rohan, green for Pinky. They wrote in English on wide lines drawn in pencil by Jyoti, who also translated the text into Gujarati.

Although she would never admit to it, Ganga Ba was secretly ashamed and rather frustrated that her grandchildren could not speak her language. Their language, too. On visits and on the telephone, conversation with them was limited to "You okay, Nani?" on their side, and "All good" on hers. While they could speak a few words, enough to get Bhraamanji to make them their favorite dishes, so much was lost to them.

Jyoti and her husband, Sanjay, couldn't see this. Jyoti, in her salvar kameez, bought specially for the trip, and Sanjay, in his American trousers, would watch proudly as the children were forced to stand in the middle of the room and "recite to Nani."

"Look, they know the Aarti by heart. Say it, children . . ." And Rohan and Pinky would sing. In tune, but with accents so white they might as well have been speaking another language. Aarti indeed! As if Ganga Ba were a village traditionalist intent on prayer and not much else. Maybe that was what old Indian women were like in America, but not here.

It was the realization of this, the distance between her world and her views on what should and shouldn't happen and that of her grandchildren—emphasized by the penciled lines, the foreign letters, and the translation—that stopped Ganga Ba from making the journey to live with her daughter. In each letter, her daughter wrote as if Ganga Ba would soon arrive for an extended visit. The implicit expectation being that the holiday would become permanent, satisfying her daughter's need to be seen as looking after her mother—whether her mother wanted it or not. Ganga Ba knew she was being a little harsh on Jyoti, but what would she do in America, in this New Jersey, where everyone worked throughout the day?

In Hastinapore she could eat what she wanted, wear what she wanted, and choose to do as she pleased throughout the day. And besides, she knew what they all got up to in that country full of foreigners. And she knew that place would diminish her even more than living with her in-laws had. In

America she would be forced, even in an Indian family, to live by American rules, where old people were put away in homes, or in dark corners, and brought out for show.

Ganga Ba had traveled both before and after Jyoti's marriage. When Ganga Ba was young and newly married, V.P. had taken her on a trip to Europe. She'd first seen snow in Switzerland and looked for vegetarian food in the middle of Paris.

V.P. spoke fluent English and a little French. From the time they met, Ganga Ba had called her husband V.P., as did everyone else. He had taught her some English. She learned the language, enough to understand the intent if not the nuance, but she didn't feel comfortable speaking anything but Gujarati.

When it was time for Jyoti to marry, Ganga Ba was prepared for her daughter to leave home and the village. After all, that was what had happened to her; it happened to all women. Getting a boy from America was an added bonus, and Sanjay was well qualified—an engineer, as V.P. had been. Ganga Ba hadn't, however, counted on such a complete separation. Not just from her daughter but from her grandchildren. While their trips to India were enjoyable, each time the family arrived, Ganga Ba found her daughter a little more removed, belonging more to her new life than her childhood. And this was only right. The minute a girl thought more of her parents than her married life, trouble would follow, as sure as heated butter turned into ghee.

Ganga Ba folded the letter back into thirds, then opened her writing desk, by the window in her room, and placed the aerogram with the others from Jyoti, all blue, all slightly crushed around the edges by the red rubber band that held them. She replaced the bundle of letters, wedging them in beside those from Kalu.

It was funny, Ganga Ba mused, how she obtained so much more entertainment from Kalu's letters, always full of life and spirit, than she did from those of her own family.

When Jyoti first left home, V.P. used to tell Ganga Ba that the distance would make the heart grow fonder, but she now knew that some things were lost in the translation from one country to another.

8

KALU HAD SETTLED into his life at Guruji's. Like new clothes, everything had been a little odd at first; an unfamiliar texture, a little itchy around the collar. But as the weeks turned into months, some differences became barely noticeable, while others remained.

For the first few months, Kalu slept on the ground on the veranda, returning to his bed in the morning. Sleeping in a room all night, every night, was difficult. Kalu couldn't see the stars and there were no sounds. It was too quiet and empty and the bed too soft. Even when Kalu stayed at Ganga Ba's, he'd slept on a mat outside where he could hear the horns or the rasp of wheels on the street.

Now Kalu's body hurt in a different way from when he was earning a living on the street. His thighs ached from sitting. His eyes were tired from trying to make sense of words rather than people. Guruji made him read all sorts of books. At the moment, they were making their way through a book on plants. When Kalu read that the roots of a tree made up a full one-third of the plant, unseen yet supporting everything above, he'd been amazed and annoyed. Until then, he'd thought that books told the truth. He was angry enough to march outside, stopping in the kitchen for a fork, to find the smallest tree to dig up, intent on proving the book wrong.

Ashwin was not amused. "Aré, baba, you'll be the death of me and this garden."

Even the mynahs squawked at him, like old women catching a child stealing buttermilk, although Kalu felt they were far more interested in the sound of Ashwin scolding him than the fate of the tree.

Guruji, hearing the ruckus, emerged through the large windows in the book room and chuckled, fine lines filling his face. "Let him be, Ashwin. It's good to have an inquiring mind." He turned to Kalu. "If you want to do the thing, boy, do it properly. Get a measuring tape from the cupboard and ask Ashwin for a spade. You'll still need the fork for the final stages, especially if you intend to tease the roots out to get a true indication of the length. And, Ashwin, bring some water. We'll need to keep everything wet. That way we can replant when we are through."

"No harm done? No harm done? My poor fork. My poor garden. These musicians. All the same. Paagal. You hear? Paagal. Crazy."

Kalu untangled and desoiled the roots until there was more mud on his hands than on the fragile tendrils that fanned out from the taproot like hair on a windy day. The book was right. The roots measured eighty-six centimeters: exactly a third of the tree.

By the end of the process of unraveling and then replanting, Kalu grinned. "At least I know it was true."

As muddy by now as Kalu, Guruji laughed. It was the first time Kalu had heard that deep, joyous sound. He looked up and realized in that instant that this man, his teacher, was the person he wanted most to be like in the whole world. Kalu took a deep breath. The thought didn't bring him much pleasure. An orphan like him could never be like Guruji.

"Now that was an adventure!" Guruji, oblivious to Kalu's change in mood, clapped his hands, sending molecules of dirt on an adventure of their own. "Who would have thought that today would result in an excavation, together with a hypothesis proven?"

Kalu noted to himself the words Guruji used so he could look them up later.

"You know, Kalu, there is a saying: 'What lies underneath and is hidden is often most sustaining.'"

"Sustaining?"

"Nourishing, the thing that keeps you strong."

"And what sustains *you*?" Kalu asked before thinking. He looked up quickly to see if Guruji's eyes flashed in anger.

But Guruji wasn't angry. "The sound of two perfect notes. First one, then a pause long enough to make you feel nothing else exists, before the other. The laughter of one who knows you better than you know yourself and . . ." Guruji's eyes refocused as Ashwin returned, still muttering, with a tray containing tea and some sweet biscuits. The musician finished lightly, "And trying to teach you, my rascal." Guruji stared at Kalu as if seeing him for the very first time. "Enough. Let us get some water running and remove this mud before reviving ourselves with Ashwin's excellent tea."

~

Malti saw Bal one drowsy morning walking on the path to the river. Although they'd never spoken, she recognized him as Kalu's friend. Kalu still spoke about Bal in his letters. She heard the unspoken request in them and knew Kalu would have liked some news. But until this moment, she'd told herself it was too difficult to meet Bal. His life was far removed from Malti's. While Ganga Ba lived high above the riverbanks on one side of Hastinapore, Bal lived on the far side, closer to the fields. The only place Malti and Bal had in common was the river, and for the most part they were there at different times.

She hesitated, slowing down to remain a few meters behind him. The boy was her height and probably the same age. His clothes were torn and his feet were bare. If the other girls by the river saw her, they'd tease her mercilessly for speaking to a laborer. Besides, if she continued to walk slowly, he wouldn't notice she was there at all.

Bal half turned to force a calf back into line. Malti looked around for somewhere to hide. Then stopped herself. How silly. This boy was a friend of Kalu's.

She straightened her shoulders and called after him, "Bal? You are Kalu's friend Bal, aren't you?" Her voice rose at the end.

The boy stopped. She saw by his stance, head down and shoulders stooped, that he was unsure of why she had called him.

"You're Kalu's friend Bal, aren't you?" she repeated. "He asks about you every time he writes."

"Kalu can write?" Bal's eyes seemed to fill his face, and Malti saw the hunger in them for news about his friend. No doubt he missed Kalu as much as she did.

"Can the buffaloes wait? Why don't I tell you what else the rascal has been up to since he left."

Bal smiled and Malti couldn't help but smile back at the joy reflected in his face. She sat on a rock by the side of the road. Bal sat on the ground and listened as Malti spoke about Kalu and his new life in the mountains.

When she'd finished she smiled at Bal. "Now tell me about yourself, Bal. I know that Kalu would be interested."

Bal looked down. "There's nothing to tell. My life is the same. Tell him . . . tell him I'm proud of him."

Malti looked away and brushed a sudden tear from her eye. "I'll tell him," she promised. "And I'll send someone to the farm when his letters arrive. That way you can come up to the house to hear them."

"Please," said Bal, hesitating for a beat. "Please can you just tell them to give me the news? I don't have permission . . ."

Malti blushed. "Of course."

Bal rose. He began to hold out his hand, only to quickly retract it before Malti could respond. "Thank you. Thank you for stopping." The boy turned toward the lead buffalo, grazing by the path, and tapped him on the back. "Come on, you lazy thing, to the river with you."

~

When Kalu heard the car coming up the driveway, he turned toward the gate. He'd missed Vaid Dada and was a little surprised that no one had let him know the vaid was returning. He reached the gate just as the car drove through, and realized the man and woman in the back of the car were completely foreign to him. Kalu turned and ran through the garden, up toward the mountain, before turning to face the house. There, wedged between two rocks, he watched as the driver stepped out, closed the gates, and opened the car door for his passengers: a round woman dressed in a green sari and a man with crumpled trousers and a wide, red turban. The car stayed there all afternoon. Kalu remained where he was. Waiting and watching.

Later, Ashwin explained, "People come from everywhere to visit Guruji. Old waalas, new waalas, you name it. They all want to touch his genius."

Kalu could tell that Ashwin was tired. After watching the older man clean the same plate three times, Kalu took it quietly from his hands. Ashwin then moved to the stove, turning a chapatti.

"Can you really touch it?"

"What?"

"His genius."

"Well, you and I, baba, know he's really just a cranky old man, but these fools think just because he stays here, away from the big city, he's some kind of god. They all want to be the person who will convince him to leave this valley and return to civilization." Ashwin placed the chapatti in a container with others. "Civilization, bivilization. You ask me, this place is much better than any other."

"Doesn't he ever leave?" Kalu eyed the chapattis as he spoke. In all the drama, he'd missed lunch.

"Never. And keep your hands away from my chapattis unless you want to feel my velen on your backside. And"—Ashwin waved the rolling pin as he spoke—"next time, I want to see you here, front and center. No more hiding in the mountains for you, baba. You are part of this family, and if Guruji and I have to put up with these bafoodhya, then so do you."

~

Guruji rolled the flute on the tips of his fingers in just the way the paan-waala used to roll his beedi, getting the same intense satisfaction from the action as the paan-waala did.

"Most flutes are lighter, made of bamboo. But this flute of yours is rosewood. Not exactly rare, but richer in tone. You won't need to oil it as much." Guruji held the instrument out between his fingers. "Now take a good look at your flute. Deceptively simple, isn't it?"

Kalu took the flute from Guruji and held it, using his fingertips to balance the long, hollow piece of wood punctured with holes—one near the top to blow into, and then two sets of three, followed by one lower down on the side.

"There are many types of flutes. Some have a lip at the top like a whistle, while others, like this side flute, only have a hole that you blow through. This makes it harder but also gives you more control and modulation range. The European flute is metal and has levers and keys. They can play more notes, but"—Guruji pointed his finger at the ceiling, then brought it down in a soft, floating, featherlike gesture—"they are one step away from the hole, and therefore the sound. The closer you are to the sound, the more chance it has of coming from the soul."

Guruji turned and placed a record on the player. "Your flute is long, like those Pannalal Ghosh played. This is one of the few recordings of his. Listen . . . an amazing flautist, with the strength to hold the longest of flutes and keep playing for hours. No one could match his skill. Can you hear the depth of sound? Strong yet delicate—like the silk from a silkworm. You know he was a boxer as well as a flautist?"

"Will I have to learn to box?" Nothing would have surprised Kalu at this point.

"No, but you will practice your yoga aasanas and you will dedicate yourself to the flute."

"When will I be able to play my flute?"

"When you can open your hand as wide as a lotus on its fourth day."

"But the lotus isn't even in flower yet!"

"Ever the literalist. Give it time, Kalu."

Kalu bit his lip to stop the protest that he knew Guruji was expecting from him. His teacher knew how frustrated he was. How much he wanted to try his flute. He wished he had at least tried it back at Ganga Ba's place when he had the opportunity.

Guruji watched Kalu's emotions play across his face, then nodded. "You can't play this flute until you can stretch your fingers out to cover the holes perfectly. Until then you'll continue to work on the smaller flute. Why waste my time and yours on an instrument your body is unready for?"

Kalu stroked the flute, tracking the deep, rich grain with his finger.

"You know, when Pannalal first started playing, he was well known as a drunkard and a flirt, until the night when a woman's husband came home too early. Pannalal didn't want to be caught in her room, so he jumped out the window, grabbed a rope, and slid to the ground. It was only when he reached the bottom that he realized the rope was actually a snake. That was the last time he fooled around or got drunk. It was, in fact, the last time he put others before his flute and his music.

"The humble flute used to be a folk instrument rather than a serious classical instrument, until Pannalal put his weight behind it. That was when the music world started to take the instrument seriously."

"Like you, Guruji. You put everything into your music."

Guruji frowned. "No, not at all like me. I wanted it all. I can teach you the theory to match your innate knowledge, Kalu. I can tell you to work all day. But I can't tell you what you will have to give up to play. But you will have to give up something. Everything in life has a price."

"I will remember," said the boy. Guruji captured Kalu's hand and turned the palm upward. "Your hands may not be as large as Pannalal's yet, but these fingers will be the making of your music."

Later, as Kalu sat on the rocks above the house, stretching his fingers and flexing them back until they shook, he recalled the rest of the lesson, in which Guruji taught him the mechanics of changing notes from flat to sharp by moving his fingers over the holes on the flute.

"It's called meend," Guruji had said. "Now watch." He took Kalu's flute and played a note, a clean, deep note. Then he moved the very tip of each finger until he had every sound between one note and the next. A smooth glide between the notes trailed in the air.

Now Kalu took a deep breath and rested his trembling hands for a moment before starting his stretching exercises again.

~

The first time Kalu spontaneously grabbed Ashwin, the man jumped. Ashwin had played up his fear, pretending to scold the boy before feeding him sweets and surreptitiously wiping "some onion" from his eyes.

It had been eight months since Kalu's arrival in the mountains, and the stiffness in his spine had slowly loosened, melting little by little. He became more used to physical contact with others, and he laughed instead of flinching when Ashwin tickled him under the chin.

Ashwin made a point of touching the boy as much as possible. Like the vaid, he realized that the child needed to heal in more ways than one. Guruji worked on the boy's brain and physical strength, but Ashwin knew it would take more time for the boy's eyes to lose their hollow look.

There were still times when Ashwin would see Kalu consciously stop himself from stepping away when someone came too close. But those times occurred less and less often, and the sound of music was now mixed with the sound of laughter.

Ashwin smiled. Although Kalu didn't realize it, he had brought life back into the house.

~

Every morning, girls walked down to the river with the washing. They stood tall, balancing flat cane baskets on their heads. Each basket was piled with clothing from their families or the households they worked in. Other girls worked as sub-contractors to the dhobhi-waala who collected dirty clothes from people in Hastinapore and the outlying district. Their baskets looked the same, but their diligence was greater, as everyone knew the dhobhi-waala docked your pay if he found even the smallest mark.

Reaching the point where the river met the town, they hitched their skirts up, high enough to stop them from filling with water but not so high as to be unseemly. Then, bracing themselves in the flowing current, they scrubbed each garment on wide, flat rocks rising out of the water like tiny islands. Some of the girls then laid the clothing on the banks to dry, creating a patchwork landscape over rocks and soil—a sari the color of sunset next to a shirt of holy yellow.

As she concentrated on the conversation around her, Malti squeezed a tablecloth tightly, half watching the water, now stained as red as pomegranate seeds by the material, seeping through her hands. Soon she would take her bundle back to Ganga Ba's to dry. In comparison to the others', her pile of washing was small. She didn't have to worry about cleaning fancy clothing; Ganga Ba had her good saris dry-cleaned in Vadodara.

Her load consisted of Ganga Ba's everyday cotton saris, bedspreads, tablecloths, and a mix of clothing from the other live-in members of the household. Still, eager for company and the latest news, Malti took her time washing the clothes. Stories flowed through the rhythmic beating of cloth. The girls spoke about new city fashions, film-industry gossip— including which girl was the better dancer and who she loved this week—or local gossip, such as whose cow generated the most milk and who was stealing it.

Today Devyani was the focus. A tall, clove-colored girl, Devyani had just been matched to a boy from a nearby village. She had been secretly worried that with her dark complexion, it would be difficult to find a groom, and now her excitement bubbled out. As she spoke she waved the blue cotton shirt she was meant to be washing in the air rather than in the water. Her man was tall, his family lovely; her mother-in-law had already told her there was no need for her to work at all now that she would be part of their family.

"Just think! I'll be a woman of leisure. Just like that witch Kanta Ben, who I work for. No more clothes washing for me!"

The others laughed, none of them begrudging Devyani her good luck. Malti liked Devyani. When Malti had first arrived in Hastinapore, she had been lonely, and Devyani made her feel welcome. She was funny, honest, and always friendly. She had shown Malti how to scrub material on the stones without tearing it and had helped her to find a free surface to claim as her own.

Everything had seemed to Malti so frightening then. Hastinapore was much bigger than her little village, and she missed her family. The other servants at Ganga Ba's were much older, and it was only because of Devyani's friendship that she came to meet girls her own age.

"And what about you, Malti? When will it be your turn? I've seen the way the paan-waala's son looks at you as you walk by. I'm sure it'll be your turn soon, yaar. Or have you already been contracted?" said Devyani.

A few of the girls had been married as children but remained with their families until they reached puberty. Their families had chosen the security of marriage and a dowry when they could afford it rather than waiting until their daughters were older.

"No, no man for me yet. My parents will wait until Raja, my brother, has finished school." Malti raised her face, taking quiet pride in her brother's progress. "He won a college scholarship, which means more study, but then he's going to be an office worker. Maybe even work for the government."

Kavita, standing on the other side of Malti, spoke up. "Hmm, leave him for me, then. It would be nice to have a salary man. None of these layabouts for me." She waved her hand up toward Kalu's banyan tree where the girls knew that at any given time at least three men would be playing cards and smoking in the shade.

Malti laughed as she wrung the final drops of water out of the clothes. She twisted them into thick ropes before placing them, and her soap, in the basket. She balanced the load on her head, waved to her friends, and walked upstream toward Ganga Ba's place. She followed the river until the bank gradually curved up toward a steep rise. It was quieter here and the sun gently dried the water from her clothes and her neck.

On impulse, Malti found a place to sit, watching the river sparkle as it flowed around the bend toward her friends. This was the same spot she'd come to with Kalu the day he cleaned the dirt from his flute. She still missed Kalu, more than she'd thought she would—at least as much as she used to miss Raja. She didn't realize how popular Kalu was, either, until he left. Everyone knew he kept in contact with Ganga Ba, so people often asked Malti about him when she went out.

"How is that rascal Kalu?" the lady serving at the sweetshop had asked her just yesterday. The lady didn't know any-thing about Malti other than that she worked for Ganga Ba, but she knew all about Kalu.

Kalu made Malti feel more than herself. When she was with him, she knew she had his total attention, and he was interested in what she had to say—not what she could do for him. She wondered how he would treat her now that he was no longer Kalu the street boy. It would be different when he returned. If he returned.

It had been almost a year now, and she hoped he'd come back to visit. Her own first trip home had been the hardest. She had been so excited. She'd changed and she'd expected everything at home to have remained the same, but her parents both had new lines on their faces and many of her friends had gone. The village itself looked so small, and far poorer than she'd remembered.

She'd seen changes in Raja, too. When she left home, he had seemed more boy than man. Since then he, too, had left to study. Now his voice had become deeper, heavier.

Malti remembered being with her brother when she was small. He'd throw her in the air, up high toward the sky, and she thought if she was lucky and he released her at just the right moment she'd be able to fly. Being a bird would be wonderful. Not a noisy parrot—loud, colorful, and raucous; Malti preferred kites. Smaller than the eagle or hawk, they were brown, neat, and, best of all, graceful. They seemed to float rather than fly through the sky, and they were nearly always in pairs. Malti had heard that kites mated for life.

Maybe she would never fly, but someday, Malti knew, she would have a mate for life. In the past year she'd felt her body changing: her breasts had grown larger and her hips a little wider. The last time she'd gone home, her mother had told her to make sure she was covered modestly at all times and had warned her about men, not pausing for breath before launching into discussions about marriage.

"Just make sure you stay at Ganga Ba's, and take care; no one wants a spoiled girl. Although where we'll get a dowry from, I don't know. Still, once Raja starts working . . ."

Malti knew there was time. At some stage her father would arrange her marriage, though not for a while yet. Raja had four years of studying to go.

9

"GURUJI!" KALU CALLED as he ran into the house, grabbing the door frame of the book room with one hand as he pivoted on his good ankle and swung into the room, only to falter and stop so abruptly he landed on the floor, spread out flat like a chapatti.

"And this is my student, Kalu. You'd think if I was to pick just one apprentice, I'd pick one with more decorum." Guruji directed his comments to the man seated on a chair opposite. A man so tall his legs were crammed under the chair. A white man.

The white man's lips twitched. "Martin. My name's Martin." He held out his hand. The gesture turned into a half wave as Kalu sidled away to stand beside Guruji's chair, hands tight by his sides.

Later, Kalu couldn't remember what the weather had been like that day, or why he had run into the house calling so loudly for Guruji. What he did recall was the way he'd sheltered behind his teacher, tracing the network of scars on his ankle with his toe.

It was the first time Kalu had seen a real, live white man up close. Tourists didn't normally make their way to Hastinapore or to the village at the bottom of the hill. There wasn't anything for a gora to see in those places. This man had yellow hair and skin the color of cheesecloth, with pink patches over his nose. He wasn't white the way Kalu was brown. He should have been called multicolored, really.

Guruji told Kalu that Martin was a musician who had been told to visit Guruji by a mutual friend. "Kalu, come away from the back of me. Sit properly. Give Martin the respect he deserves. He's an excellent musician. Started as a child prodigy."

Kalu sat in a chair and looked more carefully at the foreigner. This man was apparently a musician, but the awkward way he sat made Kalu rather skeptical. He didn't look as if he'd be able to sit cross-legged long enough to play anything.

Guruji said the spirit behind the music mattered more than the notes. A truly great musician would let this spirit, the Divine, speak through him. This man didn't look the sort. He was too eager, smiling far more than needed and speaking with a quick rhythm that Kalu found hard to follow. He used English with a scattering of barely recognizable Hindi, waving his arms until he seemed to fill the room. Even Guruji was dwarfed by this "Mati" fellow.

Kalu edged his way to the corner of the chair, torn between wanting to talk about the stranger with Ashwin and wanting to stay in the room to see what happened next.

Then Martin, at Guruji's request, picked up his violin, tightened the knobs on the instrument's neck, and started to play a "tune from back home." In time Kalu heard Martin play everything from Bach to Prokofiev, Bhairav to Bihaag. That day, Martin played a simple folk tune. It tipped this way, then that, like the roll of the ocean, a cry for home, the yearning for a loved one and for the river where it met the sea. The smell and sting of salt.

Kalu didn't realize at first that he'd bitten his lip or that he'd moved during the playing to stand directly in front of Martin. With the final notes of the tune still echoing through the room, Kalu placed a finger on the still-warm bow and felt the taut hairs that had vibrated so sweetly rest against his skin. It took him a moment to come back from the music, to the conversation between the man and Guruji.

"Why? Why do you want to learn?" Guruji asked Martin. "And what do you want to learn? There are classical Indian music teachers around the world. You are a busy musician in your own right and could be taught by the best of them. Why here?"

"Look, I was never interested in Eastern music as a child, or even as I started to perform professionally. I thought it was old hat—something of a fad left over from the sixties—until the night I saw Ravi Shankar play in New York.

"The concert was at the Cathedral of Saint John the Divine. It started at dusk and was to finish at dawn. It was a cold, gray day, with the sheen of rain. I remember feeling as dark as the mist." Martin looked up at Guruji. "The demons had visited that week. I only went to the concert because the tickets were complimentary and I wanted to see my agent, who I knew would be there.

"Only then Ravi Shankar started to play. There was something in his music that called to me. That stood with me in the darkness and gave me the courage to face my demons. I don't know what he played that night, but it was as if the five thousand other people in the space had vanished so there was only me and the sitar, the beat of drums, and the drone of the taanpura grounding the music. Grounding me.

"And in the last fifteen minutes, just as dawn broke, the rain stopped and light from the morning sun shone through the stained glass onto Shankar's face and into my soul."

Martin looked at Guruji and Kalu. "I know it sounds stupid, but there you are. There are other teachers in other countries, but you were recommended to me by my teacher."

"There is a saying in Sanskrit: Ranjayati iti Raaga," said Guruji. "It means, 'that which colors the mind is a raag.' Each and every raag is structured differently and represents specific human emotions and characteristics. However, for a raag to truly color the mind of the listener, the effect cannot be created from just technical virtuosity. The musician needs to take his audience on a journey to the very root of all things, to reach for the nectar of creation. Only a master musician trained in the oral tradition can take you there.

"What you have described to me, and what you seem to want, takes time and patience. Something I think you may not have."

Kalu waited to see what Martin would say. If Martin decided to stay and learn, Kalu was sure he would have to leave. There wouldn't be enough room for the two of them. Being evicted would be much harder to bear now than when he first met Guruji. Then, he had no idea what was at stake. Not really. Now Kalu didn't just want to play; he wanted to play well. Music, and the thought of playing well enough for Guruji, consumed him. This man with the honeyed voice and magic touch already played that way.

Martin cleared his throat. His hair looked damp, as if he'd bathed in the river. "I don't want to be a master musician in the Indian tradition, nor do I just want to learn the notes. This music has been haunting me. I want the time and space to bring some of your music into mine—if that makes sense. And I need to do it here in India. Where no one has heard of me—and where no one can access me."

Guruji raised an eyebrow. "We do have telephones here in the backwater."

"Yes—but my agent doesn't know that." Martin flashed a warm smile before leaning forward. "Look, I made inquiries. I also learned that the word 'guru' means 'dispeller of darkness.' My teacher remembers you. He says that there are many great musicians but fewer great teachers. He only met you the once but felt that you would understand and teach me in a way nobody else could. I need that."

As Martin finished, Kalu held his breath, wanting to say, "But he doesn't take pupils—except me."

Finally, Guruji replied, "Very well. I'll take you on. You can come for a few months every year, until this hunger of yours is satisfied. But"—Guruji became more serious, ignoring Kalu's little intake of breath—"there is a question of reciprocity. As I teach you our traditions, I want you to teach Kalu some of yours. I'd like him to be able to read, write, and play music the Western way. Not so that he becomes a Western musician but—and I mean this, Kalu—so he understands your world as you learn his."

Martin shook Guruji's hand. "Deal. I've got some sheet music here with me. You tell me how much and when, and I'll teach Kalu. Okay with you, Kalu, my man? We'll learn together."

So one apprentice wouldn't replace the other. And if Guruji wanted Kalu to learn with Martin, maybe that meant he would keep him after his trial time was up. Only a few weeks remained until Guruji would tell him whether or not he was to stay. Kalu held the chair tightly, worried that his legs, which felt as if they'd turned to liquid, would betray him. Learning to play like Martin, thought Kalu, could never be a bad thing. But from what Martin said, it meant learning a different language. And already he'd learned so much. All he had to do was keep up. Keep working so he could stay. He felt tired already.

Martin tugged at his pants before sitting gingerly on the thin reed mat, across from Kalu. The boy watched carefully. He smiled as Martin moved this way and that in an effort to find a comfortable spot. It had been the same all week.

"Kalu, although this is for Martin, you'll benefit, too, so pay attention. Martin needs to understand the difference between Western music and Indian music, and I think you'll be interested in hearing the theoretical perspective from another angle."

Kalu hoped Martin understood what Guruji meant better than he did. They were using the main divan room rather than the music area, where Kalu normally had his lessons. This room was larger, so the three of them could sit on the floor with their instruments around them. It was a little darker here than in the book room. Bougainvillea curled around the posts of the veranda on this side of the house, forming a canopy that kept the room cool and dim. The blue walls reminded Kalu of a clean, clear pool. Guruji cleared his throat.

"Martin, it's probably easier to start with the notes themselves rather than the raag. Once you understand the meaning of each note, we will go on to the combinations by which they make up each raag. Tell me what you know already."

Martin shrugged, the movement involving his whole body. "Not too much, I'm afraid. I know the Indian octave is called the samtak, which means . . . 'seven notes'?"

"That is close. You have the meaning correct, but not the word. Saptak." Guruji spelled the word in English for Martin, telling Kalu to write the word in both Hindi and English.

Kalu grimaced; writing in two languages wasn't his preferred option. He remained silent, however, interested in where Guruji was going to take this lesson with Martin and whether Martin's bottom could take sitting on the floor. He'd noticed the man shifting his weight ever so slightly from one side to the other, just as Kalu used to in the early days.

"The octave can be divided into sixty-six shrutis, although in practice most musicians work with twenty-two. The shrutis are modifications of the seven svars that form the scale identical with the European diatonic major scale. We call this Raag Bilaval." Now Guruji picked up the sarod, holding the instrument across his body. "I could show you on the flute, but with the sarod, I can talk and play. Here is the svar, *sa*, and now the shrutis around *sa*; they range from flat to very flat, and sharp to very sharp. Now you try."

Martin had already reached for his bow and the violin. He found the note and then played the notes around it, adjusting the sound to match the sarod.

"How can you tell it's what you want? Do you have a formula for the difference between sharp and very sharp?" Martin continued to play the notes, speaking as he held the violin in place with his chin.

"Ear and training," replied Guruji. "Our tradition is both oral and aural. And you need to sing." Seeing Martin grimace, he continued, "Don't worry, I'm not going to have you sing. You already have a well-developed ear."

"What about—," Kalu started.

"No." Guruji didn't even let him finish the sentence. "If you could play like Martin and had played for the past fifteen years like him, it would be different."

Kalu grinned; it was always worth asking.

"Although we write down notes, you need to be able to play instinctively, to create within the constraints of the raag . . . but I'll get to that another time. Let's just stick to the notes for now."

Martin placed the violin beside him, using the movement to free his legs before recrossing them. "So, do you have a base scale?"

"Not exactly. Our notes are named in a similar way to your do, re, mi. We have shadj (*sa*), rishabh (*ré*), gandaar (*ga*), madhyam (*ma*), pancham (*pa*), dhaivat (*dha*), and nishad (*ni*). Each note comes from a different part of the body. Kalu, sing the notes, and put your belly into it."

Kalu was prepared; he'd guessed the singing parts would come down to him.

"See how the sounds start deep and then move through?" Guruji nodded in approval as Kalu faded to silence.

"And is *sa* your tonic?" asked Martin.

"Our music doesn't have the same sense of key. There is no harmony, or even formalized melody, in Indian classical music. Not the way it exists in classical Western music or in the a cappella traditions of Africa. Each note, or *svar*, is felt to have an individual quality that is heard in relation to sa. Here is the first note, *sa*, and *ma*, the fourth." Guruji played the notes, nodding to Martin and Kalu, indicating they should follow him on their respective instruments.

"*Sa* and *ma* together represent tranquillity. *Ré* indicates sharp, harsh feelings; *ga* and *dha* are a little serious. *Pa* is joy, and *ni* sorrow."

Guruji placed the sarod on the floor in front of him. The instrument, with the gourds on either side, looked balanced, like a table between students and teacher. Guruji continued, "The notes have also been likened to the sounds of animals. Kalu, can you remember these? What is *ré*?"

"The mooing of a cow." Kalu mooed.

"*Ni*?"

"The trumpeting of an elephant."

"That's good, boy." Guruji turned to Martin. "The thing

you have to remember is that this music is about the heart and its connection to Mother India and to the Divine. Unlike jazz, which was formed out of rebellion—the need for the spirit to rise against the status quo—the raags are a part of our tradition and our heritage. These differences are sometimes more important than the theoretical context. Now, let's play some real music. You'll notice layers within layers in our music, Martin—and don't fidget so much. You're as bad as Kalu used to be. Kalu, fetch him a stool and a pillow or two."

"Maybe three," called Martin, unable to rise to help carry in the cushions.

Kalu and Martin sat in the back of the Jeep as Ashwin drove down the hill.

"Is this always what happens when you ask a question?" said Martin.

That morning at breakfast, Martin had asked Guruji, "So, what makes a raag—is it a key or a melody?" Ashwin had groaned and risen from the table.

Kalu could tell from the frown between Guruji's eyebrows that Martin's question wasn't an easy one to answer. Martin seemed to enjoy learning about music backward, always asking about what things were not, or what things were like, rather than simply asking for a direct explanation.

"Not quite." Guruji paused. Unlike Ganga Ba, who had a reply for everything, Guruji, like his brother, always took his time, providing an answer that would best suit the listener rather than the speaker. "A raag is a framework. An ideology first and music second. Without spirit a raag is nothing. Rather than lecturing to you, let me set you both a task. An easy one at that."

Like Ashwin before him, Kalu rose; nothing was ever simple where Guruji was concerned.

Within half an hour, both Martin and Kalu were being driven by Ashwin, to be let out of the car at Tanakpur, a town one hour away. They had been provided with the ascending and descending notes of Raag Desh and, in Guruji's words, had one day to find the raag. Guruji didn't join them on their excursion. As Ashwin explained to Martin, while Guruji was happy to receive visitors, he never, under any circumstance, left the house.

"Why?" asked Martin.

Kalu had hoped the answer would be different this time, but Ashwin's response was the same as ever. "You'll have to ask Guruji."

"So how many raags are there?" Martin asked as the Jeep flew down past the village at the bottom of the hill.

"Hundreds," replied Kalu, speaking by rote. "And more are developed every year. Guruji says each raag has a particular time and place. Some raags are affectionate and should only be played in the mornings. Others are night raags. But we practice everything all day long."

"My teacher used to do the same," said Martin. "'Practice makes perfect,' he'd say whenever I wanted to be out in the sunshine with my friends."

Kalu shook his head and smiled, unwilling to let Martin know he had only a limited amount of time to prove he was worth the effort. A few more days and the final month would be up. He had marked the days on the calendar Ashwin had given him. It was from Motilal's Sari Emporium. Kalu had asked Ashwin what he had been doing in a women's shop. "Where else do you find women?" Ashwin had replied. The red-marked day that his probation would be over was fast approaching.

Kalu unconsciously moved his hands on an invisible rosewood flute. Most of the time he let the music, the sheer happiness of learning, carry him, but other days he had to work harder. It felt like walking into a strong wind where the only way forward was to close your eyes and push against an unseen force. He'd never imagined doing something he loved would be this difficult.

"What do you do when you aren't playing or studying? Have you been to this town we're heading to before?"

Kalu looked across at Martin. "Ashwin has taken me with him once or twice when he buys rations. Otherwise I like to walk into the mountains or watch the children in the little village down the road from the house."

"Your friends?"

"My friends are in Hastinapore." Kalu didn't mention the one time the village boys had seen him. Their taunts had hurt him more than he realized at the time. Not everyone in Hastinapore had liked him, either, and when his foot festered, not many people would associate with him. But no one there had jeered at him for no reason at all, as the village boys had. He'd run back up the hill to the house and didn't return to the mango tree for a long time. He told himself it was because there was no time.

"Yes, but all work and no play . . . you know."

"No." Shadows danced across Kalu's face as they drove.

"Look, Kalu, you need to do more than study. And just because Guruji is a recluse, it doesn't mean you have to be."

"Why? Why must I? I used to do more before. I had to make friends to live. I don't need to anymore. I know enough people. I have enough friends, and they'll be with me forever."

"Life isn't like that. Things change," Martin said quietly.

"But people don't. People stay the same."

He didn't hear Martin sigh. The Jeep swung out to avoid a cyclist balancing a load of iron rods. "People change most of all, Kalu, and even when they don't, you'll find that you do. You haven't seen your old friends for a long time. Think about how much you have changed and grown in all this time. How can you expect things to stay still?"

Kalu sat ramrod straight, concentrating on the task ahead of him rather than on Martin's words. He didn't know how he was going to find a raag in the middle of a town. This was his final chance to show Guruji what he had learned.

At last Ashwin stopped the Jeep by a busy crossroad. Ashwin handed Martin his violin case while Kalu removed a single flute from the box by his seat. Then, after telling Kalu and Martin to return to the same spot before four o'clock, Ashwin made his way on foot to the bazaar, weaving in and out of the people until he was swallowed by the crowd.

"Shall we head off together?" asked Martin.

"No," replied Kalu. "I want to do this on my own."

Martin shrugged, choosing to walk in the opposite direction as Ashwin. "See you at four."

Kalu clutched his flute tightly to his chest. Around him the blare of horns merged with the call of shopkeepers and the laughter of children on their way home for lunch. Two monkeys fighting for food scraps screeched, only to be drowned out by the raised voices of women haggling over the price of plastic containers. Competing sounds encased everything he saw. Nothing reflected the notes of Raag Desh as he knew them.

Kalu sank to the broken pavers next to the Jeep, letting the cacophony wash over him. He couldn't hear any music. Only noise.

· · ·

Guruji walked into Kalu's room and sat in a chair next to the bed. The boy was lying with his face toward the wall. The room was dark, but Guruji didn't turn on the light.

Kalu heard the man enter and closed his eyes, knowing he would have to open them sometime. And it would be the end of everything.

"Kalu." Guruji's voice was soft, though the unspoken order felt as strong as a mountain.

Kalu turned over but kept his eyes closed. "Guruji, I don't need a lecture. I understand. I know I've failed. I couldn't find it anywhere. You were right. I've been here a year and a month and I'm not good enough." Kalu fought the heaviness in his eyes, trying not to let a single tear fall. It was nobody's fault but his. Had he studied harder, worked more . . . It was too late now.

"Kalu. Sometimes when you try too hard, you can't see what's in front of your face."

"I'm sorry, Guruji." Kalu opened his eyes, looking down at the soft covering on the bed.

"You need to relax and trust yourself a little. Nothing comes without patience."

"But I can't go out to the town every day, and even if I did, I don't know what to look for. Not like Martin."

"No, but what works for one person may not necessarily work for another. You can find the raag your own way. Besides, you didn't even hear Martin. How do you know what he learned? You have that advantage over Martin, this is your land."

Kalu could hear his own breathing, rough and torn in the silence. "But I don't know where my blood comes from." The words were whispered so softly that Kalu was only half aware of saying them aloud. "I still failed. I'll leave tomorrow."

The silence felt as deep as the ache in his heart.

"I see. So you decide rather than me, do you? Giving up after the first difficult task?"

"No!" cried Kalu. "Not giving up. Don't you see? My time is almost up. I failed."

"Yes, you did. But just because you have a little talent, it doesn't mean you won't have to work hard to rise above mediocrity. Why shouldn't it take you time to learn some things? If I had given up every time I failed, I would never have become a musician.

"Some raags come with living. Desh is the raag of this country. The fact that you found it hard means that you were on the right track, child. You have a lot more living to do before you truly feel that connection to our country and her spirit. If you had found the task easy, you wouldn't still be my apprentice."

"But—"

"And who said this task was the make-or-break one? You realize your greatest strength and your biggest enemy is your own desire to succeed? My brother was right about one thing: you need to be here. Your probation is over. Go if you choose to, but don't tell yourself I sent you away. That is totally your decision."

The shadow rose and moved toward the bed, speaking in a softer voice. "Now, child, finish this glass of milk, otherwise Ashwin will scold me for the rest of the night."

Kalu sat up and looked at the glass. He should have been pleased. Guruji had not thrown him out. But he'd been so sure he could find the raag. If he couldn't even do that, what chance did he have of making it as a real musician? The ache that had started in his belly now curled through his chest and he had to force himself to breathe. Long and deep. He couldn't let Vaid Dada down. He couldn't fail himself. He would stay. Regardless of how stupid he felt, he would remember Guruji's words. He would stay until he was forced away or until he transformed into the musician he wanted to be.

～

"Here." Guruji placed some money in Kalu's hand.

"But why? I haven't done anything."

"You've passed your probation, haven't you?"

Kalu opened his mouth to protest but was stopped by Guruji.

"As long as you stay here, you work by my rules. Everyone needs a little bit of spare money. What makes you think you are so different?"

Kalu wasn't convinced. It showed in the scowl on his face. He'd never before been given money without earning it. And he hadn't even started playing properly yet. Not the way he wanted to. Not the way Guruji expected.

"You rise at five and work like the rest of us, through to the night, don't you?" continued Guruji.

"Yes, but I should be paying you, not the other way around. I don't need handouts. You're already feeding and housing me."

Guruji's eyebrows came together like a thick, black stick. "When you arrived here, did you or didn't you agree to abide by my rules?"

"Yes, but—"

"You will take the money I give you each week. You will learn to save, and you will use it to good purpose. It will be paid back in full when you start working."

"But—"

"Do you have to contradict me on everything?"

"I'm not a child. I can look after myself."

"Then act like an adult and do as you are told." Guruji

turned and left the room, walking quickly so Kalu couldn't respond before he disappeared.

Kalu turned the notes over in his hand and thought about Guruji's words. He had no use for money. Not now when he had everything he needed to allow him to play. Still, there was the future to think about. He couldn't imagine living on the streets again. Even if he left here, he would find another teacher, or if he couldn't do that, he would find a job. Now that he could read and write, it would be much easier.

He rubbed the notes between his fingers. If he saved all the money, maybe one day he could buy a place of his very own. He would pay Guruji back, with interest, and he could live as he wanted, in a place he could share with Bal. Kalu smiled, wondering how many such notes he would need to free his friend. He wouldn't tell Bal yet. Just in case. It would be his secret, until he could pay off Bal's bond.

It would take time. Bal's master wouldn't let him go easily. But Kalu missed his friend and hadn't forgotten the promise he had made when they parted so long ago. Bal understood him like no one else. Maybe, thought Kalu, it was because Bal had been abandoned, too. Bal knew and loved his family, but all he had left were memories. Kalu knew nothing of his family. He had no past, nothing to return to. The boys' circumstances and loss had united them.

At least now Malti wrote to him about Bal. Knowing that someone kept an eye on him comforted Kalu. But a sentence in a letter wasn't enough. He would never be really happy until Bal was, too. They had only each other.

If Kalu could pay the bond, the two of them could live together. Bal could come here or they could find a place nearby. They would be each other's family.

It took Kalu some time before he was comfortable in the presence of the foreigners. Or any guest really.

The household consisted of the three of them for the most part, with Vaid Dada stopping by once a month and Martin's extended stays of a few months once or twice a year, depending on his touring schedule. However, students and musician friends often came to exchange ideas, catch up with Guruji and Ashwin, and, of course, meet the new student.

On a few occasions, the house was actually filled with guests from around the world. At those times, Kalu would sleep on the veranda and offer his room to whoever needed it. He met people from China, Russia, and Japan. Different people with different music—not just in the way they played or appreciated sound but even in the way they spoke. Kalu could hear the sounds of their heritage in their voices. He was struck, too, by how funny it was that the Indians often wore Western clothing while the Western people wore Indian clothing.

Martin, however, was special. After that first day, he and Kalu had become great friends. Martin was vigorous and enthusiastic. He asked Guruji questions that opened up the music in unusual ways, taking paths that led to greater adventure. As a musician he was innovative. As a person he was youthful and energetic, like an older brother to Kalu. Even their duets were fast and furious.

Martin was now an important part of Kalu's life, his visits punctuating the year. The boy still remembered Martin's parting words on that very first trip: "Look, Kalu, I understand, I really do. I know how it is, what you have to do to play. Just promise me one thing, don't cut out life in the process."

"So, Malti, is Ganga Ba pleased with you?" Her father sat by her side and stroked the very edges of her hair, where tendrils flew out from the neat, tight plait. His smell—of coconut oil, tobacco, and salt—reminded her of her childhood. He took the metal cup full of hot, sweet tea she offered and blew on it to cool it down.

"And how long are you with us this time?" Her mother took a soft sip, passing the tea through her teeth to cool it as she drank. "Don't overdo it. You don't want Ganga Ba to think she can do without you." She always worried that Malti would lose her job by coming home. That, somehow, Ganga Ba would find she could manage without her.

"Ganga Ba suggested I come as soon as she heard about the eye operation." Malti didn't mention that Ganga Ba's first suggestion was that her family ask someone else, possibly one of her aunts, to help. Her second suggestion was that the family pay someone to look after Malti's mother for a few days.

Malti finally arranged for her friend Kavita to come and work for Ganga Ba for a little while. Kavita's employer and Ganga Ba's friend, Sukenya Ben, was going on pilgrimage so she'd also extended the offer: "You'd be doing me a favor, Ganga Ba. I need to make sure Kavita doesn't gallivant all over the place while I'm away. It will be good to keep her in line; otherwise Lord knows what she'll do to my reputation." Ganga Ba couldn't refuse. Especially as she didn't have to pay for this extra help.

"You shouldn't have come, Malti; the neighbors could have helped me. Besides, it would do everyone good to fend for themselves. Then your father would know what trouble he puts me to."

"But I wanted to help, Ma. If I can work at Ganga Ba's, can't I help my own family? Especially after your operation." Malti didn't voice the question she really wanted to ask: Aren't you happy to see me? She knew they were. But her parents, particularly her mother, were cautious when it came to showing her affection. Only Raja, who handed out hugs like others gave out sweets, was shown affection in return.

"It's because we get to keep him, Malti," her mother once explained when Malti was small and wanted to know why Raja got his favorite food more often than she did. "It's a mother's burden to give away her girls and her treasure to keep her sons."

Malti kept silent then, as she did now. This was the way of things.

10

She stood straight, her body taut. Her sari yellow, for purification. The whole village came to witness the event. The women gathered around her. The men stood at the edges, closer to the fire, housed in an old forty-four-gallon drum.

He stood across from the drum, directly opposite his wife. He could smell his own sweat. The jute they'd used to secure his hands behind his back chafed. He didn't know why they had bothered to tie him. With everyone in the square, there was nowhere to run.

The village elders supervised the lighting of the fire at dawn and organized a roster of younger men to tend the fire for the next six hours. The priest had determined the best time for the punishment. One of the village elders now removed some of the glowing embers and placed them in a large, steel bowl on the raised platform a few meters away, next to the women. An old lady spat in the dust as the man passed.

The women had spent most of the night in the temple with his wife. She had fasted for twenty-four hours, taking in nothing but a little water.

The leaders of the other village and the owner of the goat

stood together, in the shade, watching from a distance. Everything was quiet. Even the children, watching from between their parents' legs and from the shelter of the mud-brick houses, were silent.

Ramanlal, the elder nominated to oversee the punishment, squinted at the sky and took out his pocket watch, rubbing its face with his dhoti. It was his, and the village's, prize possession, the only pocket watch in the district.

The accused shrugged, trying to concentrate on the feel of the ropes around his wrists rather than the ordeal ahead. He watched Ramanlal finally check the embers before raising his hand like an umpire. The elder dropped his hand and started to count.

"Sixty, fifty-nine, fifty-eight . . ."

The folds of the wife's sari seemed to catch the smoke in their turmeric-colored creases. There was a collective hiss from the women as she placed her hand in the glowing coals. The accused stepped back, almost unbalancing. The guard on his right steadied him, and then let go, his full attention on the woman in front of the coals.

"Fifty-seven, fifty-six, fifty-five . . ."

Although he tried to look away, at the ground or the crowd, anywhere, she caught his eyes and wouldn't let go. Denying him the right to escape from the smell of burned flesh.

"Fifty-four, fifty-three, fifty-two . . ."

One of the women started to sing.

> *Maari naad tamaaré haath, hari sambhaar jo ré*
> *Mujné potano jaani né hari, prabhu pad aapjo ré*
> *My pulse is in your hands, Lord look after me.*
> *Knowing I am yours, I surrender to you.*
> *Give me shelter at your feet.*

"Forty-five, forty-four, forty-three . . ."

Other women joined in with the first, one after the other, singing in time to Ramanlal's countdown.

The wife didn't flinch, nor did she acknowledge the song. Only the beads of sweat on her forehead, the dilation of her pupils, and the faint shudder that traveled intermittently up her arm betrayed the pain.

"Twenty-three, twenty-two, twenty-one . . ."

The singing became louder as Ramanlal counted down to one, raising his hand again to signal the end.

The women moved to help the wife but stopped as she raised her unburned hand, and they knew, by the straightness of her back, that while the elders may have decided on the punishment, she would choose the end, keeping her hand in the embers until she was ready to remove it.

And the man saw, in the complete stillness of her face, the contempt she felt for him. He was a coward and a thief and now the whole village knew of her shame. The shame he had brought on her. Her burned and blistered hand would be his constant reminder.

She slowly removed her hand, and the women of the village covered it in milk. The smell of roasting meat reminded him of the goat he had stolen. The goat that had led to this very day. If she hadn't nagged him, he wouldn't have had to steal the goat.

He swallowed, tasting nothing but a deep, aching dryness. He didn't know if he would ever be able to taste again.

~

It was one of Malti's special jobs, when she came home, to make the chapattis. The feel of the flour, loose to start with, firming beneath her fingers with the addition of a little oil and water, the soft, slightly gluey texture of the dough: it all reminded her of childhood. Back then Raja would take her out to the mud puddles brought by the monsoons, where they would both sit comfortably in the brown slush. Malti would make pretend chapattis and laddus, Indian sweets, out of the mud. The only problem occurred when she tried to feed them to Raja. Smiling, she remembered how as a child she had never understood why he didn't eat them as quickly as he did the ones her mother made in the kitchen.

Making real chapattis always reminded her of those pretend ones. Especially of the beating the two of them would get when their mother found them, covered in mud, wrestling in those puddles. At the time Malti thought the fun was worth the beating.

"Do you remember our mud chapattis, Ma?"

"How could I forget? The two of you gave me no end of trouble." Even though her mother had to keep her eye covered for the rest of the day and wear dark plastic glasses for another three, she refused to stay out of the kitchen. Malti didn't mind. She liked the company.

"And make extra chapattis for Swetaben. You remember her? Married to that good-for-nothing down the road."

"What happened?"

"He stole a goat from the next village, and Swetaben paid the price, that's what."

Malti stopped rolling the dough. "Is she all right?"

"When the eye doctors came, we made them check her. They made a hoo-ha over her hand and put cream on it before they left. Those doctors, they may come and help, but they really don't understand life."

"And what about him? Where is he?"

"Still skulking in a corner. Swetaben refuses to let him in the house. You should have seen her; the minute her hand touched the fire, it was as if the Mother entered her. The young girls have already started asking her to pray on their behalf. Now, go next door as well. They'll have some vegetables for her, too. We won't let the family starve."

Malti's mother placed a blue sari and some money in Malti's bag on the day she was leaving. "I've saved some money this month. Your father doesn't know the price of sugar has come down. Besides, he has too much sugar anyway. This is for you. You do enough for this family." Malti knew her mother hated good-byes. The sari was all the colors of the sky on a warm winter's day, from the pale blue just before the sun rose to the clear, crisp blue that framed clouds. It was beautiful.

"Now, be good. Work hard and don't tell your father about the sari or the money. Men have no idea. Your father will walk you to the bus stop." She squeezed Malti hard and walked away without a glance.

Malti and her father walked in silence. It was always this way. They left the house early so they could spend a little longer on their walk together.

"Are you happy, beti?" her father asked.

"Yes," responded Malti. "Yes," she repeated, realizing she really meant it. She had freedom and family. While Ganga Ba could be a handful, she was never cruel. And although leaving home was always sad, this time it felt bittersweet, like chewing aniseed.

"I'll miss you and Ma, I always do," said Malti, trying to express her feelings to her father. "But I like my work, and I have friends. School would have been wasted on me. You should see the trouble I had learning to read!" She turned her head so she could look her father in the eye. "I'm happy, Bapuji."

Her father smiled. "I'm glad." The bus stop came into view. Malti could see the yellow and green markings on the waiting bus that would take her most of the way back to Hastinapore.

"Here, beti, take this." Her father passed her a red box wrapped in orange ribbon. "I went to the sweetshop when your mother wasn't looking. They are for your trip back. Can't have my girl turning into skin and bone."

Malti took the packet, slipped it into her pocket, gave her father a brief hug, then touched his feet in respect. As she took her place on the bus, she looked through the window at her father. He never turned his back until the bus was out of sight.

~

"You can't play with us. You wouldn't know how to."

"Why?" asked Kalu.

"Because I said so, Flute Boy."

Kalu knew this would happen. He'd told Guruji as much, but the man had brushed off Kalu's concern, reminding him that failure was one of the steps to success.

It was all Martin's fault. On his last trip, he had convinced Guruji that it was important for Kalu to have some friends his own age, and Kalu hadn't been able to change his teacher's mind. Watching the children from the tree or as he drove by with Ashwin was one thing, thought Kalu; joining their games was quite another.

Instead of walking straight down to the village, Kalu had first climbed up to a flat gray rock that overlooked the valley below. He put his flute to his lips and played from his heart. He started by playing what he had seen, the sunlight and how it danced through the leaves of the peepal tree; and then as the music took over, he thought about how he felt. The music became stronger and deeper, one lone note after the next, falling like droplets into a pool of water, before fading. He played out his fear, that the young people of the village would not let him join them. And then, last of all, he recalled the confidence he seemed to have lost on the road from Hastinapore. There, he'd never worried about what people thought, whether they liked him or wanted to be with him. He just joined in until he was chased out, and even that had felt like a game. The tune gathered around him and held him tight even when he took the flute away from his mouth.

He'd carried that tune all the way down to the village. Now, looking at the circle of boys around him, Kalu made an effort to stand tall. The area in which the children played was smaller than Guruji's plot and had the air of a proper cricket pitch, where battles had been fought and won. A metal bin took the place of stumps on the far side, with three strong sticks on the other. Bowling went in only one direction.

"Why are you here, Flute Boy?" said the tallest boy, with a shadow of a mustache, almost but not quite a man. "You may have fancy shoes, but you can't give us anything we haven't already got. Go talk to your own kind!"

Kalu thought of the story Guruji had made him read of the monkey and the crocodile. The monkey wanted to get to the juicy mangoes on the other side of the river but was scared that the crocodile in the river would eat him. He convinced the crocodile to take him across the river, promising him in exchange the thing the crocodile desired most, the monkey's heart, which the monkey said he kept safe in the tallest tree. Of course, the monkey's heart was exactly where it should have been, but the crocodile was fooled, and the monkey got his ripe mango.

Although Kalu didn't want to trick the boys in the way the monkey had the crocodile, he realized that if he could give the boys something they were interested in, they would be more likely to let him play with them. They wouldn't be interested in his music, he knew. What he needed was a nice watch, like Martin's. Or maybe Martin himself . . .

"What if I bring a gora film star to meet you? He's a friend of Guruji's and I know he'd come if I asked. Maybe even film you." Kalu took care to speak to the whole group, rather than just to the tall boy, who seemed to lead them.

The boys discussed the offer. Their excitement rose like grains of wheat in the wind, moving first one way, then the other. Kalu looked away casually, pretending not to care.

"What do we want with fillum stars?" asked the boy holding the bat. "I'm going to be a world-famous cricketer."

"Maybe he knows Lillee," a voice called from the back.

"Can you get us Lillee?"

"Aré, what do we want with Lillee when we could have Gavaskar?"

Voices grew around Kalu.

"But"—the boy with the bat held up his hand—"he doesn't even know who we're talking about."

"I could learn." Even as he spoke, Kalu knew he'd lost them. One by one, the boys made their way to the dirt patch. Kalu squatted on a broken brick at the side of the area, determined not to leave until he had to. It was now a matter of pride.

As the game started, Kalu noticed other children gathering around the edges of the ground. At first, they kept their distance. Kalu shifted on the brick, trying not to attract attention, just as he did when he sat up in the mango tree looking down. He wanted to concentrate on the players, and on how he was going to persuade Martin to pretend to be a film star or to bring with him one of those cricketers the others spoke of. He didn't even know if Martin had any dark glasses or gold rings. And he would have to convince him to wear proper

Western clothes rather than odd deshi clothes—kurta tops, jeans, and champal. Martin was honor bound to help him, as this whole thing was Martin's fault in the first place.

Meanwhile, the crowd of girls and smaller children continued to gather in groups, some talking to friends, others focused on the game.

"What are you doing here?" a girl in a bright green skirt asked Kalu. She had a shadow, a younger girl, small and brown, with inquisitive eyes like a cuckoo's. Kalu listened to the sound of green-skirt-girl's voice, expecting accusation, but heard only curiosity. She was half a head taller than he was, and stood, hand on hip, watching him. "Well?"

Kalu bent his head toward the game. "I was watching."

"Why aren't you playing?" A boy with a tin-whistle voice joined them, his question cutting through the shouts of *Howsthat!* on the cricket pitch. "Can't you play?"

"Of course I can play." Kalu stood up, kicking the brick in his haste. He fought off a grimace as pain shot through his ankle.

There were now more children surrounding Kalu than watching the cricket match. "What about all of you? Why are you here?" he asked them.

"They won't let us play, either, because we're girls or too young," said a child.

"Why don't you make your own team?" There were as many children off the field as on.

"We don't have a ball, silly! A good plastic one costs at least one rupee."

Kalu looked at the other children. They weren't what he'd expected to meet when he went out to make friends, but unlike the boys his own age, these children hadn't called him names. And they didn't seem to mind talking to him. Guruji hadn't specified who he was meant to befriend.

"One rupee isn't hard to earn if we all do a few small jobs," he pointed out. "It'll be less than ten paise each. Why don't we start up our own game?"

Biddu, behind the stumps, stood up in surprise as the children who had been watching the game burst into a cheer. In the time it took for him to scratch his neck, they had disappeared after the flute boy.

"Aré, bowl, yaar!" called Nishal, their leader, from the slips. Biddu bent down again. The game seemed much smaller without spectators. And since Nishal had said no to the flute boy, they might never meet the film star now.

Maybe tonight his sister, who had been on the sidelines with the flute boy, would tell him what they were doing.

~

"What's so special about a birthday?" Kalu asked Guruji. It was always better to ask Guruji to explain things, as his answers were more accurate than Ashwin's, which always started on one path and ended up somewhere completely different.

"So you want to know about birthdays, boy," Guruji said. "Well, besides being a year older and one's hair getting grayer, I don't know. . . ." Guruji looked at Kalu. The boy had grown and was now only a few inches shorter than he was. "I think perhaps the reason they are celebrated is that they mark time. Another year of action, or inaction, as the case may be. Some people think the day itself can have consequences for the individual. On one's birthday a person is supposedly often more open to ideas. To influences from within." Guruji nodded as if coming to a conclusion. "It's a good day to think about where you have been and where you will go." Guruji ruffled Kalu's hair before turning away. "At least, that's what I think. Of course others, like Ashwin, may have a completely different view."

"Birthday?" Ashwin looked up from his television program. "Whose birthday? Not mine. Kalu's? Do you realize that it's been more than a year since Kalu came off your probation-bobation? That makes it two years since he came to live with us! Where has the time gone? And we haven't celebrated his birthday once in all this time. Guruji, I blame you."

"When is my birthday?" As Kalu said the words, he wished he could change them. No one knew when he was born.

"Hey Ram, I didn't think . . ."

Guruji ignored Ashwin and drew Kalu to face him. "Kalu, you are in a rather interesting position, but you're not alone in not knowing when you were born. Many people don't know the day of their birth. In the old days, no one really took note of it. Not like today. Even my parents had to guess their dates of birth. It was the same at the time of partition. So many people moved, so many were lost. Birthdays were the last consideration, only celebrated by the Westerners and the wealthy."

Kalu kept his head down. He wanted to know his real birthdate and there was no one to tell him.

"You'll have to do what others did and decide on a date for yourself. Only, I think you should pick an auspicious day. Once you've chosen a date, we'll have Ashwin plan a celebration to his heart's content, no doubt disturbing me even more in the process. Now, get to bed and let Ashwin scold me in peace."

~

"So, Flute Boy! Are you and the children too weak to accept a challenge?" Nishal, the boy with the mustache, stood tall, an oil slick of hair streaking across his face as he swung his bat over his shoulder, his troop positioned behind him.

Kalu raised his head. "What challenge?" A few of the younger children surrounding him turned, poised to run if need be, held by the coins in Kalu's hands that were partly theirs. The girls, however, ignored Nishal completely.

"A cricket game, of course. Your team against mine."

"How did we become your team?" grumbled one of the boys standing around Nishal, breaking rank.

Nishal ignored him. "Come on, then. You win, you can have the ground. We win, and you lot stop playing."

"We'll have to discuss it." Kalu and his friends walked toward the far end of the pitch, where the other boys couldn't hear them. The ground was cracked and compacted, having lost the battle to the elements, the cows, and the children.

"Well, what do you want to do?" Kalu asked.

"I think we should play them and beat them . . . *pa-chang!*" A small boy hit an imaginary ball right over the boundary, twisting as he did so—just like a professional cricketer. "But that's the point," said green-skirted Lata. "We wouldn't win. They've been playing for much longer than us. And they're bigger, too. I don't want to have to stop now, just when we've started to have some fun." Tulsi, the small, birdlike girl who shadowed Lata, nodded, her eyes softening with approval. Lata was her voice.

Lata had been Tulsi's friend for a long time. Tulsi's grandfather was one of the village elders. His family had been the biggest landowner until Guruji arrived. He still owned most of the land surrounding the village and, unlike Guruji, played an active role in the village's upkeep.

Tulsi's mother married a man from a larger town, but

they had frequently come to stay in the village. Lata's parents had worked for Tulsi's grandparents, and Lata's mother had looked after both her own child and Tulsi whenever the family came to visit.

Those days were now a discolored memory, leeched of their warmth by the blackest night. It happened when Tulsi was four.

She had been traveling in the new car, her uncle's pride, along with her parents, brother, and sister. It was dark. She heard the sounds of the trucks as they beeped past and saw the pinpricks of headlights reflected in the eyes of bullocks working through the night. Her eyelids must have closed as the others played antkadi, each singing a song starting with the sound the last person finished with. No one knew that the driver her uncle had recently hired had been awake for the past forty hours, making money on the side as a tourist driver. He'd closed his eyes for a second.

Tulsi was the only survivor. Apparently she'd screamed and screamed until her voice disappeared. Her grandmother told her that when they pulled her out of the metal, they left her voice behind. Vowels and consonants were replaced by hoarse, aching sounds, like a broken mirror reflecting fragments of the past.

Now Tulsi lived in the city with her aunt and her aunt's new husband. They treated her with care, like a delicate piece of china that could be easily broken. Only to be reminded, whenever she made a sound, that it was too late to protect her; all that was left were those fractured notes that hung in the air.

Every holiday, Tulsi came to the little village to be with her grandparents. They left her to do as she liked during the day, even if it meant running with the village children, who, because of Lata, accepted her as one of their own. Tulsi's grandparents would do anything to put color into her cheeks and flesh on her limbs, if not words into her mouth.

While Tulsi kept a pen and paper with her to communicate, she never used it around Lata. They'd developed a language of their own.

Now, as Tulsi listened to the other children talk, her eyes widened.

"I want to play the boys. But I don't want to stop if we lose," said Jaya.

Lata turned as Tulsi touched her shoulder. Kalu and the others waited. Lata's face split into a grin and she hugged her friend. "If we lose, we can go to Tulsi's grandparents' farm and play there."

Kalu smiled. "So it looks like we win, even if we lose. Shall I tell them?" The others nodded.

Staying where he was, surrounded by the team, Kalu projected his voice across the field. "We'll play you. But these are our terms. If we win, we can play with you whenever we want. And you stop the name calling. If you win, we'll leave the cricket pitch to you. Deal?"

Nishal thought a minute. The boys shuffled behind him. One cleared his throat as if to speak, before a glare from Nishal silenced him. "Deal!" he called. "I'll toss: you call."

⁓

"Heppy b'day to you, heppy b'day to you . . ." Ashwin's voice could be heard throughout the house. He'd been singing his version of the birthday song to various tunes on and off for the past few months. It was worse today, as Vaid Dada was returning. Kalu groaned and tried to concentrate on his practice. Every time he started to play, Ashwin's song intruded and he found himself playing along to Ashwin instead. He wanted to practice as much as possible before Dada arrived that afternoon.

Whenever the vaid returned home, the four of them would sit in the book room or the music area late into the night. Dada spoke about places he'd visited and people he had met. Ashwin would match him story for story, each tale getting wilder and louder as the night passed. Guruji, often reading, would clear his throat as the noise level increased.

Guruji was older than Vaid Dada, and Dada often called him a grumpy old man. Guruji would close his book, replying that dealing with the lot of them made him old.

Vaid Dada watched as Kalu took a second serving of dhokra. The boy covered the soft yellow squares with Ashwin's special green chutney and ate with obvious enjoyment. Kalu had changed beyond recognition in the last two years. The hard lines bracketing his mouth were gone. He sat straighter and moved with grace. He spoke with confidence and fit into their little family as if he'd always been a part of it. But it was his eyes that had changed the most. The old Kalu was streetwise but also completely open. His eyes always told the truth. This boy had learned through experience to conceal his thoughts.

"So, Kalu, have you picked a day yet?" asked Vaid Dada.

Ashwin poured more tea. "What about Janmashtami? Krishna's birthday would be auspicious."

"No," Guruji answered, instead of Vaid Dada. "Choose a day that resonates for you particularly, Kalu."

Kalu thought hard. So much had happened in his life, it seemed like an impossible choice to pick just one day. Everyone was focused on him, as if this decision was important to them. As if he mattered.

He felt an ache in his chest, as fragile as a butterfly. He

wished he could somehow translate it into music. The whisper between sadness and joy.

"The day you said I could stay."

Vaid Dada smiled as Ashwin clapped his hands. "Shabaash! The day we all landed in trouble!"

"That, my son, is perfect," said Guruji.

Kalu looked up at his teacher. Although Vaid Dada often used the term "beta" and Ashwin spoke about their "family," Guruji had never called him son before.

~

"You, Flute Boy!"

Kalu kept walking.

"Aré, wait up!" called Biddu. "I want to talk to you."

"My name is Kalu. Not 'you' and not 'Flute Boy,'" said Kalu as the boy reached him.

"Well, I didn't know, did I?" Biddu said. "You know my sister. She plays for your team, and I know you're still playing. That was pretty tricky, the bet you made."

"So?" Kalu looked straight ahead, remembering the way this boy had stood with the others when Nishal refused to let him play with them.

"Well, I was wondering . . ." Biddu's words tripped over each other in their eagerness to come out. "I was wondering if you needed a wicketkeeper. I'm good."

The boy collided with Kalu's flute box as Kalu stopped. "Why would you want to join us? It's not the best team, girls and children mainly. You won the challenge."

"Yes." Biddu rubbed the side of his head. "But your team always seems to have more fun, even when you aren't playing. And you all took a vote. I'm tired of just being the ball collector. So are some of the others. They wanted to come, too, but they're afraid of Nishal. Besides"—Biddu grinned as Kalu's stance softened just a little—"not all the girls are as pesky as my sister."

"Well, we'll have to ask the others, but if the team doesn't mind, I don't."

"A deal!" Biddu held out his hand, shaking Kalu's with the enthusiasm of a puppy finding a ball of string for the first time. Kalu smiled in surprise as he realized that this boy really wanted to be his friend.

Biddu linked his little finger with Kalu's as they continued to walk down toward Tulsi's grandparents' farm. At his touch, Kalu instinctively stiffened, hoping the other boy didn't notice his reaction. "Does my sister, Lata, get a say, too?" Biddu asked.

Kalu grinned. "She especially gets a say!" They walked in rhythm beside each other and Kalu finally relaxed. He laughed and the other boy joined him, until one voice became indistinguishable from the other.

~

Bal sat in the shadows, watching the buffaloes cooling themselves. He heard the sounds of laughter and song float across the river. The women washing clothes around the bend had started singing songs for the coming festival of Navratri. As the melody danced down the water, he could picture the women scrubbing cloth to the beat of the song.

Naagar nandaji na laal, naagar nandaji na laal
Raas ramanta maari nathani khovaani

The song centered on a village girl who had lost her nose ring while dancing to the sound of Krishna's flute. The lilting rhythm was balanced by the sound of wet, dirty clothes being beaten against river stones.

One voice was particularly strong and full-bodied, vibrant as a mynah and about as tuneful. It didn't matter, though; her obvious enjoyment carried the song more than the melody did.

> *Naani naani nathani né maahi jadela moti*
> *My nose ring is tiny and studded with pearls*
> *Nathani aaponé maara Subhadra na veera*
> *Please, Krishna, give me back my nose ring*

Bal smiled. He wasn't sure if his buffaloes twitched their ears to wave away mosquitoes or the song. His fingers tapped the sides of his legs lightly in time with the tune. Navratri always featured the dhol. The drum resonated in the heart and then, lower, in the belly.

The festival was one of the first leading up to Diwali, the New Year. The nine nights of dancing made Bal feel more alive than at any other time of the year. Something about the movement, the swirl of skirts, the beat of the dhol, and the sound of the flute soaring over voices made a fleeting curl of warmth, starting at his toes, travel right up to his calloused fingertips.

He didn't know if it was due to the music itself, or the laughter, or the atmosphere of lightness and, of course, romance that seeped through the town. After all, the raas garba dances were said to be how Krishna seduced the gopis. More than any other, this festival was played out in Bal's world, in the fields and in the evening, rather than in the home or the temple.

There were two places the village people would gather to dance. The main event was run in the paddocks next to Bal's master's home. This function was organized by the village elders, more particularly their wives. There were always loudspeakers so the city musicians hired for the occasion could be heard throughout the area. Bal preferred the smaller event attended by the poor and lower castes. It was held some twenty minutes' walk from the village, in a field nestled between a cliff and a gentle slope to create a natural amphitheater. There was no need for loudspeakers here.

Bal never participated in the festivities. Instead, he sat high on the slope, between the trees or up in the branches where no one would see him, looking down at the village singers and dancers. Nor would he attend for all nine nights. After working all day, he was tired. Once, he'd fallen asleep on the slope and received a beating for arriving home well after dawn. Master had threatened to call the police or to lock him in the storehouse during the nights to make sure he would be on time in the mornings. Bal hated the feeling of being enclosed. Any space where he couldn't see the sky made his heart thump and his body sweat. Now he limited himself to seeing the first and last nights, as well as Sharad Purnima, which was held the final night, when the dancing would take place under the full moon. Even from a distance, he would be able to see the image of Mother Amba, the goddess ringed by the dancers who called, "Jaya Ambé, Jaya Bhavaani, Jaya Ambé. Victory to the Goddess," over the songs themselves.

On Sharad Purnima the dancers wore white, reminding Bal of moonbeams. One of his earliest memories was of his mother leaving out flattened rice mixed with milk and sugar on Sharad Purnima night, for "the moon to cook." Later, as the moon crossed the sky, she would wake the children and feed them a spoonful each. The rice would be sweet and soft with milk. Bal never slept on those nights, waiting for the treat. But he'd pretend to be asleep, just so his mother would come and tickle his ear or brush his hair from his face so he wouldn't wake with a start. He couldn't even remember his brother's or sisters' faces now, but he remembered the milk and the touch of his mother's hands.

~

In Hastinapore, Kalu had loved the early mornings for their coolness and the smell of the river sliding over the town like mist. Now he loved the mornings for their peace. The chilled air was invigorating before the sun rose. As the crickets fell silent and the birds still slept, he'd bathe in water that was barely warm, rubbing his hair hard and then shaking his head like a very wet dog, watching the water drops fly.

He'd then light a diva at the little temple in the garden. The temple contained a shiv-ling, a miniature one, reminding him of his private temple, where he'd practiced Raag Bhairav on his plastic flute. Although there was a proper temple in the house, Kalu much preferred this place, hidden behind the flowers. There were no bright lights, no silken clothing or incense. This place was personal. Just for Kalu. Decoration came in the form of the fragrance of jasmine and the heat of the moist earth. The light from his diva would shine throughout the small enclosure, flickering at first and then holding still and strong, with a blue center like Dhruv-taara encased in gold. The smell of ghee feeding the flame would briefly remind Kalu of meals to come. He would pray for Ganga Ba, Malti, and Bal. He'd thank God for Vaid Dada, Guruji, and Ashwin. Most of all he prayed for music. For the strength to play and the ability to learn.

"Oh Lord, let me be your vessel, your flute."

Guruji had taught him to breathe. To close his eyes and simply breathe, starting at the belly and filling his body with air before releasing it again. Feeling the breath moving through his body and slowly out through his mouth. That breath, sometimes soft, sometimes strong, was the key to making his flute sing.

Kalu would silence his mind, and in this void, just as the sky turned pink over the mountains, he'd start to play. He played only his exercises, strengthening his breathing and warming his fingers as he moved through consecutive, then nonconsecutive, notes.

Ashwin would arrive with cups of tea for them both, often sitting to listen until the sound of chanting rose across the mountains, picked up by the microphones in the temple in the village below, and the tea developed a thin skin on its surface.

The sound, together with the call to Allah from mullahs at the mosque on the hilltop, would rouse Kalu. When he stopped playing, Ashwin would rise and stretch his joints. The two would drink their lukewarm tea in silence, taking in the promise of the day, before making their way back through the gardens and into the house.

Guruji, Ashwin, and Kalu would sit and listen to the BBC world news on the radio, drinking a second cup of tea with biscuits or thepla—chapattis made with mustard leaves. It was only as that second cup was almost empty that anyone would speak about anything meaningful.

"You know, I'll be going to Hastinapore soon, Kalu," Vaid Dada said during one of his visits. "Why don't you come with me? I get asked about you so much, I know they would love to see you."

Kalu realized with a start that it had been almost three years since he first arrived in the mountains. His first year with Guruji had passed slowly and he'd marked each day on the calendar. Now months passed without his noticing. As one day flowed into the next, time was marked only by the raag he was learning.

"He's here to work, not gallivant," said Guruji before Kalu could reply.

"Just because you don't leave this place, bhai, there's no good reason why Kalu shouldn't. Everyone needs a break, and three years is long enough."

"Can I?" asked Kalu, looking to Guruji for an answer.

"I suppose so. But mind you continue your practice while you're there. And not too long, brother. I want him here."

Kalu smiled. He'd be seeing his friends again soon.

11

MALTI WATCHED THE boy with the flute box slung over his shoulder walking toward the house. If not for his dark skin and slight limp, she wouldn't have recognized him. It had been more than three years since Kalu left.

Until she saw him, she wouldn't have believed that time could have changed him that much. Her life had just continued and she'd kept in touch with him through their letters. But he had changed. It wasn't just that he was older—she'd expected that. It was the way he held his head, the way he strode with long, wide steps. He didn't hesitate when he reached the gate. Didn't look to see if anyone would stop him.

She wondered if Kalu would bother going to the kitchen or whether he would make his way straight to the front door. She remembered the first day he came to the gate with Ganga Ba's mail. Then he had been almost delirious with hunger. He had fumbled with the catch at the entrance and then stood near the wall waiting, for someone to attend to him or drive him away.

Now he wore shoes Raja would have loved to own but could never have afforded. His clothes were ironed and new. His hair had been cut and shone with health, as did he. Kalu had grown from a child to a youth, almost a man, and had changed status at the same time. This was no beggar, comfortable in hand-me-downs, striding to the door. This was someone else altogether.

One thing she knew was that the extra mat Ganga Ba had told her to place outside for him to sleep on would remain unused. This boy would receive a bed in the house. Nor would Ganga Ba give him the bag full of old clothes that she had made Malti wash and iron.

Malti hurried into the house, just in time to hear Ganga Ba call, "Bhraamanji, tea for both our guests, please." Malti chuckled as Ganga Ba continued, "Kalu, would you mind sharing a room with Vaidji? You'll both be staying here, of course. Hey Bhagwaan, you've grown, boy, haven't you!"

"Malti! Malti! Where have you been? What could be more important than spending time with me, yaar? I only arrived yesterday, you can't be fed up with me already!" said Kalu.

Malti looked up and smiled. "Hello, big eyes."

Kalu hadn't realized quite how much he'd missed Malti until that moment. He took the pot she was carrying and placed it on the ground, feeling her warmth as he brushed against her. She looked both different and the same all at once. More grown up, a woman now, yet still Malti. He'd never noticed the contours of her face before. The clean, simple lines gave her grace and dignity beyond her years. They walked around to the back of the house and sat beneath the frangipani tree.

"So, has it been worth it?"

Kalu didn't need to ask what she meant and was glad she'd started with what was most important. "Yes, it's worth it. It doesn't seem like three years. I still can't play my rosewood flute as well as I'd like, but one day soon I will."

He remembered his excitement the day he realized his fingers had indeed stretched so the span matched the length of the lotus that grew in the garden pond. Guruji had placed his flute in his hands and watched as Kalu positioned his fingers on the holes, starting on the high notes and moving down the scale. The sound was full and deep, like a lake in the middle of a forest. He'd made it to the lower "ga" before his fingers lost their grip. He would have to wait a little longer to play that flute, but Guruji's quiet smile of approval when Kalu reached for a smaller flute was encouragement enough.

Kalu waited for Bal on a flat rock by the roadside. The morning was fresh, the sky still pink, when Bal approached, stick in hand, herding the slow buffaloes out to the river, his movements angular, like a stork trawling through water.

The boy walked past Kalu without looking up.

"Aré, Bal, yaar, forgotten me already?" called Kalu, running a little to catch up, and grabbing the other boy in a hug.

Although Bal's face was at first full of joy, it quickly settled into a frown as he stepped out of the embrace and kept walking. "What are you doing, Kalu? I'm not fit company for you now."

"Don't be stupid, Bal." Kalu looked across at his friend. "Just because my clothes are different, it doesn't mean that I've forgotten you, bhai."

"Kalu, you have changed. It doesn't take a fool to see that. And although I'm not educated, I'm not a fool."

Kalu stopped in his tracks. He hadn't expected this reaction from Bal. He felt a deep ache inside at the thought that he may have lost his closest friend. No one else understood what it was like to be truly alone.

"No!" he called. "Stop. Just because you think I'm different, it doesn't mean that we can't be friends. You've changed, too, you know. Do you think I'm not going to speak to you just because you now have a few hairs on your face? If you had a real mustache, then maybe I'd change my mind."

Bal looked back at Kalu, tears welling in his eyes, unsure whether to laugh or cry.

"Kalu, I'm not in the same class as you. You know this."

"Bal, I'm still the same flesh and blood. You were my brother. You know me like no one else does." Kalu paused. "I'd give up music before I'd give up you."

"It's too late for that." Bal brushed his eyes and stood tall. "Besides, music is the only thing you're good at." He took a deep breath. "If you really aren't going to leave, then at least make yourself useful. Why don't you play that flute of yours and make these creatures move faster?"

Kalu laughed as he took out a flute and began to play.

A few days into the trip, Bal asked him what it was really like to leave one place and try to fit into another. Kalu cried as he spoke about the last three years. Bal just held his hand as the words tumbled out. "It's all right, yaar," the older boy said. "It's all right to feel sad and happy at the same time. Most people think that it's been easy for you, that you have been given a gift—and that part's true. But they don't realize that it's never easy to change and to try to belong to a world that is so different."

"It's funny," said Kalu. "You know Jaya-shree Ben, the paan-waala's wife? She now tries to give me paan for free as if I was some sahib. And other people that Vaid Dada heals, people who wouldn't have had me near them in the past, now want me to eat with them."

"Nothing remains the same," Bal said quietly.

Kalu rubbed his thumb against his finger, now calloused from the hours he spent playing. "I thought I'd always be able to return to Hastinapore if things didn't work out with Guruji."

"You can never go back, Kalu. Only forward. If people like us focus on the past, we can never move forward. But that doesn't make it easy." Bal offered Kalu the end of his faded shirt to dry his eyes on. Kalu knew he would never forget the way Bal made him feel. As though someone understood.

He spent his last morning in Hastinapore with Bal. The boy herded the buffaloes while Kalu played the flute, the sound echoing across the river and over the cliffs.

On his last night, he sought out Malti.

"So what does it feel like being back, even for a short while?" she asked, leaning against the frangipani tree. Kalu sat beside her.

"A little odd. It's good, but it's not really the same."

"Well, I can tell you you've changed, big eyes. You're not as cheeky as you used to be. I don't know if that's a good thing or bad. You've grown, Kalu. Soon I won't be able to tease you anymore!"

"Huh, you'll always tease me, Malti."

"Well, someone has to stop you getting a big head."

Kalu laughed. This felt right. Somehow, despite the distance and the time they had been apart, things were just as they had always been.

"Want some chikoo?" Malti lifted one eyebrow.

"Maybe."

"I suppose you want me to go and fetch it?"

"Well, yaar, if you get it, I'll peel it."

"Deal." With that, Malti rose and ran into the house. In the old days, Kalu would never have expected Malti to offer him fruit. When you weren't quite as hungry, food was so much easier to obtain.

Kalu picked up the flute by his side and started to play. The sound was deep and full, as if he were translating his thoughts into music. It stayed in the air like dust floating in the sunlight, and each note held the promise of something not quite spoken but maybe heard in the darkness of a dream.

Malti paused by the door, mesmerized by the sound. Kalu had learned far more than he realized. Her brother had once told her a story he was taught at school about a man who played a pipe and lured all the children away. She wouldn't have been surprised if Kalu could do the same.

~

It was mosquito weather, ripe with the promise of rain. Kalu had originally decided to climb to the summit of the closest peak, knowing that from there he would get a view all the way to Tanakpur, but as he breathed in the sticky air and brushed away another fly, he changed his mind, heading instead for a platform of rocks surrounded by golden grass midway between the summit and the house.

"Hey!"

While the speaker was close by, the word echoed across the mountain, and the young voice sounded sharp and thin. Kalu kept walking. The fact that Nishal had disturbed the silence of his mountains angered Kalu as much as Nishal's refusal to call him by his name after all this time.

"I was talking to you. Hey!"

Kalu turned, knowing he wouldn't be left alone until he did. Nishal had grown since the first time Kalu met him, and in the past year Nishal's anger had continued to fester as Kalu slowly made friends in the village.

Nishal stood, fists clenched, chest heaving. "What reason did you have to come to our village and change everything? Things were fine before you arrived."

"Things were fine for you, you mean."

Nishal tensed with rage. "You know nothing about me." He kicked a stone so it landed near Kalu's foot.

Kalu didn't move. Nishal made him angry like no one else did. What right did Nishal have to sneer at Kalu as if he had committed a crime? Just because Biddu and then slowly the other boys chose to join Kalu's team. "And you know nothing about me, either," said Kalu, struggling to keep his voice calm and even. He turned away, continuing up the slope. He could hear Nishal following.

After a few steps, Kalu turned back and half held out his hand. "You know, we could call it a truce, be friends even."

"Not everyone needs to be your friend, Flute Boy. You have it lucky; most of us have to fight for what we want."

"You know nothing about me," repeated Kalu, balling his hand into a fist.

"I know more than you think. You're the bastard son of the man who can't be bothered spending one rupee in our town. Who thinks he's too good for us, just like you do."

At those words, Kalu launched himself at Nishal, blindly hitting him wherever a blow would land. Nishal responded, and soon both boys lost their footing, tumbling over the rocks.

Kalu's flute box fell open on the ground, the flutes scattering left and right. Kalu twisted sideways, trying to take Nishal with him, more worried about the flutes than his injuries. He had left his rosewood flute at the house but still had three of Guruji's. The boys got up at last, panting.

"Looking for something?" Nishal had a bloody lip and torn trousers. A flute lay by his feet. Kalu ran forward, just as Nishal stamped on the flute. Both boys heard the crack of the bamboo, sharp as a gunshot across the valley.

Kalu said nothing as Nishal limped away. There was nothing to say.

"Hey Ram, you need to be more careful, child. What Guruji will say, I don't know. Now don't move, and don't speak until I clean you up."

"Will say to what?" asked Guruji, stopping short when he saw Kalu's battered state and the broken flute in his hand.

"He fell," said Ashwin before Kalu could speak.

"I recognize the difference between a fight and a fall, Ashwin," the older man said.

Kalu looked up, anger still alive in his face. "I had no choice—the things he—"

"We all have choices, Kalu. I'm not going to scold you. I'll leave that to Ashwin. You are old enough to realize the consequences of your decisions. Both good and bad."

"Are you telling me I shouldn't have fought back? He was rude about . . ." Kalu stopped, unwilling to voice Nishal's accusations.

"Sometimes you may feel it's right to fight. And no one can make that decision but you. Son, I'm just telling you that the things we do in anger often don't have the results we think they will. Not everyone will like you in life or treat you fairly. And arguments can't always be won with words. But there is always a trade-off.

"When you were living in Hastinapore, would you have given up your ego or pride if a flute was involved? Did you care what others thought of you or your friends?"

"No," said Kalu, sighing. "But . . . no." He brushed a tear from his eye, not wanting Guruji to know it wasn't what the boy thought about him but what he had said about Guruji that had angered him so.

"Enough." Ashwin hugged the boy, ignoring his groan of pain. "It's finished."

~

"I won't have my house turned into a concert hall," said Guruji.

"But, Guruji . . ."

Ashwin smiled. He knew when Kalu used that tone of voice, he normally got what he wanted.

"But, Guruji, they already listen," continued Kalu.

Guruji's head snapped up. "What do you mean?"

"Well, when we play late, they often sit on the other side of the gate and listen. Given all the grass on this side, I thought it would be more comfortable." Kalu's eyes widened pleadingly.

Ashwin tried not to laugh. "It's not a bad idea," he said. "I do get tired of shooing them away. I'm surprised you didn't hear the hoo-ha last time."

Kalu spoke softly, touching Guruji gently on the arm. "It makes us part of the community, Guruji. I don't want them to think that we are somehow better than they are."

Guruji gave Kalu a piercing stare. "Do you really think I care?"

Kalu looked down. "No, Guruji, but I . . ." He stopped, unsure of how to explain himself. Although the bruises had faded, the argument he'd had with Nishal still preyed on his mind.

"We aren't better, anyone with eyes can see that," said Ashwin. "Besides, they like the music. I don't think you should stage a concert. Not yet. I think Kalu should just continue his classes. They can listen to that if they like. Lata, Biddu, and Tulsi already come in, although Biddu practices bowling more than he listens."

Now it was Kalu's turn to try not to laugh.

Guruji looked from one to the other. "I'm glad, Ashwin, that you know what's best for my student. Maybe you could run lessons and I could cook?" Guruji left the rest of his tea and stalked out of the room, his hair at right angles, like a bird with its feathers ruffled.

Kalu looked at Ashwin. "Was that a no or a yes?"

"Well, he didn't say no, and he's an awful cook." Ashwin started to clear the table. "Tell them in the village that I'll leave the gate open from now on."

12

She sang as she walked toward the well, an empty plastic pot linked loosely in her arms.

> *Paani gyaata re beni ame talaavdi*
> *We went to the lake together to get water*

Other women joined her. She loved this time of the morning, when the sun hung low in the sky and the day seemed pregnant with promise. Even the fields looked green and abundant. In a few hours she would feel as dust-worn and limp as the plants would look. But the mornings were lovely. At this moment, the lilt of the song matched the lilt in her heart. It was still early.

> *Paarethi lapsyo pag, ke beda maara nandvaana*
> *My foot slipped at the pond's edge, my pots shattered,*
>   *how shall I go home?*

They sang quietly, her friends, just as she did.

At Navratri or at weddings, with kohl-rimmed eyes, linking arms and swinging hips, they would sing out loud. Now the words were as soft as a bee's hum. They sang just for themselves, finding a rhythm that worked for their feet and the empty plastic containers. They were lucky these days. Their mothers used to carry earthenware pots. The plastic ones were so much lighter, even though you couldn't mend them when they broke.

> *Chore betha re beni taara sasraaji, kem kari gharma*
>   *jaish, ke beda tara nandvaana*
> *Your father-in-law is waiting at the gate. How will you*
>   *go past him unseen, with your broken pots?*

The well had been built many years ago. While not as large or intricate as Adalaj ni Vaav, it was still an active step well, with three full levels of steps until one reached the water. At this time of the morning it would be cold inside. As the day passed, though, she'd be glad of the shelter.

Now the sun gently heated her joints, preparing her for the day to come.

> *Laamba taanish re beni maara ghoomta re, rumjhum*
>   *karti jaish, ke beda maara nadvaana?*
> *I will cover my face with my sari, I will let my anklets*
>   *ring to distract my father-in-law, he will not notice*
>   *the broken pots!*

She turned slightly as a new sound played in counterpoint to the voices.

"Over there," a young girl said, and gestured.

The musicians sat in the shadow of the well. There were four of them. One with a flute, another with drums, and a third with a string instrument. The fourth carried a set of cymbals. The man playing the flute continued to play, even as the women stopped singing. She had to look hard to see the flute. Its color matched his skin, the shade of dried tobacco leaves. The creases on his face and the dark shadows beneath his eyes aged him. The other musicians had the same look about them, although the drummer's smile was as bright and white as fresh sugarcane.

"Play for us while we get water." The youngest girl clapped her hands, unconsciously jumping in time to the flute. "Please, play for us!"

"Get us some water, lass, and we'll play. Make it sweet and we'll play for longer." The man with the cymbals spoke slowly as he chewed on a stalk of grass. His voice was rich and thick.

As the girl headed to the well, one of the ladies called out, "Is it age or experience that makes the water sweet?"

He twisted the long stem of grass he'd been chewing around his fingers as the women laughed. "Try me. We'll drink as much as you offer."

"There's enough of us for everyone," the drummer added, stroking the skin on his drum.

By the time he had finished talking, the youngest girl was already back with water in her pot for the men.

When the child held her palms, full of water, up for the men to drink, the woman who had sung in the morning grabbed her arm, jerking it so the water spilled, soaking into the ground. "They can drink from the pot if they're that thirsty. Words are one thing, but don't go offering them your fingers like a loose woman," she said.

"So will you play?" The youngest addressed the musicians and ignored her words.

The man with the flute stopped playing to drink from the pot.

Then, after all of them had had their fill, the musicians took up the tune. Hearing in the song the happiness and energy of the morning, she joined the other women, who had formed a circle and started to dance.

The shy ones were dragged in by the youngest. "One dance won't kill you. Your husband will never know. Besides, we work too hard as it is! We'll stop at the end of this song."

Only the song never did finish. Just as one tune seemed to end, another melody wove its way through the music so there was no beginning and no end.

The euphoria turned to fear as she continued to dance. "Enough!" said her brain, but her feet continued. There was no way to stop them. Slowly the fear turned to something else. Release. As if the very fact that she couldn't stop gave her power. Salty sweat dripped down her face as the sun continued its arc across the sky. She was briefly aware of other women coming to the well, dropping their vessels, and joining in.

She realized her hair had loosened and her glass bangles had broken. Beads of blood showed on her wrists and later on her feet as she stepped on the shards of glass. The sound of the drum danced with the beat of her heart until nothing else mattered.

She felt a hand on hers trying to drag her away from the dance. She heard a voice, deep and angry, shouting at the musicians. But they were more than mere musicians. After all, who but Krishna himself could make such sweet sounds?

Then, as suddenly as it started, the music stopped. She fell to the ground, only to be dragged up by a man. The warm, heavy arms and sweet, spicy smell of her husband enclosed her. As she struggled to orient herself, she saw, in front of her, the drummer pinned to his drum by the sword that had silenced him and his instrument forever.

~

"You better watch out, baba. Playing the flute here is one thing, playing music for Navratri quite another." Ashwin scooped a mixture of spinach and dhal into his hand, then dropped the ball into the hot oil. The kitchen was filled with the sizzle of oil and the spicy tang of the pakora. "I'm surprised Guruji will let you go to play in Hastinapore. All those girls at Navratri . . . too much of a distraction for you, my fine fellow. It was hard enough when I was fourteen, and I didn't even play an instrument."

Kalu stood beside Ashwin, turning the pakoras as they became golden brown. He never tired of helping in the kitchen. Ashwin's chatter, the smell of turmeric, and the bite of chili eased the tension in his spine and the stiffness in his fingers.

"Guruji said no the first time Ganga Ba called to ask. You know how his lips firm up as if he's eaten something sour. But you can't say no to Ganga Ba for long. Finally he said yes, pretending it was all his idea." Kalu took one of the cooling pakoras and popped it into his mouth. They held just the right balance of crunch on the outside and lightness within.

"Hey Ram," continued Ashwin, "you need to watch out, you know. Those girls will start treating you like a film star if you aren't careful. And"—he poked Kalu in the stomach—"at this rate you'll be too fat to run away."

Kalu grinned, his mouth too full to talk. He swallowed before replying. "Who says I want to run away?"

"You musicians are all the same. I don't know what it is, play a little tune and women are like this dough. Watch out, though, sometimes it can backfire. Don't you remember what happened at Amiraveli?"

"They paid the musicians?" Kalu ducked as Ashwin tried to cuff him over the head. A glob of batter landed on his face.

"No, saala, they killed one! The husband of one of the women knifed the drummer—straight through his drum and into his heart."

"I don't think my friends in Hastinapore intend to murder me."

"Just watch out, music can make people crazy—and stop eating or I'll be cooking for the rest of the day!"

~

Malti returned from the market and went straight through the side door into the kitchen. She tipped the mix of peas, bitter gourd, beans, and green chilies out of the cloth bag and started to sort them. It was amazing how you could have a bag full of green things and yet have so many colors. She placed the gourd on the right and separated the beans and peas from the coriander and chilies.

"Aré, Malti! Why didn't you tell me you were back?" Ganga Ba entered the kitchen, leaning heavily on the counter. She waved her hand toward the earthen pot containing water. Malti moved to fill a glass as Ganga Ba continued, "Bring it into the other room, I have news for you. Your mother's friend Shami Ben just sent word."

Malti followed Ganga Ba into the main room, passed her the glass from the tray, and waited as she drank. If something was wrong at home, Ganga Ba would have told her immediately. Still . . .

"Such a morning I've had. Now, girl, your Shami has organized for the matchmaker to visit."

Even though she'd just eaten, Malti's stomach felt light, as if beetles were dancing on it. "But Raja still has six months of college to go." She found herself watching a small gecko on the wall. "Have . . . have they found a boy yet?" The gecko seemed to blink.

"Aré, sit down and let me tell you properly, my head hurts from looking up at you."

Malti sat on the floor, placing the tray beside her before turning to face Ganga Ba.

"They have found a family—apparently your brother knows of the boy, who went to the same college a few years before. But of course the family wants to look you over first. Fortunately they live here in Hastinapore, on the other side of town, and I've been asked to make sure everything is in order. They will come here this afternoon, after lunch. I told the matchmaker this was the best time. I need my afternoon rest.

"Now, wear the sari my daughter gave you the last time she came. We want you looking your best."

"Yes, Ganga Ba."

Ganga Ba looked at Malti sharply, taking in her pale skin and clenched hands. "Malti, you can't be getting sick now. It's the most important moment of your life. Surely you were expecting this?"

"Yes, yes, I suppose so. It just seems a little sudden." Malti took a deep breath. The gecko opened its mouth as if to yawn at the world, as if in fact everything were the same as it had been this morning. Only Malti knew differently. "I like it here. I like working. Still, if my parents have found a boy . . ." The sentence sat like a question, full of unspoken possibilities.

"More like his family found you, Malti. But, you know, the matchmaker had two proposals for you. Both from families in Hastinapore. With the matchmaker's advice, your father has picked the most suitable. Even though you've been working for me, the money your father has saved and your caste mean the family is of a good standard. Higher than you would have expected. Of course, the fact that your brother is doing well helps, too. And they specifically wanted a girl from the village rather than some city girl. All that remains is for you to be seen, and for me to do the negotiations on your father's behalf."

Ganga Ba flicked her hand in response to Malti's word-less reaction. "Yes, I know it's unusual, but I intend to be involved. I'm going to have enough trouble replacing you, I might as well make sure all the arrangements are correct. I'm sure your Shami Ben is fine, but she wouldn't have my experience. Even if I like the family, you won't be married until you are eighteen. That's still too young, but at least it's legal. I have a reputation in this town, and I can't have my servants breaking the law. Now, keep on with what you were doing, Malti, and we'll talk after they leave. Remember, the nice sari, straight after lunch."

Malti walked back to the kitchen. Bhraamanji had finished sorting the vegetables. He pointed to the tray of peas and she sat on a low stool on the floor and started to shell. She dropped the peas into a wide thaali, discarding the pods on the floor beside her. Bhraamanji worked silently, as usual.

Marriage. It was such a big step. It must have been a sudden decision: her parents hadn't mentioned an interested party when she last visited or spoke to them.

Unlike many of her friends, Malti telephoned her parents regularly, saving part of her money just for the calls. On the first Sunday of each month, at 3 p.m., she would make her way to the red phone booth on the street corner near the paan-waala. There, Suresh Bhai, who sat at the booth, would dial the number of a phone booth in a village near her parents' home. Both her mother and father would be there waiting to hear from her, having walked an hour to reach the booth. They spoke for only a few minutes, five at the most, before Suresh Bhai would roll his fingers as if winding yarn, indicating her time was almost up.

In the last few conversations, her mother had said it was time Malti thought about getting married, but Malti had just laughed, thinking her mother must have been worried about the antics of the young girls and boys—a sly word here, a sideways glance, a hand brushing past a wayward plait. It must have been the same when her mother was young. Malti knew her mother never stopped worrying. Besides, she was used to her mother talking about her future as a wife. Every scolding would start with "How would your mother-in-law think I'd brought you up if she saw you . . ."

Still, she didn't feel ready for marriage.

The mound of peas grew higher. Each green ball dropped from her fingers to the top of the pile, then rolled down until it settled, seemingly content among the other peas.

Maybe, she thought, just maybe, marriage wouldn't be so bad. She'd live in a family again. And have a husband. She wouldn't mind if he wasn't handsome, but she hoped he would be kind. And that he would grow to love her, as she would grow to love him. Then, one day soon, they would have children. Two small boys. The children would be naughty but clever, and when they were hurt they would always come to their mother for comfort.

"Our bride-to-be, yaar!" Two of the other servants entered the kitchen, grinning widely. Both girls circled Malti, singing wedding songs as they danced around her, until Bhraamanji got angry and scolded them, telling them to get back to work.

Their laughter was infectious, however, and they persuaded Malti to stop working and show them the sari she was to wear, leaving Bhraamanji to mutter alone about giddy girls.

Ganga Ba directed the servants to place seats for their afternoon guests outside, in the shade of the frangipani tree. She felt it would be better for all of them if they stayed in the garden rather than meeting in her house. Although the alliance would be a good one from Malti's family's perspective, Ganga Ba was far richer than the potential in-laws. It didn't pay to mix things around too much. Always more trouble came that way than it was worth.

Once they arrived and were seated, Malti entered with the requisite tray of water. She kept her eyes downcast, waiting until Ganga Ba told her to sit before looking up through her lashes at the people who could be her new parents. The woman was slim. Her husband a little fatter. He had a mole on the side of his face. The woman looked older than him and didn't smile.

"So do you cook, girl?" The woman's voice was thin, although her tone wasn't so much unkind as brusque.

"Yes, I do. I help here in the kitchen and my mother taught me, too." Malti tried to stay still as the soft material of her sari folded around her. She knew she looked her best—the other girls had even picked pink flowers and set them in her hair—but this woman didn't seem impressed. Malti kept her hands clasped in her lap.

"And work?"

Ganga Ba responded before Malti could speak. "She's a good, hard worker, and I've taught her to read, and write a little. She's much better educated than you would expect. I like having her here. Naturally her hours will be reduced if all goes well, but I take it you have no objection to her continuing to work here?"

The man remained silent, staring at Malti. The woman's mouth tightened. "We thank you for your generosity, but if we agree to the marriage, there will be no need for her to work. My son earns a decent wage. Her parents made no mention of . . ." She trailed off.

There was a small pause before Ganga Ba spoke again. "Yes, well, they are not the only interested parties, I have an interest in this girl myself and I believe all women should be fully educated, so Malti will come to me for two hours every week." She nodded as if what she had said was completely commonplace. "No money need change hands. I'll see her for two hours every week." Ganga Ba's tone was inflexible.

"Our women don't work," said the man at last.

"It's not work—think of it as providing companionship for me. And regardless of her role, all women should have the opportunity to learn to read."

Malti fought not to smile. These people were no match for Ganga Ba. No one was. Today, as she saw the couple's reaction to Ganga Ba, the way they deferred to her, not because of her wisdom but because of her status, Malti wished she had the strength and power to do whatever she liked, regardless of society.

Then she remembered Ganga Ba's daughter, sent all the way to America, now more Western than Indian. Ganga Ba wasn't to be envied—not when she had no one to live with. Ganga Ba was old and her family lived far away. And Malti thought about Kalu, with no family to speak of, and she knew that regardless of the decisions people made for her, she was happy to be plain old Malti.

Maybe not so plain, either. She sat still, pulling the paalav of her sari tight, waiting to hear their decision.

~

Rather than wait until his next visit, Ganga Ba decided to write straightaway and tell Kalu about the wedding. Since Guruji had agreed to let Kalu play at Navratri, they had seen a little more of him. She knew, however, that Kalu would want to know about Malti's marriage as soon as possible. She wrote the words with a strong hand, the characters as clear as they had been when she was fifteen. That was her age when she had consciously perfected the way she wrote after hearing that fortune-tellers could discern one's personality and future from their handwriting. She developed a clear, unornamented style, so that she would be seen as having a clear and focused life. No fancy frills for her.

With the letter completed, she looked out to the court-yard, where Malti scrubbed the pots. She was a good girl, Ganga Ba reflected. She would do what was asked of her. And, in turn, Ganga Ba would do what she could for her, even if it meant going through the effort of breaking in a new girl.

Ganga Ba had played quite a part in the negotiations and had decided to attend the wedding, at a major inconvenience to herself. As she told her friends, "If V.P. was still alive, it would have all been so much easier, but now I have to be the guest of honor. It's important Malti's family produce someone of status. Especially as her marriage is such a good one. Her family are so pleased I'm attending. Well, I could hardly say no, could I? It was all so much simpler when V.P. was there. Men tend to simplify life. He would have seen to everything." Ganga Ba spoke with such conviction that, by the end of the afternoon, she almost believed what she was saying.

Life had been rather dull since Kalu's last trip. At least Malti's wedding would provide some action. While it would be a nuisance for Ganga Ba, the wedding would symbolize the start of a very different life for the girl. She recalled her own marriage. The fear and the pride at being picked. The reality of living in a new family. Her name had been Gayatri, but that was the same as her sister-in-law's, so they changed her name to Ganga. She remembered the feeling of disorientation, as if the world had somehow changed; a new house, new family, and new name took a long time to recover from.

Ganga Ba chuckled, thinking about those early days.

She had been a feisty thing, no ha-ha-hee-hee miss, sure of her place in the world and the freedom she felt entitled to. She'd always been quite outspoken. Fortunately her mother-in-law was a patient woman. The same couldn't be said for her husband. They had some fantastic arguments. V.P. was as stubborn and adventurous in his own way as she was. He had chosen to follow a career out to Hastinapore to help with the dam projects rather than stay in Baroda with the family. She never regretted the marriage. And she still missed him. As much as they had quarreled, he was the first person to admire her need for independence.

~

Kalu looked up at the banyan tree. The footholds he had used as a child seemed closer together now, and the branches looked a little thinner. He walked between the multiple trunks, taking note of which new roots had anchored into the ground, forming new supports, before returning to the main tree.

He knelt down, leaning into the trunk to place his palm and ear against the tree. The bark was thick and as coarse as his fingertips. Time slowed and then stopped for one moment. He could almost feel the imprint of the younger Kalu, who used to place his palm just so. His hands had grown in the past four years, but he hadn't forgotten the boy he once was.

Kalu had learned about survival beneath this tree. Learned to sing a different song for each person he met. Learned to bury the things he didn't want to think about and focus on what was good and what would make him happy. Malti understood, but only Vaid Dada and Bal saw the whole.

A leaf, only partially brown, floated to the ground. Kalu

grabbed a long root and pulled himself up into the branches, high enough to see the women by the river. The branches held him comfortably in the folds of the tree. He brought his flute to his lips and started to play.

It was a call for Malti. His muscles slowly released against the familiarity of the branches. His body was shaded while his feet dangled in the dappled sunlight and the notes slid up and over him. He knew if he played in just the right way, she would come to him, as she always did. Raag Shree soared through the air, high and straight like a beacon.

"Hey, big eyes!"

He heard her before he saw her, and continued playing, now more consciously, until, ending on a laugh, he climbed down the tree to sit beside her in their old spot. Malti looked up, smiling. The bundle of wet clothes beside her told him he had been right, she had just come from the river. Some things were still the same. For now at least.

Malti tugged at his shoulder as he sat. "You're lucky I know where to find you. The girls down by the river have hurried up to Ganga Ba's house. Rani is the funniest. 'Kalu, Kalu is back!'" Mimicking the younger girl, Malti fluttered her eyelashes until Kalu pushed her so she overbalanced into the basket of wet clothes. "Watch out, yaar, I'll have to wash them all over again."

"Serve you right."

"So . . ." she said.

"So," Kalu echoed. "I hear there's a wedding in the air." Malti blushed. Kalu nudged her again. "Tell me, yaar, is he handsome, is he rich?"

"Kalu! I expected that from the girls, not from you." Malti turned to face Kalu but found herself staring at her own twisting fingers instead. "I haven't seen him. He won't be returning to Hastinapore until the wedding. The parents seem good. A bit stern at first, but I think most of it is show. Once Ganga Ba said yes . . ."

"Ganga Ba? I knew she was involved but . . ."

"You know what she's like. Can't resist having the final say. But once she said yes, they softened, almost as if they were worried I'd say no. Like I had any choice!" Malti smiled. "They are the right caste, though, and well-to-do. I'll be marrying up, Ganga Ba says. Apparently Raja has met the boy. He was a few years above him at college. That's what settled Ma." She released a deep breath and looked up. "That's it really."

"That's it?" Kalu examined Malti's face. He didn't think the girl he knew would have taken this decision so easily. "You're willing to marry this person just because Ganga Ba and your mother think it's right? Someone you haven't even met?"

"No. Yes. No. Because *I* think it's right." Malti looked at Kalu. "Remember when we were young, I told you I would never leave Hastinapore? It sounds like the gods listened. I won't have to go to a new town or make new friends. And I'll have a family again."

Kalu fell silent. He hadn't realized Malti missed her family that much. Enough to try to create a new one.

"It was going to happen sometime."

Kalu looked down. "Yes, but I didn't think it would happen like this."

"Face it, big eyes, you didn't think it would happen at all." Malti jumped up. "Too busy thinking about all those girls following that flute of yours. Kalu . . . oh, Kaluuuu." She ran around the tree as Kalu rose to chase her. Finally, after nearly running over the clothes basket, they stopped. Malti picked it up and they walked together to Ganga Ba's.

"Malti."

"Yes, Kalu?"

"Are you sure you're happy?"

"Yes, Kalu."

"And"—Kalu hesitated—"what about us? Will your new family accept me as your friend?"

Malti stopped. "Us? Everyone knows I wrote inviting you to the wedding. My in-laws are very impressed—famous musicians and all that! Besides . . ." Her voice became determined. "If Ganga Ba can force my in-laws to allow me to continue to visit her, then you, my friend, should be able to twist them round your finger. We are friends. Always."

"Always?" returned Kalu, taking the clothes basket from Malti's hands. "You realize that means your in-laws are marrying me, too?"

"Aré, saala!"

"Exactly!"

That night, when everyone was asleep, Kalu left Ganga Ba's house and walked toward the town center. The light of the moon was hidden by the harsh streetlights that lit each stone, each piece of refuse, and the large rats that clung to the gutters.

Kalu was reminded of how many people there were in a town, even one the size of Hastinapore. In the mountains, he had been so focused on becoming a musician, he hadn't even realized there were things he had forgotten. Things he used to take for granted, like the smell of tobacco and the continual grind of generators.

While Ganga Ba had remained the same, Malti had grown up while he was busy studying and he hadn't even noticed.

He couldn't imagine Malti married or with children of her own. No, that wasn't true. He could see her, happy and content, with small versions of herself, girls with long plaits down their backs, tugging at her sari. He just couldn't imagine marrying or raising a family himself. He wouldn't know how. Even when the girls in Hastinapore flirted with him and he flirted back, it seemed like a game. Guruji's house appeared to operate in a different time, and being there made him feel like he could remain young for longer, rather than take on responsibilities. The idea of someone depending on him in that way appalled him. Malti, however, knew what it was like to have parents, uncles, aunts, brothers, and cousins.

Kalu walked until his ankle started to ache, and then walked some more. Some people were just born loved, he concluded.

13

VAID DADA SAT relaxed in the rickshaw, his body sway-ing to the bumps and curves of the road, while Kalu rested against the metal frame. The smell and fumes of Bombay made Kalu's eyes water, but he didn't want to miss anything. He had thought Tanakpur was large, but it was tiny next to Bombay. Like a folk tune trying to compete with a big band. He remembered the old song about Bombay that Ashwin sang in the kitchen, particularly when he made bhel-puri as a treat. "Just like they make at Chowpatty Beach. But, of course, mine is much better." Kalu's favorite part had been the refrain, in which men were said to be full of spice. He hadn't smelled the spice yet, but he saw the way the gray sky melted into the slate-colored ocean and the tall buildings were sandwiched tightly together, each leaning against the next to stay upright. People called or waved to one another, focused on their tasks, ignoring the rickshaws, taxis, scooters, cars, and the carts dragged by people, cows, or the occasional horse. Kalu couldn't work out if the pedestrians were brave or just stupid.

"Flutes first, or to the house to refresh?" asked Vaid Dada. They were to stay with one of his friends near Nariman Point. Kalu had no idea where that was or whether they were close.

"Flutes." Kalu nudged Vaid Dada. "Did you honestly believe I'd say anything else?"

"Well, I believe in giving people choices. It's been a long trip." He placed a hand on Kalu's knee.

"Sorry, Dada, would you like a rest?"

"If I wanted a rest, I would have said so." The frown, at odds with the twinkle in his eye, made Kalu laugh. Although Guruji had refused to come to Bombay, Kalu knew that Vaid Dada was the next best person to have with him.

The street was narrow. Nestled between jewelry shops and a large sari emporium, the flute maker's place looked tiny and a little shabby. When Guruji said Bansubhai was the best and only true flute maker, Kalu had imagined something grander. Still, Guruji knew what he was talking about.

"Bansubhai knows what he's doing and so does my brother. There's no need for me to join you," Guruji had said.

"But—"

"Enough! I'm not leaving this house." Guruji's eyes blazed. He left the room. A few minutes later a storm could be heard playing through the house.

Now here Kalu was, ready to pick up his own personal set of flutes. Each one would have a different starting note and be a different length. These flutes would be made of bamboo. While Kalu's rosewood flute had a rich, earthy sound, bamboo carried a lighter, sweet sound, just like the wind after monsoons or the song of the tiny koyal bird.

A radio blared in the distance as Vaid Dada stepped out of the rickshaw, asking Kalu to remain for a moment. It was then Kalu realized that the metal door covering the front of the small shop was bolted closed. Vaid Dada spoke to a few of the men near the shop before returning.

"Our adventure continues," he said to Kalu, giving the rickshaw driver new directions. "Apparently it's not uncommon these days for Bansubhai to work from home. There was a bandh here late yesterday as protesters marched through the area, so he may have decided it was safer to stay away. I have the address. It's not too far. Given we have an appointment, I'm sure it's worth trying there."

"You don't think he's forgotten?"

"Don't worry, Kalu, Bansubhai keeps his word. If he took the order for the flutes, I'm sure he will have them ready for you. Besides, we can always wait a few days if need be."

Kalu didn't want to wait. These flutes were special. He had passed an unwritten test for Guruji to be comfortable in placing the order for them. When he had first started playing, Kalu would have jumped up and down or at least demanded to know what it was he had done, how his playing had improved for Guruji to consider buying him a full set of flutes. Instead, five years on, he sat, head slightly bowed, waiting for the next instruction, savoring the warmth that came from knowing he had taken yet another step on the journey.

Bansubhai's apartment block was tall and narrow. Exposed steel showed through the broken concrete sides. Vaid Dada and Kalu entered, stepping over the track for the security gate and climbing the staircase. They walked up four flights. Vaid Dada rang the bell.

A male servant answered, half opening the door, then closing it once the vaid had explained why they were there. The door opened again. This time a girl stood before them, perhaps the same age as Kalu, maybe older, dressed in a plain white salvar kameez. "Please come in," she said.

They took off their shoes and entered, following her to a small living room with a single divan.

"Welcome, Vaidji. And you must be Kalu?" asked the girl as the servant brought in some water. Her skin was pale and her eyes wide. Kalu wondered if she had been ill. He turned to Vaid Dada.

"Yes, he's Kalu. We have an appointment with Bansubhai. Your father?"

"Yes." She sat on the edge of a small aluminum stool. Her voice was low and she reminded Kalu of the simple white mogra flowers, with their rich scent, that people offered at the temple. She took a deep breath. "My father is dead. He finally passed away last night." The girl's knuckles were white as she spoke, though her voice was composed. Calm.

Vaid Dada and Kalu rose.

"No. Please sit. He told me about you. And he made your flutes. Please. He would have been most upset if you didn't receive them. Please, sit." She walked into a side room and returned with a large wooden case and a smaller brown box. They seemed too heavy for someone so small, but before Kalu could offer to help, she had placed them softly on the floor. She patted the rug beside her. Kalu, on a nod from Vaid Dada, joined her and knelt next to the boxes. She unlatched the case, lifting the lid to display rows of flutes. All different lengths, all made of bamboo.

She looked at Kalu; then, in a completely unexpected gesture, she lifted one of his hands, pressing on the muscle, checking the calluses, gauging the strength of his fingertips. She lifted out a flute. Caressed it gently before handing it to Kalu. "Play sa."

The sound was sweet and mellow yet strong. The flute balanced in Kalu's hands as if it had always been a part of him. She smiled. Her eyes glowed for a moment and Kalu knew this girl would be beautiful if she laughed.

"My father always knew. He had a knack for these things."

Kalu realized there should have been other people here, mourning her father and supporting her. He didn't want to ask her if she was alone.

"And you?" Kalu cleared his throat. "What will you do now?"

She straightened, her reserve returned. "I'll do what we all do."

He wanted to ask her what she meant but didn't know how to do so without intruding.

Closing the case, she stood, placing Kalu's new flutes in the brown flute box she had brought with her. "So this is yours. And I think you'll do these flutes justice."

"Will we see you again? Will you be okay? Can we do anything?" he asked, not knowing what help he could give.

She stood, calm and composed. "I'm fine. But in the future, when you play in Bombay, I may come and listen." Her voice broke, so slightly most people would not have picked up the sound. "And just remember my father every now and then when you play them. And use them well."

"But—" Kalu held the box tightly, knowing he wouldn't be returning to Bombay for a terribly long time. He didn't want to leave this girl made of silver and steel.

"He will, beti, he will," cut in Vaid Dada. "We've taken enough of your time. Thank you. And thank your father in your prayers, as we will."

~

Kalu looked at the flutes spread out between him and Guruji. None was exactly the same color. They all had a colored band at the top and bottom to keep the bamboo from splitting, and that allowed the user to quickly pick one in the correct scale. Every time he touched the flutes he saw her face.

"So how do they feel?"

"Heavy." It angered Kalu. What should have been a celebration felt like an added burden instead.

"That's because they aren't truly yours yet."

"What do I do?" Kalu asked slowly, knowing he wouldn't like the answer. These instruments were his and he would have to live up to them. Only, he didn't feel strong enough yet. He didn't want the song of a dead man in his head, and he felt guilty for thinking that way.

He rubbed his ankle, tracing the scars that webbed across his foot like paths on the side of the mountain. Barren and treeless, the paths wound their way up the mountain around rocks and jagged edges, bare to the elements. They must have had a purpose, though they seemed to lead nowhere.

Guruji took one of the new flutes and played a few notes before placing it on his lap. Kalu sat on his hands, wanting so much to take the flute back, surprised at the ownership he already felt.

"You take these flutes with you. And look after them, as if they were a part of you. An extension of your hands. And you polish them and you play them. Everywhere. Not just in practice, or for special occasions, but when you are walking, when you are in the village.

"You introduce them to your life. Until they understand you and can translate your thoughts into a melody. Kalu, you were meant to have Bansubhai's flutes, and you'll have to live with the fact that they were the last he ever made. But that doesn't mean you let them or anything else get in the way of your own personal melody. You need to reach the point where they become a gift in your own mind, as Bansubhai would have intended, rather than a curse."

• • •

Kalu sat under the gulmohar tree. He grimaced before picking a flute. Then, accepting the images and feelings it brought, he lifted it up to his mouth. Kalu closed his eyes and she was there.

He played. A lament to what she was and could have been. The sadness he saw in the calmness of her face and the comfort he knew she wouldn't ask for. As he played, the sounds seemed to solidify until he could actually see her, walking through the streets of Bombay and out toward the bay. The music reflected her pain as she watched the waves break, and he knew as the sound of his flute softened that she was remembering trips to Juhu with her father, his hand twice the size of hers. If she had been good, he'd pay for a pony ride. If she had been naughty, he'd still buy her some sugarcane juice. It was a time when she believed, as some children do, that he would never leave her. A time before she knew better.

Kalu didn't think about how he understood this. These were scenes he'd never experienced in real life. Rather, he kept his eyes closed and continued to play, as if by doing so he could transfer her heartache to his hands for a short while. He played of growing things. The slow uncurling of a new leaf. The first signs of a tadpole's budding legs as it transformed into a frog. The half croak of a fledgling crow. Those things that made him happy. And as he did, she raised her face to the sky and, for an instant, smiled.

Kalu stopped. Shaken by the vision and the tears running down his face. He didn't know if he was crying for her loss or his.

In that moment, high up away from everything but the wind and the sun, Kalu knew she would no longer haunt his flutes, but they would, if he let them, play true.

Bal walked across the fields. The moon cast shadows over the ground. Once the sun set, the colors in the fields changed from green, brown, and gold to black or gray. The shape of a tree or a lookout post took on more significance than the tree or post itself. Without color, details were invisible and a new world evolved, populated with shapes that were almost, but not quite, familiar.

The air was still. Even in the dark, Bal knew his way, not so much by sight as by scent and sound. The rhythm of the music seemed to beat beneath his feet, guiding him to the right place.

"Bal! Where's that Kalu, yaar? The girls are getting anxious. They want their Kalu playing the flute."

"Coming, he's coming," said Bal without stopping, waving at the boy who had called to him.

He still found it surprising when someone called out his name. That people even knew his name. He was used to being invisible, the person among the buffaloes. There was a time when he thought the little birds that sat on the buffaloes' heads received more attention than he did. The last few years, however, had been different. Now, whenever Kalu returned to Hastinapore, Bal, too, felt like a hero.

Kalu was famous not just because of the way his foot had healed but also for the fact that Guruji had taken him as a student and, perhaps, most important, for his flute playing. Kalu wasn't worried about class or status: he'd play for the buffaloes as comfortably as for Ganga Ba or Master's friends. Kalu seemed to know everyone. Or rather, everyone knew Kalu and, through Kalu, Bal.

Bal had thought that when Kalu settled into his new life, he would lose his friend. Instead the opposite had happened. Navratri was a good example. Whereas before Bal sat on the outskirts, now he was drawn into the inner circle.

Kalu returned to Hastinapore for Navratri each year. It had become a tradition, allowing the town to boast that it featured the best musicians. Kalu would normally start the night playing at the larger function, attended by the upper classes from Hastinapore and nearby towns. However, just before midnight he would leave to come to the fields where the poor met.

Everything was a little brighter, and even the air seemed charged, when Kalu played. It was like having Krishna playing the flute.

Bal sat next to Kalu on the stage. He played the bells or the cymbals, surrounded by a flood of music and dance. In the old days, seated above, high on the hill, he'd never felt the heat that rose from the women and men as they danced in circles around the image of Ambaji, the goddess. He'd never experienced the tension and release as the dance flowed, gaining speed and momentum until the dancers sang, "Jaya Ambé, Jaya Bhavaani, Jaya Ambé. In praise of the Goddess."

Kalu had made him feel a part of the music. A part of his life.

"Martin will be back in the next few days," Guruji announced at breakfast. His voice was slow, rusty at the edges. Kalu and Ashwin knew the sound. It meant Guruji had spent too long playing through the night and not enough time sleeping. They also knew not to ask questions.

"Martin baba. Excellent. There's a man who knows how to eat," said Ashwin, focusing on Guruji's words rather than his tone. "If I didn't know any better, I'd think he was the incarnation of the Paandav Bheem. Does he have four brothers as well? If he does, I'm sure he could carry them away from harm on his shoulders at the drop of a hat. And he could definitely finish off a cartload of sweets like Bheem did when he killed that demon Vakaasura."

"I don't know about the killing part," Kalu responded, trying not to laugh as Guruji raised his eyebrows. "I think rather than wrestling it to death he'd probably mesmerize the demon with his violin playing." He took a mouthful of spiced rice as he finished talking. It was no wonder Martin liked Ashwin's food; the man was a genius. Even the simple rice tasted special.

"Well, given that Martin insists on calling me Ash—as if I were as black as you, Kalu—I think it's time I changed his name to Bheem. It certainly fits better. Fancy calling me Ash! As if I was in need of that Fair and Lovely cream the women are so keen on to lighten my skin."

"Ashwin, rather than casting aspersions on Martin, I suggest you organize to have a room ready. He'll be here for a few weeks. So you can make him peda and whatever other sweets you wish until he bursts." With that, Guruji rose. "Five minutes more, Kalu, and I expect you at practice. Continue your work on Raag Khamaaj. I think it's a good one to trial with Martin."

"No doubt there'll be a few late nights with Bheem around," quipped Ashwin.

"Bheem indeed," muttered Guruji, and he left the room.

The pair remaining at the table were careful to avoid each other's eyes, knowing one look would start them laughing. And laughter would end in grief should Guruji hear when he was in this mood.

At the sound of a double horn, Ashwin and Kalu went out to meet Martin. An old Jeep, dusty from travel and rusty with age, rolled through the gates. It had been at least eight months since Martin's last visit. It didn't seem that long, though. Between letters, phone calls, and recollections, Martin was a firm part of the extended family.

"Hey, Kalu, my man. Christ, you've grown!"

Kalu realized that, for the first time, Martin was at eye level. "It's Ashwin and his food. He's been cooking for you, too, so watch out, or you'll be leaving with a belly."

"You mean a bigger belly." Martin tapped his stomach. Although it was large and square, Kalu knew Martin carried more muscle than fat. "I've been starving myself so I can fit it all in. Lead the way, Ash."

"No problem, Bheem—I've been preparing for you." Ashwin smiled serenely as Martin raised an eyebrow, directing the unspoken question at Kalu.

"I'll explain later, Bheem, my friend. Maybe over a snack, and definitely when Guruji isn't listening. Besides, there's news to catch up on."

"Not more cricket," groaned Martin.

"No. You're coming to a wedding this time," replied Kalu. "And you'll be the guest of honor. I promised them you would attend." Kalu lifted Martin's bags, and Ashwin led the way while Martin collected his battered black violin case. They knew better than to offer to carry that. Martin, like Kalu, always took responsibility for his own instrument.

They walked into the hall together before separating, Kalu to the bedroom, Ashwin to the kitchen, and Martin to the book room, to pay his respects to Guruji.

Kalu sat cross-legged next to Martin, who was sprawled under the gulmohar tree. This was Kalu's favorite tree. It had been since he'd dug it up as a child to see its roots. Since then the tree had grown even more than he had. He loved the way it reflected the change in season. The buds were out now, ready to erupt into a riot of flame-colored flowers in the coming months.

"So, Malti . . ." Martin played with a blade of grass. "How do you feel about her getting married? She is quite young still, isn't she?"

"Some would say she's quite old. Many girls in her village get married long before eighteen."

"Well, I think anything under thirty's too young," said Martin. "What's her village like?"

"I've never been there before. It'll be a new experience for both of us, Martin. I'm looking forward to meeting her family." Kalu turned to look at the other man. "Where'd you grow up? You spend so much of your life traveling."

"I don't really have a home anymore. Not in the conventional sense. But, you know, I love having corners around the world that I can crawl into when I need the time and space. People have always been more interesting to me than places or things. As long as I have my violin, I can live pretty much anywhere."

"What about your family?"

Martin watched as a ladybug flew onto the grass, reminding him of the old rhyme his mother would say for good luck whenever she saw one. "I didn't really get on with my parents when I lived with them. They wanted me to get a real job. You know, doctor, lawyer . . . hell, bus driver would have been more acceptable to them than musician. It wasn't very comfortable. For any of us, really. They didn't understand me any more than I understood them. I must have picked up the music gene from a distant ancestor or something."

"Or something," repeated Kalu. "Do you see your parents at all?"

"At Christmas, when I have to. But other than that, we

go our own ways. I'm quite happy this way, and it's less arguments all around. You know, after all these years, my father
still asks me when I'm going to get a proper job."

"You have to make an effort, my friend," said Kalu. "Do
you know how lucky you are to have them? Don't wish them
away or you'll regret it."

Martin laughed. "How things change. When you were
a young boy, I used to lecture you. Now it's the other way
around."

~

Malti kept her head bowed as required. The weight of the
sari pinned to her hair helped. The medley of chanting, camphor, and smoke from the fire dulled her mind. She was tired
from late-night preparations and her twenty-four-hour fast.
Confused by the sounds of people laughing and the drone of
the priests, she couldn't immediately bring herself into the
present.

She was the bride. Beside her sat her groom. *Please, God,
don't let him be ugly,* she thought.

The first part of his body she saw were his feet. The skin
was even in tone, the color of brown sugar or jaggery. Long
hairs sprouted on his toes, which were short and squat like
a gorilla's. No, not a gorilla's. Malti stopped herself. More
like a film star's. All men had big, strong toes. She turned
her eyes up to the man sitting next to her, mindful her sari
didn't move so no one realized her eyes weren't appropriately
downcast.

Everyone knew what happened to happy brides. Happy
bride, unhappy marriage. She tilted her head just a little more
to see her husband and repeated, *Please, God, don't let him be
ugly.* His face was turned away. All she saw was a silhouette,

set against the paper flags fluttering on the houses around the wedding site. She noted thick, black hair and a slightly curved nose.

They sat side by side, tied together with a piece of red cloth. Malti tried to concentrate on the ceremony, but her mind wandered as the priest continued to chant. She didn't understand the words; only the old women did. She did, however, know when to stand, when to sit, and when to throw offerings of ghee or popped rice into the flames. She gauged her groom's height and bulk as they walked around the fire. Three times one way, one the other. His foot was warm. It covered hers on the betel nuts as they took the final seven steps to make them man and wife.

The ceremony dragged, and Malti found herself becoming more and more agitated. After three hours, she had glimpsed the sum of his parts but had no sense of the person within. All she needed was one look into his eyes, but even that had been denied. Malti turned and smiled at her family, seated to her right. There, next to her brother, was Kalu, smiling back. He was now taller than Raja and sat straight and composed, watching the wedding.

Kalu's eyes hinted at maturity, but they still held the familiar seeds of laughter. And, most of all, strength. Those eyes told her she could do anything, and everything would be all right.

She nodded to her mother, who fixed her sari and squeezed her shoulder before returning to her seat just in front and to the right of Ganga Ba, Kalu, and his white friend.

Martin's attendance had been the talk of the village. Her mother had worried about what to feed her prestigious guests even while exclaiming at her daughter's good fortune. "God must have listened to my prayers and fasts, Malti—this is the biggest wedding in ten years!"

Finally the bride and groom stood to a cascade of cheers and rose petals. Malti watched one as it landed gently in the embers of the wedding fire. The petal shriveled and turned to dust.

She felt a tug on the material joining her to her husband. He bent to touch first his father's, then Malti's father's, feet for their blessing. Malti joined him. She remembered her mother's words: "Do as you're told. Help your new mother and don't cause trouble."

She still hadn't seen her husband. Not properly. Nor had she spoken to him. There would be time for that later. They had the rest of their lives.

~

The sun had only just risen after a night of rain. The day felt clean, freshly washed, when Kalu and Bal met at the curve of the river. The two friends walked down the pathway with the buffaloes to the field beyond. There was no need for words.

Whenever Kalu returned to Hastinapore, his days were filled with people. After Guruji's house, he found this quite difficult. Although he now had friends in the village at the bottom of the hill, and the house was often full, things ran at a different pitch. Slower, and more melodious. In Hastinapore, Ganga Ba and her friends would organize meals, tea parties, and outings as if he were their special property. Then there were people whose feelings would have been hurt if he didn't spend time with them. Only, this didn't leave much space for music or for himself.

He'd formed a habit of joining Bal in the early morning so he could practice out in the quiet of the fields. He'd come to appreciate the silence, especially after nights of playing for Navratri.

For his part, Bal enjoyed the company. He didn't think he would ever be able to cope with living like Kalu, with people constantly wanting to talk to him or to listen to what he had to say. He wasn't used to chatter, but Kalu's companionship and his music were special. Every year, Kalu's music grew and deepened, serious one minute, joyous the next. And each year the sound of his flute took Bal to places far away. Places he wouldn't normally let himself dream about.

Often they just sat quietly. At other times, Bal would light another beedi, exhale the smoke, and question Kalu about his life. He held these stories tightly inside so he could replay them when Kalu left. His friend had grown into everything Bal wanted him to be. Kalu, the one person who cared for him, had found direction and a way to bring out music so gentle and tender that Bal felt emotion again; this made his own life worth living.

Kalu had changed, although not in the ways Bal would have thought. Of course, both boys were now taller and bigger. Like Bal's, Kalu's voice had deepened and he spoke a little slower, thinking before he voiced his opinion. The years had been kind to him. He filled out his clothes, and his face had completely lost that pinched look Bal remembered so well. Although Kalu was still full of life, these days his impulsiveness and joy didn't show as much, until he played his flutes. This morning felt a little different from normal, however. Kalu seemed full of suppressed energy, much like when they were young.

"So, yaar, what are you thinking about?" Bal asked.

Kalu started. "Nothing, nothing. Just thinking of the day."

Kalu had suddenly realized that what he had to say to Bal would perhaps be harder than he had originally thought. He would need to take care. He waited until they moved off the track and into the fields. The boys, now young men, sat on a rock, solid but softened enough by the years to make a comfortable seat, as the buffaloes wandered nearby. Kalu, however, made no move to pick up his flute. Bal sat and waited.

"Bal?"

"Yes."

"How would you like to leave here and live with me?" The words spilled out as Kalu turned to Bal, eyes lit with excitement.

Bal blinked, taking a moment to work out exactly what Kalu had said. He brought his hands together to stop them from trembling. "With you? Away from here?"

"Yes. I've spoken to Guruji, and he doesn't mind. Neither does Ashwin. Says he'd be glad of the company." Kalu crossed and uncrossed his legs in quick movements. "At first, I thought that we could find a place for the both of us, but I've grown used to Ashwin and Guruji. I think you'd like them too. You'd have to share my room, but it's big enough for two. And . . ." he paused. "And I've saved my money so that we can pay off your bond. Bal, you can be free." Kalu spoke in a softer voice, although the words flowed just as quickly. "I didn't want to tell you before. Just in case I couldn't do it. But I was sure I could. Now you can be free to do whatever you want. I told you when I left I'd help you. Now, finally, I can."

Bal didn't know what to say or think. Since his mother died, he had thought of himself as a slave. This defined him. The inevitability of his role. The fact that he would never escape. Kalu's words were at first incomprehensible. Bal felt like his insides were melting, bone by bone. Like his life was falling apart.

"And I could stay with you?"

"Yes. Ashwin wanted to give me money to help, and

Guruji had been giving me money, too—but I didn't use that in the end. I wanted to do it on my own so that we wouldn't owe anyone anything. I haven't told anyone here. I wanted to find out if you were okay with it first."

Kalu looked at his friend's dazed face. He knew he should have brought this up slowly, but he couldn't wait. In a way, he had forgotten some of the lessons he'd learned on the street. Expect nothing. Bal wouldn't have expected this. Not really. Not in a million years. No wonder he was quiet. Kalu waited for a cue from his friend.

"Does . . . does Guruji have buffaloes?"

"No. But there's plenty more you can do."

Bal was silent. Tears fell from his eyes. "But there is nothing else I can do. I'm not worth anything else."

Kalu waved his hand as if shooing away a mosquito. "You can learn. Just like I did."

Bal lit a beedi, holding it like a fragile flower before taking a deep drag. "But, Kalu, you learned those things a long time ago. I'm not a child anymore. I'm too old to learn. I'm like an old elephant. You know, the ones that sit outside the temple. There was one I used to watch. Her name was Rupa. They painted her yellow. The color was much brighter than her eyes. She was made to stand there, day after day, collecting money and blessing the people. One day her chain broke. She was free. The village children started to yell, waving their arms, encouraging her to go. She didn't move. They thought she was silly, just standing there waiting until they chained her up again. But I knew. I looked into her eyes. They were just like mine."

"But—"

Bal's voice broke. "No, Kalu."

• • •

Kalu walked away from Bal. He walked until his feet hurt. When he could walk no more, he looked up and realized that he'd walked around the town, past the fields, and back to the temple where as a child he'd first woken up alone all those years ago. Kalu bent briefly to touch the ground, as he had done then.

He looked back at the long dirt road. It was a quiet place, desolate. Once again, he wondered who it was that had left him here and why. Whether they knew that no one would see them drop a child here, or if it was a decision made in a moment. Questions he knew could never be answered. As a child, he'd wondered who his family was and what made them discard him. As he grew up, he realized that his family would be of his own making. And Bal was as close to a family as Kalu had found. He would never leave Bal. But he never thought that Bal wouldn't want his help. That Bal would refuse him.

The tree was still there, deep and wide, its branches stretching across the road like a canopy. However, the hole to the underground room, when Kalu finally located it, looked much smaller.

He pushed through the roots to enter. The smell of damp earth encased him, as did the cool breeze that somehow found this place below the ground.

Kalu sank to the floor. He remembered his joy in playing his flute all that time ago. It had never occurred to him then that while he could fly on the wings of music, others would be left behind. That his choice to play would change things forever. Bal had chosen his life in Hastinapore over Kalu, and Kalu didn't understand why.

Taking out his flute, he started to play. Raag Bhairav. The raag he had played so long ago. As with all raags, the tune was different each time and transient; the only permanent thing was the structure, the raag that the music flowed through. It would be heard just this once, this sound from the heart, by no one other than Kalu. This time, the sound was deep and heavy. And yet, as he played, the notes changed, from loss and longing to comfort and love. Kalu realized, but only half acknowledged, that the music brought him some peace and a little understanding. The notes couldn't move out of their framework any more than Kalu or Bal could.

As the notes faded, Kalu slowly stretched. There was still an ache in his heart, but he knew he wouldn't walk away in anger.

~

The smoke rose as the sun set, bringing with it a haze of memories mixed with the smell of dung and wood. Embers lit the whites of eyes and cast shadows over the faces of small children gathered around small fires on the footpath. Malti, returning home after visiting Ganga Ba, marked the distance to the house by the changing light. Her steps slowed when she neared the light cast by the bare bulbs within the shops. She found herself noticing the bronze and green wrappings on the sweets in the shop on the corner and the way the paint peeled on the wall near the paan-waala's.

It was rare for her to walk out after dark these days, but Ganga Ba hadn't been well lately and requested, or rather ordered, that Malti make herself available to read to her. Her mother-in-law understood. "These women with nobody to look after them. It's no wonder she orders everyone about. I don't see why she doesn't go to live with her family. She's probably lonely. You keep her company for a few hours, Malti, just until the sun sets." The words that should have come after were left unsaid, but Malti knew to follow them anyway. She would return home before her husband did, and she would help with the evening meal.

She would stand quietly behind her husband to pass him hot rotis. She would make sure his bowl was exactly three-quarters full of dhal. She would see to Papaji, her father-in-law, the same way. Then, after her mother-in-law, Vimu Ba, sat, she would, too, keeping an eye on everyone's plates, ready to offer more vegetables or dhal.

The conversation between the men would wash over her as she poured the warm dhal over the rice, careful not to make any sound as the liquid ran from her fingers to her lips. The first time she'd made a sucking noise, her husband's jaw tightened and he looked at her with distaste, as if he'd swallowed something small and bitter. She was more careful after that.

Now, as she passed the bazaar, Malti slowed again. Being married wasn't quite like it seemed in the movies. In the films, regardless of the problem, by the end the man and woman overcame everything. And they cared for each other—so much that their love became the overriding story. Sometimes she thought she'd prefer the triumph and tragedy of those film stars.

On the eve of her wedding, Malti had sat quietly on the back porch of her parents' house. The night was warm and still. Her mother joined her, tucking her sari around her waist before sitting a few steps behind. Neither spoke for a long time.

Her mother sighed. "Be like Sita." Then, "Be like Sita," she repeated, placing her hand on Malti's head in blessing before returning inside.

Malti had repeated the phrase to herself every day for the past year. "Be like Sita." Lord Rama's virtuous wife followed him into exile and was so beautiful even the demon Ravana wanted her.

Malti shook her head. Although everyone loved Sita, that love hadn't helped her find happiness. Malti remembered her mother telling her the story of Sita, how no matter what happened, she had stayed pure and good. A good wife and a good mother. Malti had always believed this to be true. Now she wondered how Sita had coped.

After being forced to live in the jungle, Sita was then kidnapped and kept in Lanka in a house with female demons. Then, when Lord Rama rescued her and took her home, his countrymen forced him to question her purity after having spent so much time as a captive of the demon. Sita called on Mother Earth to help her. With tears in her eyes, and trembling with rage, Sita asked to be taken back to the earth if she was pure. At that moment, the earth opened and took Sita away. Away from her sons. Away from Rama, who she loved and who, in that moment, realized just what he had lost.

Malti turned the final corner before her house and took a deep breath. All of life couldn't be like in the films, nor would she ever be as good as Sita, although she would try.

She saw Jasu, the madwoman, coming toward her and muttering as she walked. Jasu had once had a husband and she'd been a good wife. Then one day things changed. It wasn't a slow, gradual change. She just went mad. She started talking to herself. Hitting herself. Even tore out her hair. Finally, her husband left her and moved away from Hastinapore, leaving Jasu with the house and a wallet full of money. Only, Jasu never stopped talking to herself. Now she laughed or smiled lopsidedly as she sang.

Ganga Ba told Bhraamanji to make sure he gave Jasu food if she ever came by. "People come in all types, Malti. God knows each of us could have become just like Jasu if fate decreed. Still, I'm sure you have a stronger mind. I know I do.

If she'd come to me for advice, I'd have helped her to manage her life better."

But sometimes, thought Malti, life managed you. She remembered her wedding night, when she was left alone until dawn. At the time she had been angry. Now she took that night as one of reprieve.

14

TULSI OPENED THE gate and made her way through the garden. The others were in the field playing cricket. Kalu still came down to the village to join in the fun, but his music practice had increased and he hadn't played a full game in a long while. Tulsi sat quietly against the wall closest to the window where Guruji's and Kalu's music floated directly out to her. The flute, taanpura, and Guruji's voice calmed her, made her feel secure.

This was where Guruji finally found her, curled up, half asleep, fingers and feet softly tapping in time to Kalu's flute. "So you like the music, do you?"

Tulsi jumped. She reminded Guruji of a fawn, too scared to run, too scared to stay.

"Well, then, come in. No use sitting out here when the music is being played inside." Guruji held out a hand and, tugging gently at her little finger, guided her inside.

Kalu half rose as Guruji brought Tulsi in. "Guruji! It's only Tulsi. She just likes the music, she can't—"

"I'm well aware of that," said Guruji. "This child has the good taste to enjoy our music. I intend to take advantage of that. Can you sing, girl?"

Tulsi shook her head.

"But, Guruji—"

"Kalu, I'm talking to the girl." He turned back to Tulsi, patting her on the arm. "Don't worry about him, he's a tad testy at times." Tulsi smiled. Kalu groaned but decided to keep quiet.

"Now, Kalu, I want you to play. Play Raag Yaman, which we have been practicing. And I want you to put your heart and soul into it. Tulsi, I want you to listen, and if you ever feel ready to make a sound, do so. It doesn't matter if you don't catch all the notes or the tune. Kalu won't be distracted." Guruji speared Kalu with one look before turning back to Tulsi. "It's not a test, my dear. Just close your eyes and relax into the sound."

Kalu also closed his eyes and began to play. The music, light and bright, flew out of the flute. As she listened, Tulsi flew over mountains, all the way to the sea. It didn't matter here that she couldn't speak; she'd never felt so free.

The girl stayed for the whole lesson, leaning against a pile of cushions by the sarod. She traced the intricate pattern work between the drum and the neck of the instrument, careful not to touch the strings. It was quiet here, and peaceful. She didn't have to do anything or make herself heard in any way. The pen and paper she always kept by her side stayed on the ground. She could just listen to the music and learn about why the notes were played a particular way.

Guruji never indicated that he knew Tulsi had a problem, and he treated her as if there was nothing of note in her silence. He told her to come at least once a week if she was really interested in music.

In time, she was able to recognize the different raags. Each emphasized a particular note and had a unique quality to it. Sometimes the smallest of changes could affect the whole mood of the raag. She found her mood changing, too, when Kalu played well. As she learned, she also became far more discriminating, smiling when the lesson was on track and shaking her head or frowning at an awkward phrasing or a hitch in tempo. She never felt awkward when she was with Kalu and Guruji and looked forward to the times she could forget herself in music.

~

Kalu closed his eyes. He took a deep breath and held it, then released it slowly through his mouth. A crow in the distance marked his time with its call. He opened his eyes, lifted a flute to his lips, and started to play.

It was a process he repeated whenever he practiced. Whether in a field, in the garden, or at the roadside, Kalu always closed his eyes prior to playing. He let the air wrap around his body and sink into his skin, until he could almost taste the quality of the day or night. Soaking in the place, he called it. Guruji called it immersion.

Even here, an hour away from Hastinapore, Kalu repeated the ritual before starting to play. He could feel the heat and smell the bite of petrol radiating from his motorbike. The scooter was a present from Ashwin, Vaid Dada, and Guruji, along with a passport. They had entered his date of birth as 27 September, the day Kalu first arrived at Guruji's house and was accepted as a student. The passport was his prize possession, after his flutes.

He preferred the motorbike to the train and bus. It meant he could travel easily from Guruji's house to Hastinapore. He could stop when and where he liked and there was the added bonus of speed. The new highway helped. The scooter allowed him to weave through traffic in silence, without the constant chatter of other travelers and train vendors selling their wares. On the scooter, he could continue to play music in his mind. He normally chose a raag at the beginning of any trip and played with it for the duration.

Kalu opened his eyes as the sound of the flute drifted away, and realized he was no longer alone. Children had appeared, sitting quietly around him, drawn by the spell of the flute.

"How do you play like that?" asked one child.

Kalu could see the boy's ribs through the holes in his shirt and was reminded of himself when he was young. He removed a shorter flute from the flute box and gave it to the boy. "See, here, this is where you blow. Now try, softly."

The boy took the flute with both hands, his fingers leaving a trail of dust over Kalu's, who turned the instrument to position the hole correctly under the boy's mouth. The child blew and the sound, loud and clear, made him jump in surprise.

"Easy," Kalu said, laughing. "That's a good start."

"But I didn't sound like you."

"That takes practice. At least you can hear the difference." Kalu paused. He looked at the small hand holding the dust-covered flute. "Why don't you keep the flute?"

The child's chest expanded as he nodded. "Can I really? Just for me, not my brother, too?"

"Just for you," returned Kalu. "Now, all of you," he said, looking at each child in turn. "You are all witnesses that this flute belongs only to . . . child, what's your name?"

"Tushar."

"But we call him Tambu!" The children laughed.

Tushar scowled, only stopping when Kalu shook his hand, and then, ignoring the others, showed him how to moderate his blowing. The children finally left at the end of the lesson, promising Kalu they would make sure that Tushar kept the flute and that they, too, would help him to look after it.

Kalu clapped the dirt from his hands and rubbed the hardened skin around his fingers. They were as much his instruments as were his flutes.

Packing away his remaining flutes, he returned to his bike. He'd be in Hastinapore soon. That's when he would tell his friends he was leaving India. Not for good but for three whole weeks. Martin had asked Guruji if Kalu could join his next tour, and to Kalu's amazement, Guruji agreed. A trip to America and perhaps Canada.

"I thought you wouldn't let me play professionally until I knew everything," he'd said to Guruji.

"The day you know everything is the day you die. It's my job to decide where and how you perform. I don't know if the wider audience is ready for you yet, my son, but you are ready for your first taste of the world. You need exposure and practice. The West is a good place for you to start. They, like you, are still developing their ear for our music.

"I want you to try your hand at performing in an auditorium rather than in the open air. Use your eyes and ears as much as your hands. Listen to Martin and"—Guruji's frown softened; his hands stilled over Kalu's—"play from your heart and from your soul. Remember there are two kinds of music, one for the public, for entertainment, and the other private, for the spirit. Practice both. Perform for the people listening, for yourself, and for God."

Even now, Kalu wasn't sure if the feeling in his stomach was excitement or dread. Of course, the bike would stay behind while he traveled. He'd decided to ask Bal if he could look after it for him.

It had taken him time to get over the hurt of Bal's rejection. Guruji had helped him, however, telling him to stop thinking of himself and to think about what Bal wanted and why he had said no. Then Vaid Dada had suggested something that Bal had finally agreed to. It still upset Kalu that it was Dada and Guruji who found a solution that suited Bal better, but he realized that Bal needed to find a place that was his own. Now Bal was settled, still in Hastinapore but with a wage-paying job and a small room of his own. The place was a few meters wide, with just enough space for a mattress and a gas stove. But Kalu understood the wealth it represented. He wondered if he'd ever feel like a place was his, the way that Bal did in his single room. While he loved his own life, Guruji's house was still Guruji's and he was still the student.

Kalu shrugged, shaking off his negative thoughts and focusing on how pleased Bal would be to have the Kinetic. Knowing Bal, he'd probably store the bike in his room for safekeeping, lock the door, and sleep outside, rather than ride it!

~

Bal put his arm around Kalu's shoulders. "I need to thank you and Vaidji for finding me a job. It's good to have real paid work. The sun's hot in the fields, and I don't get as much time in the shade or by the river. But the company is good. And, thanks to you, I finally have my freedom. If you and Vaid Dada hadn't paid off my bond and found me this job . . . I wouldn't have had anything."

"The women?" Kalu looked sideways to see Bal's reaction.

"The company." Bal had grown in confidence and size since the last time they met. Five months of working in the fields had pumped energy and vigor through his chest and down his arms. He stood tall, more a man than a boy, unafraid of anyone or anything. "And I've learned a lot. Soon I'll know enough to . . ."

"To what?" Kalu asked, curious. He had never before heard Bal speak of his dreams.

"Well . . ." Bal ducked his head, rubbing the side of his face. He spoke in a rush, only stopping as he ran out of breath. "Maybe own my own farm one day. Of course, it's a long way away, maybe when I'm old, and if the land was cheap enough . . ."

"You'll make it happen, I know you will."

"But . . . I don't . . . Kalu, I don't want any help, yaar."

Kalu looked injured. "Me? Did I say anything?"

"No, but I know you. Yaar, you are my best friend. More than a friend. You are my brother. Bhai, I would be less than nothing if it wasn't for you." He held up his hand as Kalu started to speak. "This job, being paid, being part of a team, being respected for what I do—it's all because you had faith in me. But I need to do something for myself. So that I know I can. I don't need anything big. And I can wait. I have all the time in the world to find the perfect place."

"And who will you share that perfect place with, yaar? I've noticed you making cow eyes at that pretty girl with the black shirt and blacker hair at garba."

"No one." Bal's cheeks burned. He took his time rolling tobacco into a small, white wafer, twisting it, then finally lighting it. "What about you, yaar? I've seen the way those girls run to you," he said. "They sound like little birds as they dance around you."

"More like crows. I don't like the ones that squawk."

"It's the ones that don't that you have to worry about."

~

"Isn't she beautiful?" Raja looked across at his new bride as she made her way to the well.

Malti had originally been the one carrying the water pot, but Anju stopped her, taking the container herself. "I know you'd like to talk with your brother," she said. "You don't have much time before you have to leave again. Your brother would love to spend some time with you instead of me."

Raja disagreed, but Anju had gone, leaving brother and sister behind. Raja's face had matured in the last few days. His wife had changed him already, simply by being there.

Anju was shy, as were most new brides, but Malti sensed the girl's gentle strength and, most important, a genuine desire to please both Raja and the family. It took time to get used to a new home and a bride's place in it, but Anju already seemed like part of the family—more so even than Malti. Her mother was right: brides belonged to their in-laws.

Vimu Ba and Papaji were good to Malti. Vimu Ba had mellowed in the years since the marriage, relaxing in Malti's company. She was the one who insisted they all attend Raja's wedding, even when Malti's husband argued he was too busy.

"Beta, you have to go," said Vimu Ba. "How would it look?"

"Worse if I lose my job. Is that what you want? Haven't you got enough from me?" Malti's husband protested.

Vimu Ba had forced him to attend, just for one day. She doted on her son, as did Papaji; sitting against the warm clay wall, Malti wondered how such kind people could not see the coldness in their son.

Part of Malti wanted him to attend, the other willed him to stay away. He hadn't been to Malti's village since their wedding. She knew her parents would be happy to see him, to show off their well-married daughter, but she worried about what he would say to his friends on his return. It was bad enough that he laughed at her and treated her the way he did, making cruel remarks to her in private about the fact that she was frigid and infertile. She couldn't stand him being rude to her parents or about their village.

Vimu Ba had also given permission for Malti to stay longer, both before and after the wedding. "Heaven knows your mother could use the help, even if it is the bride's side that does most things. Besides, how would it look if we all stayed for such a short time?"

Malti nudged her brother. "So, are you happy?" She already knew the answer but just wanted to see his grin.

"It's not what I expected. Not at all. I just want to look after her. She is so delicate and small." Raja rubbed his ear. "And don't you dare tell her I said so. Or anyone else."

"No, sir. Can't have anyone thinking my brother has turned to mush."

"Now, don't go teaching her any bad tricks, will you?" Raja poked his sister in the waist. "I want her to look up to me, not laugh at me."

"She's shy, but she's not crazy!" Malti quieted, reminding Raja of the solemn child he used to tease into laughter. "Treat her well, bhai."

"I intend to. I never thought I'd be so lucky. Our parents picked well."

"Yes, they did," replied Malti. "Pity she has to live with you, though!" She leaped up as she spoke, before the conversation could turn to her marriage.

"Ma, I'd like—"

"Yes, we know what you'd like, Raja, now go!" His mother rolled her eyes as she waved him out of the kitchen with a spoon.

Anju blushed.

"Don't worry, beti, he's not normally under our feet like this. I remember his father doing the same thing when we were first married."

The other two women laughed as Malti grabbed a pot and left the kitchen to fill it with water. She felt more like crying than laughing.

When she was little, Raja would let her come and watch as the boys played cricket. They had used a treasured yellow plastic ball. The stumps were sticks dug into the dirt. At the time, he wanted to be Viv Richards and worshipped the West Indian cricket team, just as she worshipped him. Raja's team always played against India. That way, he was happy regardless of who won. The boys played on the outskirts of the village, before the dirt turned into farmland.

Malti would sit on the ground and watch her brother. When the ball hit the tree on the far side, the boys yelled "Six," and a cloud of birds would rise from the branches, chattering to one another. The game ended at sunset, when the colored cricket ball became hard to see. She wished she could return to that time. Of course, she knew she couldn't. And tomorrow she would have to return to Hastinapore.

She thought of the way Raja looked at his wife, the way his eyes followed her, even when he spoke to someone else. After all this time, Malti wondered if her husband ever looked at her the same way. Really looked at her.

On warm, balmy nights, his two best friends from college often visited. One now worked in a factory. The other, like her husband, had a government job. All three valued their positions, often talking to Papaji about their responsibilities and potential before making their way to the rooftop.

She recalled the first time they had visited. Vimu Ba sent Malti, the new bride, up after them with drinks and bhajiyaa, the potato cut thin, lightly battered, and fried crisp. As she walked up the steps, she remembered her mother's advice: "Be good, obey your new family, make yourself useful to your mother-in-law, and care for your husband."

"Yes?" her husband asked as Malti stood in the doorway. "What is it?" Ganga Ba treated her servants with more respect.

Malti lowered her eyes so that he wouldn't see them well up with tears. She placed the food and drink on the table. Laughter followed her down the stairs.

Sitting in the stairwell for a moment to compose herself before returning to the kitchen, she had still been able to hear the conversation above.

"How did they pick her, yaar? Does she ever talk to you?"

"Aré, she doesn't need to talk. She's attractive enough."

"There is nothing to talk about, yaar. Malti does as she is told. She was my parents' choice and they can have her," her husband had replied.

She had thought that things would change with time, but they hadn't. This thing they were caught in had nothing to do with love. Or even respect. You couldn't grow to love someone who refused to look at you.

She knew her husband would rather have married someone else. Perhaps someone who could communicate with him. Who had the same experience. Who could talk to his friends and love the way he wanted to love. Not someone simple, like her. With no education.

Malti brushed her eyes hard with the back of her hand. It wasn't even worth crying about.

Raja and their father walked Malti to the bus stop.

"So, ben, when am I going to be an uncle? Give me plenty of warning." Raja ruffled her hair as he spoke.

"You'll be an uncle for my children just as soon as I become an aunt for yours."

Their father grunted. "Both of you better make it quick if you want me to be alive to see my grandchildren." The words took Malti by surprise. Her father wasn't that old. Was he ill?

"He's joking, ben. Father, you know how serious Malti can be. Don't scare her like that."

Malti's father took her hand and squeezed it gently, pushing her toward the bus. "Keep well, beta."

Malti looked out through the barred window of the bus. Her father and brother seemed a part of another place. A different reality. She ceased to be the daughter, her body taking the form and weight of the daughter-in-law. A wife. She thought about her husband. She never called or thought of him as anything other than "him" or "husband." They were the only words that held together their relationship. He sat at the table every morning, reading yesterday's paper, as she served him and his father tea. Never looking up, only turning to comment to Papaji on the rise in petrol prices and the increase in import tax. Things he had learned, no doubt, at college. The same college Raja went to. Her brother had seen him in the corridors and knew he was a good student. "If Raja knows him, and he comes from a good family, then . . ." her parents had said . . . But who really knew a person until they lived with them?

Vimu Ba made sure Malti learned to cook her son's favorite foods and told her friends her son had married well. "She may come from a poorer family, but she is very well behaved. You know, even though we would prefer she stay at home, old Ganga Ba won't let her go. She likes her company. No cleaning, of course. We put a stop to that."

Malti bit her tongue. She couldn't complain about her in-laws. When she was sick, Vimu Ba would scold her before making her a glass of milk and turmeric. Papaji would smile as she served him rice. Her husband, however, behaved as if she didn't exist.

. . .

Tulsi sat to the side of Kalu, resting against the wall by the bookshelf, listening to the music. Guruji had turned on the lights to compensate for the lack of sunlight. The day was stormy, and Kalu's practice had not been going well at all.

"No, boy. Put your heart into it. Your fingers are moving, but that's it."

Kalu stopped playing, struggling to breathe. "You're lucky my fingers are moving at all. This doesn't work." His fingers hurt, the muscles in his back hurt, and nothing Guruji said made sense. "Can't we go out for a while and stretch before the rain comes again?"

"Tulsi seems quite happy here. You're the one who's distressed." Guruji pressed his fingertips to his eyes. "Let's try again. Something different but the same raag, please. Tulsi's raag, Raag Yaman."

Guruji had never before called it Tulsi's raag, but it was the raag she always thought of as her own. The one Kalu played the first day she came to his class. She closed her eyes and settled by the cushions next to the sarod, making herself comfortable. Kalu chose one of his newer flutes, a smaller one that would have a bright sound. Its brown binding reminded Kalu of Tulsi and the little brown bird he often thought of when he saw her.

Kalu stopped to breathe before lifting the flute to his mouth. This time he played the girl. He imagined her singing and speaking. The love of her uncle and aunt as well as her grandparents, the strength of Mother Earth that held her while the others died.

And as he played, a small, faint sound could be heard. Tulsi, her cheeks soaked with tears, shuddered convulsively.

Guruji held her tightly as she followed the sound of the flute all the way back to her own sound, her voice.

Tulsi threw pebbles into the stream, humming softly to herself. Coming back from the fields, her grandfather stopped, listened, then ran to the house to call his wife.

He didn't tell her what he had heard, just asked her to follow him, quickly. He kept ahold of her hand, pulling her down the path toward the stream. His wife followed, half scolding, half laughing, until he motioned for her to keep quiet, leading her toward some bushes by the stream.

They both stood in the shadows listening to the sweet sound. Tulsi's tone was soft but confident. Crickets buzzed along with her while the flowing water provided additional accompaniment. She sounded as if she had been making sweet sounds forever.

Her grandmother made a move toward her, then stopped, worried the dream would turn into a nightmare if she did.

She pulled out her necklace of holy basil, the basil that had the same name as Tulsi, and prayed, "Lord, if you love me, let her keep humming." She didn't ask for words. Not yet. It was too soon.

~

The last notes faded into the dark night. The only sound remaining was the low hum of the generator. The villagers sat quietly.

Many of them had come out of curiosity. Through the years they'd heard the children talk about the flute boy who played cricket with them. They all knew that the musician who adopted him had been famous, even if he was a little mad. They hoped the famous musician would be at the concert, but he wasn't. Just the flute boy, a tabla player from another village, and Tulsi, the girl who couldn't speak.

Tulsi's grandparents had put on the concert as a celebration after the havan—five days of prayers as thanks for the miracle that had happened. Together with Tulsi's aunt and uncle, they thanked God for Kalu. They still couldn't believe their girl could sing. While she didn't speak yet, she sang the taraana. Sounds without words. The Moguls had made it popular because they couldn't remember the words to Hindu songs. The sounds worked for Tulsi, and with them she could finally express herself.

The vaid believed Tulsi would speak when she was ready. The fact that she not only made sounds but also sang in syllables was a good sign. Her vocal cords were fine and were being used. This was the most important thing.

Tulsi's grandparents walked up to the stage and bowed to Kalu.

"Please don't bow to me." He pulled them up. "Tulsi is the one you should be congratulating."

"But you, you are the reason she has a voice."

"Please, it wasn't me at all. Thank Guruji or Dada."

Tulsi smiled at his discomfort and added to it by touching his feet and looking up at him with eyes so bright they could have eclipsed the moon. She handed him a crumpled piece of paper. "Tonight," it said, "you were my guru."

Kalu looked at Tulsi, properly, and realized that she was no longer a child but a young woman.

Part 3

BOL BANDH

The third part of the raag is the culmination of what has come before. Here the rhythm has primacy and the original melodies are broken up and regrouped— each answering and creating a counterpoint for new rhythmic and melodic cycles. The bol bandh demands fast, spontaneous musical improvisations. The interplay between the musicians brings about a sense of immediacy, force, and momentum.

—GURUJI

15

MALTI WIPED THE sweat from her forehead with the back of her hand. Those small droplets of salt evaporated at the touch of her knuckles. The handle of the jute bag, which contained eggplant and broad beans, rubbed her palm, distracting her for a few moments from the unceasing heat.

It was meant to rain. The man on the television at Ganga Ba's had been talking about it for days. It seemed as though everyone else had been talking about it for months. As the heat continued, everyone became short-tempered.

Malti moved the bag from one hand to the other, wiping the freed hand on her sari as she walked, thinking about rain. Stopping, she raised her nose like a deer, checking the wind for a scent. For a second, she thought that underneath the diesel and the dust she had smelled the soft, damp rain.

Malti remembered the first time she recognized it. A sweet smell that sat at the back of her throat so she could almost taste it. That first time she thought it was the perfume of a rare flower, like the mogra flower but earthier, heavy but still fresh.

She continued walking, breathing deeply enough to catch

the exhalation of wet earth under the dust that rose from the road on waves of heat. She scanned the sky for rain clouds, knowing how fast it could change from blue to black.

Finally, as she passed the bus shelter, the rain came. People walking around her slowed to a halt. Beggars looked up rather than down, raising their hands as if to ask the sky for money. Even the shopkeepers walked out of their stores, hastily pulling down awnings or dragging in produce from the footpath so that it wouldn't be ruined in the downpour.

And it fell. Green, curving rain, falling in sheets, sliding down banana leaves and over lime-washed buildings and old brickwork. Cascading in large, heavy drops. Children laughed, mouths wide open, trying to catch those drops before they landed on the dry, red earth. The rain changed the color of their clothes, their hair, and their skin into something brighter and richer.

Malti dropped her bag. The broad beans scattered and the eggplant rolled down the street as she raised her hands, feeling the rain wash away a year of dirt, both inside and out. It made pathways and rivulets through her hair, over her face, and down her neck. For the first time in a long while, Malti laughed, feeling the heat from the ground dissipate through her body, mingling with the thick, wet rain.

Later in the year, as the monsoon season continued, the rain would become a hindrance. But in that moment, those large, fat drops of rain falling like rose petals reminded Malti of who she was. Not a servant or a wife. Not a sister or a daughter, just Malti. She felt someone behind her and turned, still laughing. By her side was a man, just as wet as she, with a matching smile. He held up a sodden hessian bag.

"Madam, your vegetables."

Kalu leaned over the hotel balcony in yet another city, watching the night lights fade as the sky turned to gold in the early hours of the morning. This life of traveling and playing still felt unreal. His first trip, the year before, had been overwhelming. The fear and magic of it all. While the journey on the plane had been exciting, the thing that struck him the most was the number of white people at the airport when they landed. He thought he was used to seeing people from different countries. But seeing so many people, all wearing Western clothes, was something he'd never encountered before. It wasn't uncomfortable, just different. He realized how Martin must have felt when he first came to India.

During Kalu's initial trip, Martin was always beside him, ready to help as needed, while still letting him find his own way.

The best part of it was the music. Even though he played only a few pieces at each concert, it was a joy to play onstage with Martin. To feel the expectation build around him. The silence before that first note.

His first concert in India, in Delhi, had been more frightening, as the audience was much more knowledgeable. It was a fund-raiser for victims of an earthquake. The organizers had asked for Guruji, and he'd sent Kalu. Now, though, people asked for them both. Guruji allowed Kalu to perform at the events he deemed appropriate, although he never attended himself. He had agreed to a few performances, but not too many. Kalu liked that people liked his music. And that he could finally contribute to the household. But he loved the music even more.

When Kalu played by himself, the world disappeared. When he played with Martin, with the dhol and tabla, sometimes a keyboard or cello accompanying them, he forgot the audience and was immersed in the music. He felt he had been created for this and only this.

Their piece together on this trip was always last on the program. It would start with Western notation—an Irish air or a jazz number—and slowly, as the energy built, they would move, note by note, beat by beat, into a formal raag structure, missing the aalaap and entering with the antara and later the jugalbandhi.

Their music wasn't fusion in the normal sense; it was combustion. As the music leaped from one continent to another, members of the ensemble joined in, adding their force to the sound, only to have it scooped up and thrown out to the audience by the flute and the violin. Sometimes the performance went on for one hour, sometimes for two. Either way, performing was like being in the eye of a storm.

Afterward, Kalu and Martin would walk or ride to the closest bar or club to listen to more music and somehow release the charge that had built up inside them. Other nights they would return to the hotel and sit, silent and exhausted, as the euphoria slowly descended into deep peace.

The last of the night air brushed Kalu's face. After one trip abroad, he'd thought himself a seasoned traveler. But this tour was longer and covered more cities. Six weeks of hotel, auditorium, music, then airport or coach again. Each city felt the same, with no space in between. He missed India and his friends. He wondered what they were doing now. Tulsi would be back at school, living with her uncle and aunt. While it was early morning here, Ashwin would be halfway through the day, as would Malti. Kalu was looking forward to seeing her on his return. It felt like a long time since they'd really talked.

Martin was still asleep. Kalu picked up his flute box, left a note, and closed the door behind him. He wandered down through empty streets until he reached the docks. Men with faces half hidden in woolen hats lifted trays filled with flailing fish from boats, throwing heaving sea life into large, industrial crates coated with ice. The ground was wet, the air crisp from the ice and salt. The men's thick-soled boots and large bodies covered in rain jackets seemed immune to the cold. They shouted and laughed, and the noise, energy, and smell of fish reminded Kalu of the fish bazaar in Hastinapore.

The men worked hard and fast. Kalu found a milk crate across the road and sat down to play. The chill in the air lessened as the sun started to warm the bitumen surrounding him. Kalu ran through his morning practice before closing his eyes. He played a tune that was hard and fast and rolling, like the sea. When he opened his eyes, the docks were quiet. The men stood in a circle around him. A pile of gold coins and a small ice pack containing a fish lay at his feet.

~

"Malti, we need more dhaana and chilies; there isn't enough for the chutney. Can you go back to the market? Govinda always gives discounts when he sees a pretty face. See him, and make sure that the coriander is fresh."

"Yes, Vimu Ba." Malti kept her head bowed so that her mother-in-law wouldn't see the heat rising up her cheeks. She would have to go out after all.

When Malti got married, she'd expected to find a husband who cared for her and a mother-in-law whom she would have to learn to like. But as they'd spent more time together, she saw through Vimu Ba's sternness. On bad days, Malti decided Vimu Ba liked her only because she was obedient. At other times, Malti knew her mother-in-law liked her, even loved her, as a daughter. Malti filled the gap menfolk couldn't and wouldn't.

She often wondered how a kind woman like Vimu Ba could have possibly given birth to the man Malti was married to. She used to get angry just thinking about how he duped his parents. Still, no one would find out. It was a woman's job, her job, to keep everyone in the family happy and to keep the family together, no matter what.

Malti searched for a cloth bag to carry the chilies in. She willed the color to leave her cheeks and wondered if she was just as bad as her husband. A lie was a lie, after all. Finding the yellow cloth bag and taking a long, slow breath, she straightened and smiled. "I'll be back soon."

"Take your time, beti, you've been inside all day. It's not often you get some time to relax. But don't stand in the sun! We don't want you to get too dark."

Malti brushed her hand over Vimu Ba's cheek, dusting away invisible flour in a gesture close to, but not quite, a caress. "I get more than enough time to relax. You should try to rest yourself."

Vimu Ba laughed and waved her out.

Malti blinked. The sun was bright after the darkness of the kitchen. The small windows and thick, lime-washed walls sealed with cow dung repelled mosquitoes and kept the house cool, just as the marble floors and ceiling fans did in Ganga Ba's more modern house.

The bazaar wasn't far from the haveli, but she walked slowly, one step to every two heartbeats, head tilted so she would hear Anand's call if it came. The heat seemed to clean her skin, burning away the past, leaving it new and fresh. She caught her breath as she heard a male voice singing, then released it, realizing it came from a radio.

She didn't notice the houses or shops crowded on top of one another, each vying for space. She didn't even wave to Jaya-shree Ben in the paan shop. Jaya-shree Ben went to call out to her but, seeing a customer, turned back. It was obvious Malti had her mind on other things today.

It was almost monsoon season again. It didn't seem like a year had passed since she first met Anand. He'd smiled at her when he handed her the rain-soaked bag, then brushed her hand as they collected vegetables from the ground. He lived in a town three hours away and worked for the camera suppliers, so he came to Hastinapore only when local businesses needed more stock. Three, maybe four times a year. Their meetings were, she told herself, innocent. They only ever talked.

However, if Vimu Ba had not asked her to go to the bazaar, Malti would not have left the house. Earlier that day, returning from the river with the washing, she'd seen Anand's truck on the roadside and had resolutely passed by, joining Kavita for the walk home in order to avoid him. She knew this was what her mother would expect of her, regardless of how much she enjoyed his company. She was married now, and married women acted with decorum. Still, her mother had no idea of her life.

Ganga Ba insisted that letter writing was as good an exercise for Malti as reading. In her usual high-handed way, she gave Malti the time and material to write home, and paid for the postage of the letters. Malti wrote to Kalu and to her parents every week. Now that Raja was home to read the letters, her parents could get news without having to walk all the way to the phone booth. It occurred to Malti for the first time that maybe Ganga Ba felt guilty asking Malti to read the paper to her every second day, and insisting on the letter writing was the old lady's way of thanking her.

At Ganga Ba's she forgot for a while that she was no longer a girl. It was funny how learning to write and read had become useful after all. As she became a better writer, however, her letters had become less open. Malti wrote about what she did each day, the kindness of Vimu Ba and Papaji, the gossip in the village—all the things that took place around the edges of her life. These were things she knew her family wanted to hear. She forced herself to write about her husband so that they wouldn't wonder why he featured so little in her letters.

Stopping at Govinda's stall, she sorted through the chilies and coriander, the content of each piled gunnybag. She pressed the long, green chilies to find the freshest.

"They are all good, ben, the very best in the market—in the whole of Gujarat, even." Govinda had known Malti since she first started working at Ganga Ba's. Every day, he said the same thing. Every time, Malti smiled and continued to test his produce. She picked the best bunch of coriander and placed it together with the chilies in the bag.

It must have been fate, thought Malti, that on the very day Anand was back, Vimu Ba would decide to make chutney, and fate that led to a shortage in coriander. She walked down the alley toward the Muslim area. Somewhere behind her, someone started to sing: "When I first saw you, I had no idea that my world would change."

She stopped. Raised her head, then continued walking. His voice was as warm as his smile. Soft-spoken and gentle, he made Malti feel that she mattered. Not because of what she did but who she was. She took the longer road home, down through the town and around the riverbank, knowing that he would follow at a safe distance. Soon, the village was left behind and they could talk.

16

Adalaj was a desolate place, forsaken by the gods of fertility for centuries. Rubha Devi, together with her husband, would have changed that. Now she would have to change it alone. She walked out of the small temple and up the few steps to the entrance of the step well. Sultan Begda stood there smiling, his excitement betrayed by his eyes as much as by the small bubble of spit teetering on the side of his mouth.

He watched her glide up the steps, heavy in the bridal finery he had bestowed on her. A queen fit for his kingdom. The wait had been worth the twenty years and the disposal of her husband, Veer Singh. It was always worth it in the end. He walked beside her into the first level of the vaav. The heat of the day disappeared. Here, even just one level down, the stones radiated coolness.

As they descended to the second tier, the villagers, standing in the alcoves surrounding each level, led by the priest, began to chant.

Om trayambakam yajaamahe sugandhim
pushtivardhanam.

Urvaarukamiva bandhanaan mrityor mukshiya
  maamritaat.
Meditate on the three-eyed reality that causes all life
  to flourish.
Just as the gourd is cut from bondage to the plant,
  may the soul be liberated from the body at death,
  for the soul is immortal. Fear not death.

In the future, travelers would use the alcoves to trade in and as shelter from the heat of the day before continuing their journey through the night. Now the space was filled with his subjects, waiting for the queen to plunge the blade into the sand at the bottom of the well, finally filling the lower levels with water.

She had been clever, this woman beside him, making him promise to bring water to the land and to complete the vaav in memory of her dead husband before remarrying. The well had taken twenty years and still wasn't quite finished. The masons promised him it would finally yield water.

As they moved down another tier, the sound of the chant deepened and echoed.

Om trayambakam yajaamahe sugandhim
  pushtivardhanam.
Urvaarukamiva bandhanaan mrityor mukshiya
  maamritaat.
Meditate on the three-eyed reality that causes all life
  to flourish.
Just as the gourd is cut from bondage to the plant,
  may the soul be liberated from the body at death,
  for the soul is immortal. Fear not death.

As she listened to the song, her nerves steadied. She'd known this day would come eventually. It was a terrible promise that she'd made, caught between wanting water for her people and praying the well would remain barren, just as she intended to be without her husband.

Rubha Devi hadn't believed Sultan Begda, that bastard, could do it. This well at Adalaj was seven levels deep. Deeper and more beautiful than any other. The designs and murals decorating the walls became more delicate as she moved deeper into the well. Rubha Devi remembered her husband as she walked. The touch of his hands on her breast. The softness of his lips. The strength of his arms. It was as if only part of her had been alive since he had been killed.

They finally came to the lowest balcony.

She could no longer hear the words of the chant, just the sound that encircled her and held her, like her husband had.

Rubha Devi raised the sword, and her voice cut through the song. "Jai Devi," she called, just once, before plunging the knife between her breasts and falling into the pit.

Water rose where her blood met the sand, covering her body and taking her back into the earth.

~

Ganga Ba waited for the others to disembark before stepping out of the minibus. She rested one hand on the sliding door to stop the ground from moving. She should never have let her daughter talk her into this trip.

Having the family visit was one thing. Traipsing all over the country was quite another. Although she would never admit it, the journey had tired her more than she expected.

Adalaj ni Vaav, the famous underground well, was only an hour or two from Ahmedabad. When her daughter asked the driver to make the detour, Ganga Ba didn't comment, even when her daughter explained that she wanted the children to see their heritage. Since when had this well, in the middle of the parched countryside, built by a Muslim king lusting after a Hindu queen, ever been part of their heritage? she wanted to know.

She could have said something then but didn't, not wanting to see the wounded look on her daughter's face again. Ganga Ba sighed as she hobbled up to the well. With V.P., she never had to hold her tongue. It wasn't something she was used to. She was famous around Hastinapore for speaking her mind.

The children raced down the narrow steps into the vaav, followed by their parents carrying a video recorder and camera.

"Careful, Pinky, don't go too fast. We don't want any nasty accidents. Ba, are you coming? Do you need help?"

Ganga Ba waved them ahead, feeling the stiffness in her joints more than the humidity. She knew the steps within the well would be small and damp. Instead of following the others, she walked past the small temple dedicated to Jai Devi, the bringer of water, to the far end of the vaav. On the surface, the step well looked like a one-meter-high slab of ornamental stone, perhaps the structure for a building that had never been built rather than the roof of a well.

The heat eased the stiffness in her joints. She sat, resting one foot on some stonework on the side of the vaav, and looked out. The sky was covered in gray smog, darkening the flat, brown, empty land. She could see the hole in the center of the well's roof. She knew if you stood close, you could see down into the many levels of the well. From where she sat, she could smell the musty dampness of water on stone.

The smell took her to a distant memory. She could hear her sister's voice as it had been all those years ago, whispering in her ear each night until they both fell asleep. Ganga Ba was the noisier second daughter in a house where one daughter was already one too many.

The child Gayatri, as Ganga Ba had been known, loved to drink milk. Her mother said Gayatri would drink them out of house and home. Then came the day her big sister saw their mother place powder in Gayatri's milk. The sister quietly tipped it over before it was drunk and watched as the poison slowly seeped into the ground.

Later, as the dry season started, her father had nudged the child Gayatri into the well when the sun was high and everyone including her sister was asleep. She fell, not into the water but onto a small ledge a few meters above. Luckily, a young boy had hidden near that well rather than have a nap inside the house. He heard her cries and helped her to climb out.

She'd been called lucky then by the villagers, who often asked her to rub their good luck charms. And her parents, afraid of the consequences, left her alone after that. But Gayatri never forgot the murky smell of damp stone and deep water. The same smell that covered Ganga Ba now.

A crow cawed in the distance, dragging Ganga Ba back to the present. Ganga Ba rose and pushed her sister's voice back to the deep recesses of the past. Looking around again, she thought that the land, dry and barren, probably hadn't changed all that much since Rubha Devi coerced Sultan Begda to build the well. Ganga Ba snorted. Men could be so stupid. Women, too. Nothing was worth that much trauma. Life was meant to be lived.

She turned back toward the van. Hopefully the family would return soon. Maybe they'd finally feel connected to India, through the walls of the well, and she could convince them to head back for a good meal and a comfortable bed in Ahmedabad.

Next time, she'd know better than to agree to anything more than a shopping expedition.

~

Kalu saw Malti slip through the trees and run back past the river. He waited for her to come up the road to the banyan tree, but she stopped, licking her hand and running it across a fly-away hair. She turned twice before following the path toward the main street. He watched from within the banyan tree as she continued, head down, stepping around people in her rush.

He smiled, and the rosewood flute inched its way into his hand. Malti always came when she heard him play, and from here the notes would travel in her direction.

Eyes closed, he started to play. He was tired from his trip and let his mind wander. He thought of the women he'd met along the way. Seductive lips, painted red like their nails. Confident eyes, with none of the clarity he saw in Malti's. He thought of her ready laugh, the sway of her hips, and the way she teased him.

A quiet longing slipped into his song. For companionship, and something more. Belonging. Need. A hunger that could be satisfied only by another. Kalu continued playing until the sound cooled to a whisper. He sat still, hoping to steady himself before moving. He looked down and realized the one person he expected, the only person who would have known immediately he was back, wasn't there.

It was the first time Malti hadn't come to him when he played. It upset him. It also worried him. He decided to visit her after dinner. Although he hadn't seen much of Malti's husband, he knew her parents-in-law would welcome him.

"Kalu!" Malti rose at the sound of the flute. Soft in the distance but with a lilt that was Kalu's alone.

"Stay." Anand's fingers tightened around her arm, pulling her down into the furrow between the tobacco plants.

She knelt next to him, her face a dance of sunlight and shadows from the sheltering leaves. "I haven't seen Kalu in such a long time. Not since his last trip. Ganga Ba only returned yesterday, so I didn't expect him . . ."

"Aré! Kalu, Kalu, Kalu—that's all I hear. Give me a few minutes, Madhu, my sweet—you can spend all evening with your precious Kalu."

Malti saw the anger and longing in his eyes and realized she had put that look there. She smoothed the creases on his brow with her fingertips. It was the first time she'd spontaneously touched Anand rather than waiting for him to touch her. She was keenly aware of his hand still around her arm. The music changed, slowed, twisting around her until it merged with the sound of her breath. Lowering her eyes, she lay down in the furrow. She felt the heat of the sun on her shoulder but made no move to bring it into the shade.

Malti sensed rather than heard Anand as he settled beside her. His breath caressed her face. He smelled modern, a mix of hair cream and aftershave. Malti knew if she opened her eyes, they would meet his. They lay together face-to-face.

Anand's hand moved to the sound of the flute, fingers making small circles on her skin. Lower than her sari blouse. Higher than the skirt. His palm rested near her waist, and his fingers were warmer than the sun.

He seemed happy doing just that. So different from her husband, who made her face away from him and hiked up her skirt before entering her. If she made a sound, he'd cover her mouth with his hand. Sometimes he'd slip a hand under her blouse and press it against her breast. She'd know he was climaxing by the smell of his body, a sour, fermenting yogurt smell, and by the sweat that would collect on his hairline, spraying her with drops of salt. He'd finish as suddenly and quietly as he started, and then turn his back, leaving Malti to straighten her skirt.

The sound of the flute and the feel of Anand's breath wrapped around her. She kept her eyes closed. The heat and music relaxed her, until there was just his touch and the music that became her own. She forgot who she was or who she should have been. She left behind the night before and the many nights before that and reveled in the curling tightness starting between her legs and unfurling over her stomach, beginning and ending with Anand's touch.

She took his hand and moved it lower, smiling as he gasped as if drowning. She tightened her grip and took him lower still, until she couldn't tell whether the heat came from her or from him.

Kalu sat on the chair, drinking tea. Malti stood to the side.

"Sit down, beti," Papaji said. "He's your guest."

Malti rarely spoke to her in-laws of friends or had visitors. Through the years, most of her old friends had married and moved away. Those who hadn't left were caught up in their new lives. Besides, her in-laws weren't comfortable with girls who worked for others. In their eyes, Malti had moved up in the world.

Kalu watched Malti and knew something was different. She had changed in a way he wouldn't understand until he spoke to her. But he knew they wouldn't get the opportunity now.

"How is your son?" asked Kalu, directing the question to Malti's mother-in-law out of politeness.

"He's well," replied Vimu Ba. "He had to work late again. At this rate, we won't see him until tomorrow. Poor Malti didn't have a bite of dinner. Waiting for her husband, no doubt."

Kalu looked across at Malti. She sat straight in her chair. Too straight. He cleared his throat. "I wonder if Malti could be spared for an hour or so tomorrow? Ganga Ba has—" Kalu wasn't sure what Ganga Ba had planned, but he was certain he could organize something.

"No, I couldn't," Malti interrupted. "There's too much to do here. I couldn't possibly."

Vimu Ba smiled. "She's so good to us. You know, Kalu, I don't know what I'd do without her. I've forgotten what it was like without a daughter. And I wanted one for so long. Malti was the answer to a prayer. Go, beti, it's only for a little while," she said softly, wiping her face with the end of her sari.

Malti curled into a ball in her bed. She forced a hand into her mouth so no one would hear her cries. Her body shook under the bedspread. Normally, when her husband was away, even for one night, she relaxed. Tonight she felt nothing but remorse. She had done exactly what her mother and Vimu Ba trusted her not to do. Already she felt Anand's absence. She knew she would feel this ache between her ribs as long as she lived. God had punished her by showing her what she knew she must never, ever have again.

~

Kalu and Bal walked on the path at the top of the cliffs. Bal danced about while Kalu stayed quiet, his mind half on his dinner with Malti.

"Kalu!" called Bal, waving to him from a few meters ahead. "Hurry up, yaar!"

The ground was muddy, still damp from monsoon rains. Kalu grinned and waved back. Bal was just the same. Actually, thought Kalu, there was a difference. Bal was happier. He strode rather than walked, and held his head high.

"Wait for me, bhai, and watch the mud . . . don't want to ruin your new clothes," Kalu called as Bal turned quickly to watch the girls below with their laundry baskets.

"Kalu, get that flute ready. Now we'll have some action!" Bal waved his arms about and started to imitate the dancing girls. He spun around, only to slip and fall on a laugh that turned to a shout, ricocheting down the cliff face as he disappeared.

"Bal!" Kalu called, racing to the edge of the cliff. The men under the banyan tree ran over when they heard the boy's shouts. "Call Vaid Dada. Anyone. Get help!" Kalu slid down the cliff face like a runaway rivulet of water, changing course each time he hit a hard outcrop of rock. He landed on all fours, winded. "Bal?"

Bal lay faceup. Kalu crawled down to his friend, ignoring the sharp pain in his ankle. "Bhai, are you all right?" He shook Bal's shoulder, then held his hand over Bal's nose. There was breath. Light and erratic, but there.

Bal slowly opened his eyes. "Kalu?" His voice sounded chalky, as if rocks had taken root in his vocal cords. "What happened?"

"You fell. But you'll be fine." Kalu looked down. Bal's face had suffered only a few scratches, but a deep, red stain covered his torso. Blood seeped from the back of his head and his legs. His right leg was twisted beneath him.

"I feel awful. I think this is it."

Kalu took a deep breath, willing himself to relax his face. "Don't be silly, yaar. One small fall and look at you!" He forced a smile.

Bal mirrored a ghost of a smile. But said nothing.

There was silence for a few minutes.

"The others are coming. You'll be fine in no time." Kalu lifted Bal's head into his lap, raising it so Bal could breathe a little easier.

"Play for me, Kalu. I'd like to hear you play."

"Idiot. I told you. You'll be fine in no time." Kalu gripped Bal's shoulder, feeling his collarbone. Although Bal lay still, Kalu could feel his body quivering through his shirt.

"Play."

In those few moments, Bal's voice had deteriorated, become weak, and sounded as though it came from far away.

Kalu looked at the mute appeal in Bal's eyes and, with one hand, unclipped his flute box from his back. There was a crack in the wood near the box's opening from Kalu's hasty descent down the cliff face, but the flutes inside were fine. Taking off his shirt, he placed it over Bal to hide the stain and started to play. Long, slow notes, bringing life to the music and into Bal.

Bal's hoarse breathing took on the rhythm of the music. Kalu had intended to play a song from Navratri, the lilting garba Bal loved. But his rosewood flute was deep and rich in tone. Instead, the raag soared and keened. It bound the two of them until Kalu lost track of time; he was unaware of his energy feeding Bal's still body. There was only music, stanching the flow of blood from the wounds.

Kalu heard a gasp. Opening his eyes, but still playing, he looked down, hoping Bal would be better and smiling. Bal didn't move.

Vaid Dada placed a blanket over Bal's body. He shook his head at Kalu's mute appeal. "You can stop playing, Kalu."

Kalu wouldn't stop. He shrugged off a hand that rested on his shoulder and kept playing, knowing that as long as he did, Bal's heart would beat. The music reflected the defiance in his own heart. In the story of Savitri and Satyavan, Savitri cheated the god of death to save her husband. Kalu, too, would save his friend. Bal would not die today.

Kalu played. As the music took over, the pain disappeared. Vaid Dada sat next to him. The people who had come to help lit fires and gathered around in vigil. As he played, more people came. Kalu didn't see them. His world had diminished to the circle that held his friend. Bal's chest barely moved; his face was ashen. Still Kalu played. He licked his cracked lips to moisten them, moving only as a drop of sweat from his forehead fell on Bal's face.

A lone red tear ran down Bal's cheek. He slowly opened his eyes. "Bhai, it's time," he whispered.

Kalu kept playing.

"Please, bhai. Let me go."

His flute wept.

"You promised me the world. Now let me see it. It's time."

Vaid Dada put his hand on the flute, pressing it down and away from Kalu's lips. "Enough."

In that instant Bal stopped breathing.

Kalu twisted, crying out as he flung his flute away. "Bhai. You don't understand. I need you. Bhai." He lifted Bal into his arms and cradled him.

~

Kalu's body hurt. Walking was the only thing he could think of to keep the pain away. Things would never, could never, be the same. He wished the last few days had never happened.

Goats rummaged through the round concrete encasement full of refuse by the side of the road. Crows joined them, some on the ground, others perched on the backs of goats who balanced on their hind legs or sat in the waste in order to reach more food.

He remembered the time he and Bal had gone hunting goats. It was before Kalu hurt his ankle. Long before he'd gone to live with Guruji. Bal was angry at the goats for walking between the legs of his buffaloes, causing them to bellow and scatter. He was sure the goats followed him just to find the sweetest shoots.

"Never mind," said Kalu. "We'll hunt them down and teach them a lesson. Then they'll never steal again."

"Yes, but we have nothing to hunt them with, yaar. And what do we do once we have them? Their stupid owners will catch me, and then we'll be in trouble." Bal flicked a long stick over the ground. Kalu skipped beside him.

When they were young, Kalu never walked; he only skipped or ran. Bal, on the other hand, only walked. He'd seemed so tall and experienced to Kalu. His friend had a job, shelter, food, and he still took time to talk to a boy like him. Even as a child, Kalu had sought refuge with Bal, knowing that the older boy understood the emptiness he felt deep inside but chose never to acknowledge.

That day, the two of them stole half-baked dung patties from a house by the road. Kalu distracted the girl living in the house while Bal collected the balls in his shirt. The girl even waved them good-bye. The boys hurried down the path trying not to laugh.

They spent the afternoon bowling the dung at the goats, cheering each time one burst apart on contact with the creatures. Kalu was sure no goat would ever follow Bal after such an indignity.

Now, as he watched the goats, Kalu recalled the earthy, solid smell of cow dung mixed with straw. The smell had always reminded him he wasn't alone. Now there was no one with whom to share that memory or so many others. He was on his own. Kalu collected some pebbles and flung them in a wide arc at the goats, then walked on as they bleated.

Malti found him by the river a few hours later. She offered him his flute. The one he'd found in the temple. The one he'd thrown away as Bal died. He didn't ask her how or why she had it.

"Keep it," he said, staring out at the dried, rough banks, his eyes passing over the water to the cliffs rising high on the other side. The color of jaggery where the shadows were and flame where the sun hit the ragged edges. He looked away, realizing it was all now one big grave site. "I don't want it anymore."

"And what am I going to do with it?" she asked, squatting next to him. "I can't play it. No one else can, either. It's yours, Kalu." Malti placed the flute on the ground in front of him. He didn't look at it or her.

Malti realized the silence would be broken only by her. "Look, you need to keep going."

"Why?"

"What do you mean, why? Because that's what you do. That's what we all do. People don't have a choice." Her voice rose. "Count your blessings. Bal would have wanted you to, and so do . . ." Malti left the sentence hanging in the air.

Kalu remembered he needed to talk to Malti about something; it had been important. But it was all too far away. Her words were as unreal as everything else around him. She stood and squeezed his shoulder, hard enough that he could feel each of her fingers.

"I'm late. I need to go. Remember, no one made you God. You can't take responsibility for everything. Bal died, and you lived. Make it worth something." Malti walked away, missing the tears rolling silently down his face.

"Kalu."

His head lifted as he heard his name; only one person used that tone. He felt bone-tired and knew he must have imagined that voice. Guruji couldn't be in Hastinapore. There was nothing that would bring him here.

"Kalu." Guruji collected Kalu in his arms. The man held him tight, willing life back into Kalu's trembling body. "I'm here to take you home, son. Your bags are packed. Vaid Dada will stay and finish his work. I'm taking you home."

"Why did you come? You never leave the mountains."

"I came for you, son, because you needed me." The boy folded into the man, who bore his weight, lifting him and helping him walk back toward the town.

~

Kalu sat in the back of the Jeep. His scooter remained with Ganga Ba. Guruji sat silently next to him. When they stopped for a break, Guruji studied the boy beside him. The child had grown into a man.

When he heard what happened at the cliff face, he understood that Kalu would have gained something as a musician when he lost his friend. His music must have changed, as he put his entire heart into it, making it more than just sound. If this was the case, Guruji knew it would be something Kalu would never forgive himself for.

Guruji remembered the boy who had come to him, so full of hope and bravado. Kalu was no longer that student. He had learned his final and most important lesson at the base of the cliff. The one that would make him a true musician.

Guruji held out a cup of tea. "Love doesn't come without

pain, Kalu. In both music and friendship, you will experience happiness and anguish. It's part of what makes us whole."

Kalu warmed his cold hands against the glass. The idea of drinking was too hard to contemplate.

"You did something special. You kept Bal alive for enough time so he could feel your love. So he wasn't alone."

Kalu shook his head.

Guruji placed a hand on each of the boy's shoulders, holding him still. "Listen." His voice was quiet, for Kalu's ears only. "Play, or don't play. That is up to you. But don't kill your capacity to love. Don't distance yourself from people. Don't make my mistake. Take time to decide, listen to your soul. Don't let power or pain fuel you. If you never play again, that's okay. You will always have a home. A place with me."

"Your mistake?" It was the first time Kalu had spoken since leaving Hastinapore.

Guruji looked out through the trees. "I was young and stupid and arrogant. More interested in the accolades of many than the love of one. She cried in my brother's arms, calling out my name, as I played on one of the finest stages in the world. It was to have been my greatest hour. Instead, it was the worst. She left me that night and so did the music."

"You stopped?"

"No, Kalu. The music left me. I couldn't play in front of an audience, on a stage, again. All I would see was her face." Guruji shook the memory away. "Don't punish yourself for something that was written before you were born. You can't change the past. You will never forget Bal. You will never forget this pain. I know nothing I say will truly make a difference to you at this point. But you can take your experiences and choose how they change you."

The room was dark. The sandalwood paste only partially masked the sweet, sticky smell of sweat filling the room. Kalu rarely got sick, but the fever was in full force by the time Guruji brought him home. Together the guru and Ashwin had carried Kalu indoors. Ashwin was sure it was a fever of the heart as well as the body. "All we can do, Ashwin, is tend to his body and make sure that we are here when he needs us," Guruji had said.

Now, Ashwin stretched and yawned. He opened the shutters just a little, to let in some light and fresh air. It was finally sunrise, and Vaid Dada would arrive soon.

"Tell me a story." Kalu's voice was soft and heavy, the consonants smudged around the edges, reminding Ashwin of the boy who'd arrived at the house in the mountains all those years before. He pressed his hand over Kalu's still-burning forehead as Guruji quietly paused at the bedroom door.

"I'll tell you the story, son, while Ashwin takes a break." Guruji straightened the crushed blanket. "Ashwin, get some rest. I can manage."

Sunlight filtered through the room. Guruji lifted the mosquito net, rolling the sides and tying them to the canopy so that the early morning air could wash away the odor of sickness.

"Guruji?"

"I'm here." He placed a cool, wet cloth on Kalu's forehead.

"It's so hot."

"You have a fever, son. Relax. Let me tell you Tansen's story. He burned with a fever, too."

"A story," repeated Kalu. Guruji hadn't told him stories since he was little; the one about Tansen had been a favorite. "Start at the beginning, Guruji, when he was born, not with the fire." Kalu's voice cracked.

Guruji raised the boy so he was resting against the pillows

and brought a glass of water to his lips. Then he cleared his throat and started to speak. "This story starts in Gwalior, a town in the center of India." Guruji's voice was quiet and soft.

"In this town lived the poet Mukund Mishra and his wife, who desperately wanted a child. Mishra went to obtain the blessings of the famous saint and musician Mohammad Ghaus. The saint tied a holy thread on Mishra's arm and blessed him with a son. Nine months later, the boy, Tansen, was born.

"This," said Guruji, "we know to be true.

"Tansen grew up, as boys do. His favorite activity was to go to the nearby forest with his friends, where he would imitate bird and animal sounds. Once, a group of singers were passing through the forest. Tansen hid himself in some bushes and roared like a tiger. It was so convincing, the singers became frightened. When the boy showed himself, the leader of the group praised his tigerlike roar. Encouraged, Tansen made more animal and bird sounds. The leader was the famous music teacher Haridas. He was so impressed by the performance, he offered to take Tansen as his disciple. 'He has great musical talent,' said Haridas to Tansen's father. Tansen was sent to Vrindavan to study under Haridas. He stayed there for almost ten years.

"Like you, Kalu, he started with the basic musical notes. He learned to sing and play the taanpura. He learned about the different raags and how each raag created a different mood. This we know to be true.

"One day, Tansen received a message from home that his father was dying. He went straight back to Gwalior but arrived too late and was told his father's last wish was that he study with Mohammad Ghaus, the saint-cum-musician who had blessed his father with a child.

"Of course, Tansen had other things to think about, most

important his mother, who was now alone. He remained there in the village to look after her; however, she died within a year.

"Now Tansen was free to fulfill his father's dying wish, to go to Mohammad Ghaus, who still lived in Gwalior. His new teacher introduced him to the ruler of that region, Ramchandra. He met Husani in Gwalior. Husani means 'the beautiful one.' Tansen fell in love with and then married her. I do not know whether she loved him back, or if she was as beautiful as her name, but I like to believe it is true."

Kalu closed his eyes. His breathing became more even.

"Tansen became a court musician. Then one day, the emperor Akbar came to visit. The emperor was so pleased with Tansen's musicianship that he asked to take him back to his court. Ramchandra, being the lesser king, couldn't afford to displease the powerful Akbar, so Tansen went to Agra. There he received a royal welcome, and Akbar included Tansen in his navratna as one of the 'nine jewels'—the most outstanding talents of the royal court.

"Tansen's fame spread far and wide. However, being a favorite of Akbar had its drawbacks. Many courtiers were jealous of Tansen's fame, and they began to plot his downfall. They suggested Akbar command Tansen to sing Raag Deepak for him. Deepak was, and still is, one of the most difficult raags to sing. The courtiers hoped that either the raag would not be sung appropriately, thus shaming Tansen, or so much heat would be created by a perfect rendering of this raag that it would cause not only lamps to light but the singer's body to burn to ashes.

"When Akbar asked Tansen to sing Raag Deepak, Tansen pleaded, 'Sire, Deepak can set the singer himself on fire.' But the emperor would not listen. 'If you are the greatest singer in the land, you must accept this challenge,' insisted Emperor

Akbar. 'Then give me a few days to prepare, sire,' replied Tansen, bowing low.

"Tansen knew singing Deepak was dangerous, but he also knew that if the Raag Megh, which brings the rain, could be sung at the same time, he would be saved from the fury of the fire.

"On the day of the performance, the court was packed with courtiers and royal guests. Unlit lamps were placed on the walls. Tansen was waiting with his taanpura in hand, and as soon as the emperor entered, the great musician began the aalaap, the first portion of the raag, before moving on to the song."

Guruji paused, hearing the sound of a car in the driveway. He didn't move, knowing his brother would come directly to Kalu's room. Taking a soft breath, he continued with his tale. "As Tansen sang, the air got warmer and warmer.

> "*Jeevan ka path ujjval karo, jalaavo jalaavo, raag Deepak se jeevanjyot jalaavo.*
> *Light up my life, flames ignite, from Raag Deepak's notes, flames ignite.'*

"The audience started perspiring. Leaves and flowers in the garden dried and fell to the ground. Water in the fountains began to boil. Birds flew away to escape. The lamps suddenly ignited, and flames appeared in the air. People fled from the court in terror. The emperor stood, listening with awe, as the rose he held in his hand wilted and then died.

"Tansen's body was hot and feverish, but he was now so absorbed in singing, he didn't notice. And this. This is where it gets interesting. You see, until this point, all the stories are the same, but here, as Tansen burns, we have divergence. There are a few ways—four, in fact—the story could have played out."

Kalu opened his eyes for a moment. He thought he was seeing double, then realized the shadow behind Guruji was really Vaid Dada. Guruji moved aside, continuing the story as Vaid Dada checked on his patient.

"The first ending hinges on the extra days of preparation Tansen had asked for. In this tale, Tansen asked Haridas, his old teacher, to send him a student. Rupa was already a very good musician, and Tansen used the fifteen days to prepare her. At the end of the two weeks, Rupa had perfected the singing of Raag Megh, the monsoon raag.

"As Tansen sang Deepak, Rupa's voice, at first a little tentative, grew stronger and soared.

> "*Garaj garaj kar barso, Megh raaj ko megh raag se bulaavo.*
> *Thunderous rain pour down, invoke Raag Megh to call the king of rain.*'

"The sky became dark with clouds, and down came the rain. As the rain covered the ground, people showered praise on Tansen's genius. Though the emperor was very pleased, he was shocked he had almost lost his greatest musician to the fire of the singer's own music. Tansen's fame now spread like the flames of Deepak."

"But," cut in Vaid Dada. He smiled at Kalu, then nodded at his brother, reassuring him of Kalu's recovery before taking up the story. "But what if Rupa didn't exist? She could have been a pretty piece of fiction, made up, perhaps, by courtiers or by Husani, Tansen's wife.

"The second ending revolves around Tansen's childhood friend and sweetheart, Taani. A pretty girl from his hometown, Taani felt the heat of the fire and the burning of Tansen's body all the way from Gwalior. Perhaps she

smelled a hint of acrid smoke and caught a searing brightness from the corner of her eye that heralded her lover's
pain. She sang the same song, but Taani didn't just sing for
rain; she begged the gods to save her sweetheart, calling the
monsoon to heal her beloved."

Guruji sang again, this time with more power and passion.
Even the morning birds were still as he completed the couplet.

> "*Garaj garaj kar barso, Megh raaj ko megh raag se
> bulaavo.*
> *Thunderous rain pour down, invoke Raag Megh to
> call the king of rain.*'"

"Yes," said Kalu. "But there are still two more endings."

Guruji smiled and took up the tale while Vaid Dada made
a paste from the powders in his bag. "In the third version,
Tansen left Agra with a high fever. You see, the fire, although
calmed when he stopped singing, was not quenched.

"Tansen left the court and traveled back toward Gwalior.
It was hot. Finally, unable to walk, drawn by the smell of
water, he collapsed by the side of a well. Fortunately, Banno, a
low-caste woman, saw Tansen half comatose next to the well.
A musician herself, she recognized the symptoms of Raag
Deepak. Banno didn't know the person beside her was the
famous Tansen. All she knew was that he was burning with
fever. She sang Megh to ease the pain. She would have done
this for anyone in pain, for that was her nature."

This time Vaid Dada sang. His voice was higher than his
brother's, and not as well trained, but still melodious.

> "*Garaj garaj kar barso, Megh raaj ko megh raag se
> bulaavo.*

Thunderous rain, pour down, invoke Raag Megh to
call the king of rain.'"

"But that isn't the end," said Kalu, his eyes on Vaid Dada, who took his turn as narrator.

"No, beta, as you know, that isn't the end of the story, either. Here in Gujarat, there is another version. Not so popular these days. Tansen, unable to bear the heat within him and the heat of Delhi, traveled down toward Gujarat, to the town of Vadnagar. A Brahmin musician offered Tansen shelter. The Brahmin's daughters, Tana and Riti, sang for Tansen. They sang Megh so beautifully, the heat within Tansen died as if quenched by the rain itself."

Two voices sang, Guruji strong and Vaid Dada sweet.

"'Garaj garaj kar barso, Megh raaj ko megh raag se
bulaavo.
Thunderous rain, pour down, invoke Raag Megh to
call the king of rain.'"

The refrain comforted Kalu as much as the honey-coated medicine Vaid Dada placed on his tongue before continuing to speak.

"Overjoyed, Tansen returned to the court. Akbar was so impressed by the tale of the two girls, their voices and their beauty, he sent a special envoy to bring them to court. However, unlike Tansen, they declined the offer. Akbar was so angry, he ordered his army to attack Vadnagar. The girls saw the approaching force and chose to set fire to themselves rather than be captured.

"Every year in Gwalior, near Tansen's tomb, a music festival is held. Musicians come from all over India to perform and pay homage to Tansen and his virtuosity in playing Raag Deepak until there were flames."

"But what about the girls?" asked Kalu.

"Well, every year in Gujarat," answered Vaid Dada, "a music festival is held to remember Tana and Riti.

"And even today, Punjabi pop musicians go to the temple built by the well where Banno sang to Tansen to make a wish before releasing a new song. And there, next to Tansen's tomb, is a small tamarind tree," said Vaid Dada, now speaking so softly that the words seemed to come from within Kalu's mind. "If a singer eats a leaf from this tree, their voice will become strong and sweet.

"But there is no sign, to my knowledge, of Taani, the childhood sweetheart, or Husani, the wife. There is no story of the anguish of the father or what his daughters may have felt as they burned because of the beauty of their voices."

Kalu closed his eyes and turned onto his side, the song still playing in his mind. His breath moved into a soft, gentle flow, and his chest stilled to sleep.

Ashwin came and sat down beside Kalu in the small temple in the garden. The sky over the mountains was stained pink, but the flame on the diva glowed as brightly as the midday sun.

Kalu had finally been allowed to leave his room and he felt as weak as a baby bird first leaving its nest. Ashwin clasped his hands together and bowed his head. Kalu prayed sitting very straight.

When blue edged out the rose and orange in the sky like a rising tide, they stood. Ashwin's legs cracked as Kalu helped him up, holding him for the first time since he'd returned from Hastinapore. The two walked back to the kitchen, arms linking waists. Neither had the heart to put out the flame.

. . .

Kalu climbed up the mountain, stopping only when his legs began to shake and his breath shortened. The day was cool, but the heat generated by the climb encased him. It was the first time he had felt warm in a long while. Below him was Guruji's house, and even farther away was the village. He sat under a small ledge in the cliff face, took his flute box from his back, and, almost unconsciously, removed the rosewood flute from the case.

The ground was damp. The clouds above heavy. He sat in the silence. The air around him thickened, and he wasn't sure if it was only the strength of his desire or the spirit of his friend joining him.

He started to play. The tune was light, the gentle yearning of a flower waiting to be pollinated by a bee. The cry of a fledgling left alone for the very first time. The sound grew around him. As he played, Kalu finally acknowledged and accepted that his pain was not just because of the loss of his friend but because in that moment, between life and death, Kalu's music had changed, had soared and taken Kalu with it. In that knife edge between ecstasy and despair, he had felt blessed.

The world was still as he played. Then, as the first drops of rain fell, the music changed to the scream of the rabbit just caught by a hawk, the desperate call of a mother who has lost her son in the crowd and fears she will never see him again, loss and longing knotted fast together.

Kalu didn't know if he would ever have surrendered completely to his music if Bal's life wasn't at risk. But it was a price, if he'd had a choice, he would never have paid.

He faltered when he heard the sound of Bal's voice in the music. Bal's words when he had first returned to Hastinapore echoed around him. "You can never go back, Kalu. Only forward." He knew Bal would always be by his side. Whether he played or not. Whether Kalu wanted him there or not.

Kalu played until his mind was as tired as his body. Until he accepted the gift he'd been given. Then, as the clouds thinned and the raindrops gentled to a light fall, he stopped. His body shuddered as he placed the flute back in its case and began the slow, wet descent home.

Tulsi watched him from a cave above. She sighed and whispered his name before taking the wider path back to the village.

Kalu lay in his room and heard the sarod being tuned. He could see the crescent moon in the sky, thin enough that the surrounding dark made the stars look brighter. Shivbhagwaan's moon, the thin crescent that was tangled in Lord Shiva's hair. The sound of the sarod filled the air, and Kalu waited.

Only, this time Guruji's music was different, just as strong and rich as ever, but quieter. The sound of the wind flying through the mountains, causing the smallest flowers in alpine meadows to sway. The sound of a woman's laughter, of friendship, hope. Kalu had never heard Guruji play like this before. He left his bed and walked to the music room to quietly sit on the floor beside his teacher.

The man was so immersed in the sound he didn't notice Kalu's presence. He played. And as he played, tears ran down his face, and a smile, revealed only by the light of the stars and the thin moon, illuminated his face.

The last notes finished. Kalu took the instrument from his master. "I never said thank you to *you*. For coming to get me, for giving me what you have. For being there when I needed you the most."

"You gave me more than I could have hoped," said Guruji, grasping Kalu's hand and placing it against his cheek.

Kalu, feeling the warmth of Guruji's cheek and the wetness of his tears, having lived through the music he just heard, understood.

17

"SHE'S GROWN JUST as much as her voice has, hasn't she?" Martin asked Kalu.

"Who?"

"Tulsi, of course, idiot! She only just left, so you can't have forgotten her already. I wasn't expecting that voice. And she's grown since I was last here. I almost didn't recognize her."

Kalu, still full of music, took a hot chapatti and added it to his plate. As they grew up, Kalu had almost forgotten Tulsi didn't speak with words. They communicated so easily, it had never been an issue. Then, when she started to hum, then sing, and later speak, it seemed as natural as her growth from a child to a tall, slim girl who came to visit for the company just as much as she came to learn.

"Martin, Tulsi has always spoken. She still speaks more with her eyes than her voice. All you have to do is look."

"Ha." Martin took some cauliflower before passing the vegetables across to Kalu. "Talks with her eyes, does she? I'm sure you're the only one who sees it." He raised an eyebrow at Kalu, who was still deep in thought.

Tulsi, more than anyone else, had offered Kalu comfort when Bal died. She recognized both the anger and the sorrow in him and knew what it felt like to lose someone close. He found himself looking forward to the time he spent with her. When she sang, Kalu heard her pain and her longing as well as her joy in living. She chose her words well and used them only when needed. This quietness provided solace. It reminded him of the silent companionship he had shared sometimes with Bal.

Kalu knew Vaid Dada was still upset that Kalu had refused to help find Bal's father to inform him of Bal's death. But Kalu was too old now to be forced into doing something he didn't want to, and this time he stood firm. Regardless of the reason, Bal's father had sold him into slavery. Tulsi understood, and when Tulsi supported Kalu, Vaid Dada stopped arguing.

~

It started when he saw her in the market. Haggling over the price of eggplant, as if nothing had changed. A gust of wind tugged at her paalav so the sari shifted, briefly showing part of her thickened waist. A small movement that paralyzed him. The wind flirted with her clothes like she had flirted with God knows how many men. His knees bent under the weight of his anger, and he used the stall beside him for support.

She was his wife. How dare she do this to him? Make him a laughingstock. He was the one who brought in the money. She was just a village girl, uneducated, uninformed. His wife. And his alone, whether he had wanted her or not.

At first he thought to confront her in front of all the people in the market. Expose her for the whore, the raand, she was. But the wind seemed to have taken his voice with it. His throat dried and shriveled and no sound came out of his open mouth.

He watched her walk through the market and then back to the haveli, taking in every movement of her head. The quiet laugh as she saw people she knew. They were probably laughing at him. She had no right to do this to him. None at all.

He'd heard the whispers, of the flute man and others, but had discounted them as the jealous ramblings of his friends. But then she changed. In the past few months, she'd pushed him away. She'd started to look him in the eye, something that she'd never done before.

He had never wanted her, and she was lucky that she had him at all. He was the one who had to put up with an uneducated village girl. And he was the only one who should have touched her. He owned her, no one else; that was what marriage was.

He followed the sway of her hips, moving to a rhythm of their own, until she disappeared through the crowd. His anger grew. Then he turned and walked back into the town, resolving to stay away that night. He'd make her sorry.

~

Something was wrong. Kalu knew when he smelled the air that morning. It was in the quality of the light and the way his face looked in the mirror. It was as if he was alone, watching the world rather than taking part in life. The feeling continued throughout the day, building until he felt separated from things around him. Apart from everyone else.

"Thinking about a girl, are you?" asked Ashwin, placing more food in front of him. Kalu stared into the faded white wall, ignoring both food and Ashwin's questions.

Later in the day, Kalu also failed to focus during his session with Guruji. "Something is wrong," he said, looking up for the first time that day.

"Yes, I'm well aware of that, son, but maybe if you paid more attention, we could rectify the problem."

"No, something is really wrong."

Guruji looked closely at Kalu. His eyes seemed almost blue. Cloudy, as though he'd taken bhaang. "Do you know what it is?"

"No."

"Then I suggest you find out. You won't be much use until you do. But don't wander too far. Not in that state." Guruji wasn't sure Kalu even heard the end of his sentence as he got up and walked out, flute still in his hand, through the long windows, onto the veranda.

Kalu sat quietly under the gulmohar tree, his back resting lightly on the trunk. Normally, he would have rubbed his back against the bark, releasing the tension from his shoulders. Now he sat straight, gently stroking his flute, trying to make sense of the discomfort that started near the scars on his ankle and finished somewhere behind his eyes.

He looked out over the garden to the small diva he kept lit for Bal. The flame flickered, and the sun stained the clouds red as it started to descend. The rich color reminded him of Malti's wedding sari. He hadn't seen Malti since Bal died. Kalu knew he would return to Hastinapore one day, but not for a long while. It hurt too much. Ganga Ba continued to write to him and they'd spoken by phone just the other day. Malti was there but refused to talk, saying she needed to hurry home.

Kalu tucked his ankle beneath him and started to play. Raag Shree. Stately and quiet, the meditative raag reminded him of Malti.

The notes guided him to the first time he met her. She brought him milk after his first errand for Ganga Ba. She'd held his shoulder, feeling his bones, before forcing him to sit down and drink slowly. It was the first of many times she'd held him that way, her fingers looking for reassurance that Kalu was healthy. Even now, after all these years, she continued the practice. For a long time, Malti and Bal were the only people he allowed to touch him.

The notes lifted.

Malti the girl had been fun—never crazy like Ashwin but always quick to smile. Malti the woman was quieter. Almost too serious. Even her letters carried an absence in them, a lack of spirit. He knew the sound of her voice—the way she spoke when she was happy and when she was sad. Her tone in the letters was too measured. Too correct. There was no real joy or excitement.

When he was younger, Kalu thought it was to do with being married. It was after her wedding when things seemed to change. As he grew older, he realized her behavior didn't match that of other married women he knew. It was as if she had closed in through the years rather than grown out.

He thought things would improve over time. But his music seemed to know better. Things were worse. When he saw her, Malti spoke about her in-laws, her parents, Ganga Ba, and even her friends. The one thing missing was mention of her husband. Kalu wasn't sure what to do. How to help Malti. Or even if she really wanted help.

Heat, building from his toes, rose as he played, suffocating him until even the notes became short and sharp, ready to combust.

He willed himself to take deeper breaths so the notes softened, cooling the air. Slowly, the music took over until nothing was left but the interplay between flame and water. Light through the darkness. He sent her courage and strength. Power. The power of Shree, of the mother. Hands that would hold tight even in the monsoon he conjured. He played on until the fire within him died down and his skin stopped burning.

Kalu slumped back against the tree, feeling its strength through his sweat-soaked shirt. The sun had finally set. Dhruv-taara, the star Malti told him about all those years ago, sat in the sky. He hoped that whatever he had done had helped Malti or would help her when she needed it. And he prayed she would never need the strength he had called down for her.

~

"Whore. Raand. Whose child is it, mine or some other fool's? Was it the flute player? Or one of the others?" He pulled her up to stand before him, his words hitting hard at her face, before flinging her across the kitchen toward the back door. There she stayed, cowering, the woman he had been forced to marry. The woman who'd been barren, despite his efforts, until this year. "Raand. Just who do you think you are? You are nothing. Do you hear me? Nothing!"

She leaned against the doorway for a moment, drawing on its support before turning to him. Her hand covered her belly in an unconscious gesture that fed his anger. He lifted a tin of fuel from the shelf.

"Please. Stop. You don't understand. The child. It's yours."

"Mine?" He took a step toward her, laughing as she moved back, hitting the door frame. "As if you could produce anything of mine. When they first found you, I knew what it would be like. I wanted nothing to do with you. Ask my mother. How they whined and nagged. 'Pick a girl from the village,' they said—'easier to mold . . .' until I finally agreed. Now my friends tell me you've been with that flute boy—as if he would know what to do with you."

"Don't speak like this. It's not true. And don't tell Vimu Ba." Malti's voice was low but she spoke fiercely. A tremble indicated her passion. "She doesn't deserve to hear such lies; it would only hurt her. And besides"—she drew herself up, facing him for the first time—"she loves me, even if you don't. If it wasn't for her, I would never have stayed with you, put up with you for all this time."

"Ha! After the gossip I've heard, she won't think much of you anymore. And don't you mention her name again. Or that of anyone in this house. You don't deserve to be here. How dare you make a laughingstock out of me. How dare you! You wanted freedom—" He pulled the lid off the kerosene tin and threw the liquid at her. "Here. Here it is. Have it. Have it all."

Malti gasped as the fuel hit her clothes, soaking the cotton sari. In a vain effort to save her child, she bent over to stop the liquid from touching her belly. As she did so she saw him pulling a small box from his pocket.

She closed her eyes and prayed for help. Then, in the distance, she heard the sound of the flute. In that moment, as she fought to breathe above the pungent fumes, Malti changed from the young girl he had been forced to marry to someone completely different.

"Enough!"

Before now, if anyone had asked him if he believed in the goddess, he would have laughed. But here, in front of him, was the incarnation of the Goddess Kali. Her eyes flashed. Silhouetted in the dull light that fell through the doorway, her red sari, darkened to the color of blood, clung to her figure. A halo or haze encased her form so that all he was aware of was the strength and power behind her voice.

"Enough," she said again. "Light that match, little man, and I will curse you. Curse you so that the ground you walk on will be poison. So sores on your body will fester and reflect the type of creature you really are. No one will hurt this child."

She turned and strode out the door, head high, only to break into a run when the house was out of sight. That change in rhythm turned her from the Goddess Kaali back to Malti again.

He flicked the match out through the door in her wake and watched the flame arc into the air as he sank to the ground. The tip glowed for an instant before withering to ash.

REPETITION OF THE FULL
COMPOSITION ONCE

The ending can change depending on the school you belong to. Some repeat the mukhada or sthaayi one last time. Others finish with tihai—three equal repetitions of a rhythmic beat. I believe the last part is more than this. It's the release of breath that the audience makes as the last note dies away.

—GURUJI

18

KAVITA WOULD LATER tell Malti how people stopped and turned to follow the petrol-stained, sari-clad woman with wild hair and bare feet striding through the streets. At the time, Malti noticed only the sound of the flute, playing over and over in her mind, until the moment she opened the gate to Ganga Ba's house. She stumbled over the steps, suddenly empty, and slid down to rest by the side of the door.

Later, she recalled the feel of hands on her arms, exclamations at the state of her dress, then the sharp voice of Ganga Ba pushing through, providing space and air. Ganga Ba dispersed the onlookers with a few choice words while Bhraamanji carried Malti into the house rather than around to the back, where the servants stayed.

Ganga Ba took her to her own bathroom. Malti sat on the cold, hard tiles while someone filled a bucket with steaming water. Her teeth chattered while a girl rubbed soap into the fuel-slicked skin, washing her gently with hot water. She felt cold. And dirty. Nothing anyone could do would change that feeling.

After Malti's bath, Ganga Ba gave her some warm, soft clothes, took her to bed, and told her to sleep.

"But it's my fault. It's all my . . ."

"Shhh." Ganga Ba's voice was quieter than Malti had ever heard it. She placed her hand on Malti's head. "It doesn't matter now. Sleep."

"But the baby . . ."

Ganga Ba's hand stilled. Then, "The baby is fine. Hey Bhagwaan, I'll call Vaid Dada just in case. You need to sleep now, more than anything. You can trust the vaid. He will know what to do. Just as I do."

"Beti, come home. Please." Vimu Ba's voice shook as she spoke.

Malti sat on the divan, dressed in Ganga Ba's daughter's clothes. Forgotten garments too worn to keep but too good to throw away. She knew her in-laws had come yesterday evening as well, but Ganga Ba had turned them away. "It's not that they weren't worried," she'd told Malti in the morning. "I just didn't want to wake you. You'd been through enough for one day."

She didn't know what she would have said had she seen them yesterday. And the night hadn't made any difference to her state of mind. All that remained inside her was an echoing emptiness and an overwhelming tiredness, as though the struggle had suddenly become too hard.

Vaid Dada had arrived earlier and together with Ganga Ba, stayed with her when her in-laws returned.

Malti saw the stress lines on the faces of both Vimu Ba and Papaji when they entered the room. Lines that hadn't been there two days ago. Vimu Ba sat on the edge of the chair, all angles and stiffness. "We'll fix it, beti. We'll fix everything if you just come home. You don't know what people are saying. Please."

Malti focused on Vimu Ba's hands, wringing the paalav of her sari, and Papaji's feet, crossing and recrossing. "I have no home. Not anymore."

Vimu Ba gasped. "But how can you say that? I love you. We love you. You are like a daughter to me. Haven't I looked after you? Did I make your life a misery like some mother-in-laws do?"

"No . . ." began Malti, before Ganga Ba interrupted.

"What would you tell your daughter if a man, her husband, tried to set fire to her . . . for whatever reason? Would you tell her to return?" Her voice rose in disapproval.

"I'd tell her to return," Vimu Ba said. "We'll fix it. You'll see, I promise."

"I'm sorry." Malti could barely be heard over Vimu Ba's sobbing. She forced herself not to look away. "I'm sorry," she repeated, as if the words would make a difference.

"Tell me," said Papaji as they stood. "Is there anything we can do? Anything to change your mind?"

"No, Papaji. I . . ." She faltered and started again. "I won't stop you seeing the child if you wish it. I'll stay as close as I can. But I never want him near me again."

Vimu Ba's body shuddered. "My grandchild?"

Papaji looked down at Malti. "And is it? Our grandchild?"

Malti looked him in the face for the first time, realizing that perhaps this question and her possible infidelity were more important to him than what their son had done to her, not just in the past few days, but throughout her marriage.

She'd always assumed that her in-laws didn't realize what he was like. Now she understood that in a house that small, they must have known. She rose and walked away without responding.

When Malti arrived back at her parents' village, her family spilled out of the house, joyful and a little confused to see Malti and the vaid. Especially when Vaid Dada ushered them back inside, leaving Malti in the car.

Even through closed windows she heard her mother's wail. Her brother appeared at the car door, opened it, and pulled her out. He rushed her to the back of the house and across the fields, where no one could hear them.

Raja saw the darkness under his sister's eyes and the softness of her belly. He held her tight. She didn't relax against him until he rubbed his hand across her hair as he used to when they were children.

"You could have told me. You should have told me." His voice was rough with anger and emotion.

Malti's eyes filled slowly, like water held to the breaking point, before tears spilled down her face. "I didn't think you would understand. That anyone would understand. It's all my fault."

Raja held her face. "You are my sister. No matter what happens. No matter what you do. I am your brother."

"Ma?"

"Ma is upset. Leave her to Anju."

"Our father? Will he forgive me? The disgrace."

"Ben, you know he loves you. Leave him to me."

"Better I had died; then they wouldn't face any shame."

Raja shook her. "How dare you say that. Don't you think we have the right to stand up for you? You and your child. Why didn't you tell me?"

"Tell you what? That my husband hated me and hurt me, or that for a small time I turned to someone else?"

Raja stepped back as her words struck him. A hard, fast fist to the gut. "I'm your brother."

"Yes. And I'm a whore. I don't deserve to be here."

"Malti, if you say that again, I'll take a tin of petrol to you myself."

Malti stood, shocked that her brother would say something like that, before the laughter bubbled up and would not stop. The thought of her brother ever treating a woman that way was inconceivable. She leaned against Raja, just as she'd done many times as a child, and looked out across the fields, some in green crop, others bare. They had remained as she remembered. Only she had changed.

"Will you stay here?"

"Will Ma . . ." Her voice broke. "Will Ma want me?"

"We will always want you." His voice was strong. He sighed. "We almost lost you."

"You know, I thought I'd hate the child. With everything that happened, it was the last thing I wanted. But somehow, when he pushed me, my baby was the only thing I wanted to save. The only thing that mattered."

Raja's hand tightened over her arm. "Then don't talk about what happened. Ever. Unless you want it to touch your child. Do you understand?"

"I don't want to lie."

"No lies. Just silence, at least until you feel your child is ready to hear the real story. Not for your sake, Malti, but for your child."

Malti nodded. "I'll stay for a while. And also return before she's born. I want to stay in Hastinapore until everything is settled. Ganga Ba can deal with this better than we can. She's offered me the outhouse to live in. Once I work out what to do, I'll leave and start again somewhere else. But for now, Hastinapore is all I know."

"But that's not what I meant. Your place is here, with your family. Not in some rich woman's outhouse." Raja dislodged the flies that had settled comfortably on the back of his shirt.

"It's not fair to our parents, Raja. You know what people will say. I don't want to make it harder for them. Besides, I want to stand on my own two feet, even if it's just for a little while. For a few months, I don't want to be someone's daughter or sister or wife. I just want to be me. I want to work out what I can do with my life for me and my child."

Kalu arrived at Malti's parents' house that afternoon, after traveling nonstop. He organized for Vaid Dada to stay with him in the closest hostel rather than in the crowded house. The vaid had already spoken to the local police and wanted to stay close for a few nights in case there was trouble. He had seen too many cases where young hotheads tried to finish the job one man couldn't. Women burned for showing spirit or for talking back. Some men wanted to teach all women a lesson.

Malti sat looking out across the fields. She heard voices inside but didn't move. Neighbors visited throughout the day, a continual stream of voices, each taking a piece of the story with them. Malti refused to speak to anyone but her family.

Her mother had made her favorite food. Her father had put his hand on her shoulder, saying, "I should have realized they weren't good people, Malti. This isn't what I wanted for you." He left the room before she could respond. She didn't know how to respond. Neither parent could look Malti in the face.

Kalu found her leaning against a pillar, looking as frail as a crushed stalk of wheat. "Malti . . ." He looked broken, as if everything she had been through was marked on his face. He took her hand and gripped it. "Malti."

He smelled of sandalwood. The tightness in her chest

released as he held her to him for a moment, then moved away. "I'm sorry, Malti."

"That's my line, big eyes."

As Kalu sat beside her, Malti suddenly recalled that the fragrance of sandalwood and the sound of the flute had echoed in her mind from the time her husband had doused her in fuel until she reached Ganga Ba's house. She looked down at Kalu's hands and saw that his fingertips were tender and raw, as if he'd been playing through night and day.

"You knew?" she said.

"No, I just knew that something was wrong. And that I should have asked you when I first realized. When I last saw you, the day . . ."

She finished the sentence in her mind . . . the day Bal died.

"Malti, will you come with me?" The words tumbled over one another. "I'll look after you and the child. You won't need to worry anymore."

He saw her stiffen. "Kalu, you have your whole life ahead of you, you don't want to be burdened with me."

Kalu turned, seeing not the woman beside him but the girl she had been. "Don't you realize, we are tied together, you and me. You made me feel special when no one else did. Now I can help you. Let me help you."

Malti plucked at the hem of her sari. Life would be easy with Kalu's support. She knew he could look after her and give her child a better life than she could. The house in the mountains sounded big enough—even bigger than Ganga Ba's house. Yet while her child would have many advantages with Kalu's protection, she knew she would never be at ease in such a fancy place. Even staying in Ganga Ba's house made her feel uncomfortable.

"I'm sorry, Kalu. I have to do this alone. I need to know I can do this alone." She reached over and grabbed his hand as he moved away from her. "Please, I can't lose you, too. I need you. But I can't live your life. I need to find a place of my own. Just as you have done."

"Fine," said Kalu, turning away. "That's fine."

She heard the sound of his motorbike fade as he rode away.

~

Kalu returned to Malti's place late that night to collect Vaid Dada. He waited outside and looked straight ahead when Malti came to the door. She whispered her thanks to the vaid before disappearing inside.

Kalu and the vaid sat in their hostel room. "Why?" he asked Vaid Dada, starting the conversation in the middle. "Why wouldn't she come?"

Vaid Dada looked up at Kalu. The boy's eyes were bruised. The vaid knew Kalu hadn't eaten in the last few days.

"Why won't any of my friends take my help? If Bal had stayed with us . . . and now Malti refuses me." He kicked a small stone inside the room, sending it bouncing across the worn and cracked concrete floor.

The vaid got up and stood in front of Kalu. "You need to let go of your anger, Kalu. This isn't about you. Everyone should be allowed to make choices, just as you made yours. You can help her more by being her friend than by chastising her because she won't do what you say. Malti has decided, perhaps for the first time, to do what she thinks is right for herself rather than listening to what others tell her. Allow her that privilege."

Dada was right. But it didn't make him feel any better. The man sat next to him and hugged Kalu as he had when Kalu was little. "Malti told me to tell you she needed you. She asked if you would be willing to take her back to Hastinapore. I will come with you, of course. There's been enough talk about that girl as it is."

Kalu looked out into the dark night. "I think I can do that. And then, Dada . . . I think it's time I left, too."

"To go where, child?"

"It's not about going somewhere but leaving something behind. I need to leave you and Guruji, to find my place in the world. Just like the others have. I need to, as well."

The vaid was silent, as if realizing that this time there was nothing he could say that would change a thing.

~

Guruji came to meet Kalu down in the village at the bottom of the hill, and the two walked back to the house together. Guruji wanted to speak to Kalu before Ashwin heard that the boy was leaving.

As they walked, Guruji realized that Kalu was actually taller than him. He realized that he, too, was getting old and thought with a pang of the things he had missed by hiding in his home. However, if he hadn't done so, he would never have met Kalu. And Kalu was the greatest gift of all. They took the long way, around the back of the village. The small dirt track was just wide enough for the two of them to walk side by side.

"It's not that I don't value what you have given me—" started Kalu.

"It's all right," interrupted Guruji. "It's all right, son. You don't have to apologize. It's a good thing to find your own way in the world. Just don't forget us."

Kalu looked across at the man who had become so much more than his teacher. "I couldn't forget you."

Guruji flashed Kalu a look. "And don't think that you

can leave without promising to keep in touch—with Martin, too. I expect to know what you are doing and where you are going, young man."

"I'll do that, and maybe now that you don't mind leaving home . . ." Kalu looked at Guruji.

"Yes, yes, I may come and see you, but no performance, mind."

"But—"

"No, Kalu, I've been there already. I have no need to perform. As long as I can play, I'm happy. And I like the life we have here. But I'll come and see you perform, son. When you are ready."

"I'd like that." Kalu paused. "But I don't want to come back for a while. I need to be on my own."

They'd almost reached the gates, and Kalu remembered that first day and his fear and anticipation when he had approached those gates.

"It's all right," repeated Guruji. "I don't like it or want it. But"—and his voice took on the tone of adult to adult—"I understand it."

19

MALTI FELT THE baby move as she finished sewing a long strip of fabric to the bottom of a sari. The soft, green cotton matched the color of the silken sari and would protect its delicate border from the grease and dirt of the ground. The more she sewed, the more she was paid. While she wasn't paid much, no one told her what to do, and the money she earned was all hers and the baby's.

The baby kicked upward into her ribs, hard, creating its own separate space. She smiled. This child of hers would be strong, and it—no, *she,* Malti corrected—would be hers. Hers alone. This should have worried Malti, but it didn't.

She willed the child to kick again, to draw strength from her flesh, and reveled in the child's very aliveness, its energy giving her a cramp in the back.

Her in-laws had tried to fight the divorce, but it didn't work. It helped that only his parents were interested in the unborn child. The matter didn't even go to court. Ganga Ba had too many connections. Her friends had taken up Malti's cause with passion and vigor.

"Malti is more than capable of looking after this child by herself. I've taught her all she needs to know." Ganga Ba waved her hands, sounding younger than she had in a long time.

The vaid saw Malti whenever he was in town. She kept in touch with Kalu by phone or letter and spoke to her brother each week, when he gave her family news. And whenever she heard on the radio one of the songs Anand used to sing, she wondered fleetingly what would have happened if he had known about the child. Telling Anand to leave, however, had been the right thing. Although he had been upset, he had never returned. That decision felt like it had been made a long time ago, by a different woman from the one she was now.

She wondered who the woman was that would wear this sari. What her dreams were. As she sewed she wished that woman good fortune.

As the baby became heavier, Malti became quieter and calmer. She studied the papers Ganga Ba had given her for the school in Adalaj, for women like her who wanted to be teachers. The school helped the women find jobs afterward, as well. With the money she had saved, she would just be able to afford to study there.

Adalaj was closer to her family, too. When she told them about it, her mother had offered to look after the babe while she studied. Then she could stay at home and travel to school each day. Malti rested her head against the glass of the phone booth as her mother spoke. Now was not the time to cry. She would never be able to repay them.

That night, as her baby kicked again, she smiled. Swapana, she would call her. The child of her dreams, her heart, and her body. Malti knew she would be fearless when it came to looking after this child of hers. She had to be. And this time, for the first time in her life, Malti knew that her decisions were her own. And whether they were right or wrong, she would never regret the fact that she could now choose for herself.

. . .

He still watched her, the man who used to be her husband. He often followed her between the tailor's shop, where she collected garments, and Ganga Ba's.

It was the same on the way back. He'd start at the banyan tree and walk to her house. Always a hundred paces away. Always intent. Focused on Malti alone.

Even though she stayed on the far side of the town, he seemed to find her. She held her head high and made sure the roads she crossed were crowded. She never took the shortcut by the river. It was too dangerous. The baby made her body awkward and unbalanced. She would be in the town for only a little while longer. She didn't want to stay where he could find her so easily. Soon, very soon, she would start afresh.

~

Kalu sat on the grounds of an old Buddhist temple in Tokyo, filling his lungs with the scent of cherry blossoms and incense. A small flower landed on the yellow scarf that Guruji had given him. The pink blossoms, thin and fragile, would never have survived in the heat of his home.

Earlier that day, Kalu had walked across Jingu Bridge, trying not to stare at the youngsters with their made-up porcelain faces, wearing clothes from an old Gothic novel. They looked like dolls but had an energy and an effervescence that was exciting.

He'd turned a corner and found this small, very beautiful temple. He wondered what Guruji had made of Japan when he first played there. The country would have been different then, still reeling from the aftershocks of war.

The Japanese people were small and the cities crowded,

just like in India. But the place was so clean and neat. He could almost hear Guruji's voice: "In a country as great as India, you would think we could manage to get the sewerage system to work."

Kalu smiled at the thought; and his smile grew wider as he thought about how the boy he had been could now be in a place like this. During his stay, he listened to songs about the sweet cherry blossoms and fell in love with the haiku his friends taught him. Even here there were people who wanted to hear him play. He tried to imagine what his life would have been like if he had not met Vaid Dada under the banyan tree so many years ago. It was as hard as trying to imagine what he would see tomorrow or in the next few months. He'd been traveling for five months already. He still remembered the day he'd left. Guruji had told him to remember that first test—to find Raag Desh. Kalu realized that through the years he'd stopped thinking of that raag, the raag of his country. Like many other things, he'd buried that moment of failure, hard and fast.

He'd had a letter today, from Malti. Her baby was to be born soon. And he wanted to visit her, at least for a little while.

The smoke drifted out from the very tip of the incense and across the formal garden. The smell reminded him of his room back in India, where the same incense coated each surface. Ashwin had told him that his room would be kept in preparation for his return, no matter how long he was gone. He remembered how large and empty the room had seemed when he first arrived at Guruji's. Now he could touch the top of the door with arms bent.

He listened to the sound of the long Japanese flute coming from the temple as one cherry petal, and then another, swept across the sky, and Kalu thanked God for his good fortune.

. . .

Vimu Ba always turned to the right, avoiding the corner of the bazaar where the tailor's shop was. At first she had been angry, shocked at the girl's temerity at staying in Hastinapore. Belly large, the girl decided to earn a living. In the past, she would have been stoned out of town. Instead, for a while, she seemed a living goddess. It would have been better for everyone if she had stayed with her parents. Then she would have been out of sight and perhaps people would have forgotten the whole incident.

Her son talked of moving. To somewhere no one knew them. So he looked for work in other places, far away. Away from the few friends that she had left. Away from the streets she knew. Away from her home.

As the months passed, Vimu Ba stopped talking to her boy. There was nothing to say. Her mouth filled with the taste of bitter gourd. Her belly tightened as Malti's grew. She knew the events of that day would fester forever.

Even though she blamed Malti for coming into her life and giving her pleasure, then taking it away, leaving the family in disgrace, her anger at her son increased over time.

When she asked the jeweler to melt her wedding bangles so they could be turned into jewelry for the baby, who she knew would have her eyes, no one noticed—neither her husband, who loved her, nor her son, who loved only himself.

~

"So, are you going back to Guruji's house, Kalu?" asked Malti, cradling her daughter in her arms.

Kalu shook his head. "Not yet. I want to go back to London first. I have a concert there. Besides, I hear that Guruji isn't at home at the moment—he's gone to visit some very old friends in Bombay." Kalu smiled at the thought.

Malti placed her baby beside Kalu on the bed. He lifted his hand a little, just to watch the tiny fingers tighten around it. He couldn't describe the feelings he had when he first saw this child. A child who was calmed by the sound of his flute and laughed when she saw him. He had never seen anything this small or vulnerable before.

Malti was already making a life for herself and the little one. She had been right in refusing his help. Malti was now more of a woman than she had ever been. Her child had given her the confidence that had been missing.

Kalu recalled the girl who'd told him about Dhruv-taara and realized they now had a little star of their own. Swapana would have the best he could give her. Not just because she was Malti's, or because Malti called him, along with Raja, the child's mama—that is, the maternal uncle—but simply because the baby loved and needed him.

He held Swapana's tiny hand and thought of the people in his life, those who loved him and those who must have been there when he was born. This child would be treasured.

Malti saw the seriousness in Kalu's eyes as he started to sing. A quiet little song she'd never heard before. A song full of promise and joy.

20

He walked across the bridge, looking down at the boats and the swirling brown water. The Thames was cleaner now than it had been in a hundred years. Apparently the fish had returned. He had no idea why he knew this. All he knew was that he didn't care. Not for the river or the fish or himself. The boy who'd grown up in Mumbai and the adolescent who'd made an effort to forget the world he'd come from had both disappeared the day she said she didn't want him anymore. Because of the color of his skin.

This was his London. He spoke, ate, and drank just like the other lads. When he went home, to North London, that world changed. He had mamas and kakas instead of uncles. His mother harassed him to find a nice girl. He loved his family but knew his interest in white girls would cause a problem one day.

He overtook an Indian man carrying the type of flute he hadn't seen since he left India, then paused to look out across the water. He'd always thought his parents would be the difficult ones. The ones who wouldn't understand. It never occurred to him that it would be the other way around.

The man with the flute stopped a few meters away from him and started to play. He didn't look like a busker, a street performer. The melody was haunting. It carried a mix of the East and the West. It reminded him of the music playing the night he first saw her, sitting across the pub talking to a girl he knew at university. Norah Jones's sultry voice had floated across the room. Another mixed kid in a mixed-up world. He wondered how Norah had dealt with it.

He'd become a London cliché. White boy, black girl, Hindu girl, Muslim boy, Anglican versus Swami Naaraayan . . . Romeo and f'ing Juliet. Now, on this bridge, the only thing that made sense to him was the water below, the same gray as her eyes the last time they made love. He remembered her tears when she said good-bye, still amazed she could say it. The one thing he could never have said to her. He leaned over the rail and wondered what it would be like to let go.

The sound of the flute grew louder, surrounding him. Now it mocked him in his sadness, forcing him to think about the impact of his choices. Moved him to anger, buffeting him with sounds from his childhood he had chosen to forget. Laughed at his self-absorption, and then, calming him, helped him to see, through the long, slow notes, that grief was a part of living.

He pushed away from the rail, away from the water, and made his way back to the city he called home.

The man with the flute stopped playing, took a deep breath, and continued the other way, his yellow scarf waving in the wind.

~

Kalu decided to return to the South Bank one last time. He knew the place well, having played there the night before. It had been the biggest, perhaps most formal, concert he'd held on his own. But without Guruji in the audience, it had felt like a hollow victory. Today, he wanted to be nearer to the river rather than in the concert hall itself. The wind blew against Kalu. He shivered and pulled his coat around him.

While so different from the Narmada, the gray Thames still took him back to India. Lit by a pale sun, the old stone buildings on the opposite bank of the river reminded him of their far-distant cousins in Bombay. These buildings by the Thames were graceful, looking out over the gardens and the river. The ones in Bombay never looked so solid, their brick-work crumbling with the heat and rain. Here plants grew in every crevice and the buildings' color was faded by the sun and the dirt. They had become almost Indian. Just as the Indian boy he had seen on the bridge yesterday on his way to rehearsal had seemed almost English. He wondered what had hurt the boy so badly. Whatever the cause, Kalu knew that the music had helped.

Kalu tightened the yellow scarf around his neck, watching as a man in a tattered coat and pants with holes collected discarded cups of coffee from tables scattered in the courtyard outside the concert hall and carried them back to a table near large glass doors. He continued his collecting until his bench was covered in a mosaic of half-full cups. Then he sat and systematically started to drink. First the cups holding latte and cappuccino, then the straight black coffee.

Kalu found a spot nearby. He took out a flute. Last night he played inside for the wealthy, the knowledgeable, and the critics. Afterward, Martin had called to congratulate him, as had Ashwin and Guruji. He could hear the love and pride in Guruji's sharp voice, though more in what he left unsaid than in what was said. It was Ashwin who'd asked him when he would finally return. He'd been very close, that last trip back to India, but had chosen not to go home. Today, however, he wondered what was holding him back.

His thumb rubbed the dark rosewood, and the spicy scent

of the rich, wet earth he had smelled nowhere else but in India rose from the flute. This flute was meant to be played outside.

As he played, the sound spoke of the sun and summer, the spirit of the river, and the madness of the kite festival, where the wind flung a million kites at one another, the warmth of Tulsi's smile, her understanding, and the small hand of Malti's little girl. He felt the cold diminish and he realized this was Raag Desh—as it was meant to be played. The music of his country, rooted in his soul.

This was what really mattered. The gift Kalu had received from Guruji. He recalled the silences between Guruji's words on the phone and realized that Guruji missed him as much as he missed the man.

Now he played Guruji, sharp-eyed and sharp-tongued, who he knew was waiting for him to return. Who loved him. Guruji had become his father in all ways but one. He played his longing and belonging, and in that moment Kalu found both, realizing that the what he'd received wasn't only the flute but the way it had helped him to find the people he needed most.

The cup man stepped away from the table; he lifted his hands like the wings of a bird about to fly for the very first time. He started to dance. First a slow, shuffling gait, then faster, then still faster, round and round, a dance that took him back to a place of warmth, a place with mangoes, rum and Coke, and hot coffee. Really hot coffee.

It was midweek in London and no one asked Kalu to show them a busker's license. No one stopped him, but they listened and they left coins in front of him. Kalu watched the cup man, who was full of joy, surrounded by sound yet so alone. Kalu knew that wasn't the life for him.

As the sound died away, Kalu turned and hugged the cup

man tight. He didn't notice the dirt or the smell, just the light in the man's eyes. Kalu knew he had given and received a gift that day. He took the yellow scarf from his neck and, with a half bow, presented it to the man along with the money he had received while playing.

Kalu wouldn't need it. He was going home. He walked back toward the bridge, playing again, leaving the laughter of the cup man behind him.

Glossary

A

aalaap: musical term, first part of the raag structure, without beats or count

Aarti: ritual offering at the end of a religious ceremony

aasana: yoga posture

agarbati: incense

antara: musical term, second part of the raag structure, the melody

antkadi: a song-based game

aré: idiomatic expressive term: "oh!"

B

baba: young boy, pronounced "baa baa"

babu: term of address to a man of education

bafoodhya: term used by Ashwin to mean "fools"

bandh: literally "close"; in this case a strike

barfi: Indian sweet

beedi: hand-rolled cigarette

ben: sister

beta: child

beti: child; girl

bhaang: marijuana

Bhagwaan: Lord; god

bhai: brother

bhajiyaa: fritters

bhel-puri: snack made with puffed rice, vegetables, and tamarind sauce

Brahmanji: caste name, in this case the name of Ganga Ba's cook, who is a Brahmin by caste

C

chai: tea

chai-waala: person who makes or sells tea

champal: sandals, known in Hindi as chapal

chapatti: flatbread

chikoo: Gujurati word for sapota fruit

D

daacter: idiom for "doctor"

deshi: from India

dhaana: coriander

dhobhi-waala: person who launders clothes

dhokra: savory dish

dhol: drums

dhoti: men's clothing, a loose cloth wound around the waist to cover the legs

Dhruv-taara: polestar

diva: flame, known as diya in Hindi and other dialects, pronounced "divaa"

Doordarshan: state-run television network

G

gaanda-giri: playing the fool
Ganga: the River Ganges, pronounced "Gangaa"
garba: folk dancing, mainly at Navratri
goonda: criminal, thug
gora: white person
gulmohar tree: royal poinciana
gunnybag: shopping bag made of jute

H

hai: exclamation, pronounced "high"
Hastinapore: fictitious town
havan: symbolic offerings through fire, cleansing of negative attributes
haveli: communal residence
hera-feri: playing around
hey Bhagwaan: Oh Lord!
hey Ram: Oh Lord Rama (incarnation of Lord Vishnu)

J

jor: musical term, first part of the raag structure; no drum, but in rhythm
jugalbandhi: musical term, third part of the raag structure; term for a performance involving two musicians

K

Kaali: goddess, the destroyer of evil
Kalu: also pronounced "Kaalu"; another name for Krishna, meaning "the dark one"

khichdi: rice dish mixed with turmeric and lentils, often made
from broken rice
Krishna: god, the incarnation of Vishnu the preserver
kurta: shirt

L

laddu: Indian sweet

M

maasi: maternal aunt
mandir: temple
masterji: teacher
matric: idiom for "matriculation"
meend: musical term meaning "glide"
mogra: jasmine

N

Naaraayan Bhagwaan: Lord Vishnu
Naaradji: son of Lord Brahma the creator
Narmada: river in Gujarat
Navratri: festival for the goddess held over nine nights
NRI: nonresident Indian

P

paagal: crazy
paalav: the decorative part of the sari
paan-biddi: betel nut and cigarette
paan-waala: betel-nut vendor
paise: currency worth one hundredth of a rupee

panchayat: assembly of elders
papaji: father
peda: Indian sweet
peepal: sacred fig tree, also known as pipal tree
pundit: scholar

R

raag: a musical form or a composition in this form; the word
  "raag" means "mood"
raat-ni-raani: flower with a strong night scent

S

saadadi: floor mat
saala: brother-in-law, also form of jest, endearment
saambelu: drums
salvar kameez: style of clothing consisting of a long top, pants,
  and a scarf
sapota: known as "chikoo" in Gujarati—sweet, brown fruit
saptak: musical term meaning "seven notes"
sarod: a stringed musical instrument known for a deep, weighty,
  introspective sound
shabaash: congratulations
Sharad Purnima: festival of the full moon in autumn, directly
  after Navratri
shishya: student
shiv-ling: object of worship for followers of Lord Shiva the destroyer, and creator of sound and music
sthaayi: the refrain of the raag

T

taanpura: four-stringed drone instrument used for accompaniment

taraana: musical term meaning singing without words

thaali: rimmed metal plate

thepla: kind of chapatti containing rice and mustard leaves

V

vaav: a step well, a well in which the water is reached by a descending set of steps. These wells are often of architectural significance.

Vadodara: city, formerly known as Baroda, in the State of Gujurat

vaid: traditional healer

velen: rolling pin

Vishnu: god, preserver

Y

yaar: friend or mate

Acknowledgments

I acknowledge the Aboriginal people of Australia, and elders past and present, as the traditional owners of the land on which I live and work.

A special thanks to my gurus, and all those people who have helped to make this novel, my first, a reality. This book wasn't written in isolation, but with the support of so many.

Devleena Ghosh and Cathy Cole, along with many others at the University of Technology, Sydney, provided words of wisdom for the first draft of this work, as part of my PhD thesis. Varuna, known as the Writers' House, and Peter Bishop provided me with the space to write. My inspirational and feisty writing friends—Rachael, Helen, Karen W., Karen F., Robyn, Dianne, Kerry, Barbara, Deborah, and of course Roanna—provided fierce discussion, clarity, and the courage to keep going. It was James who told me the real story of the woman who put her hand in the fire. Pat Skinner and Prue McKay would have cheered me to the finish line with this book; I wish they were still here to see its fruition.

My family; from Shaan and Jimmy, the youngest, to Mani Ba, the eldest, and each and every person in between—this one is for you. Especially my father, who plays the flute and who edited all my Gujarati and found songs just when I needed them; my mother, who told me stories, many of which are in this book; and my sister Janaki, who listened to those first few paragraphs. Sunanda Foi, who read and checked the work and shared it with my cousins, and Shailini Kaki, who took me to the school near Adalaj. My grandmother, who provided a voice over the phone and Tulsi's name.

Selwa Anthony, I won the lottery when you agreed to represent me. Thanks to you, Linda, and Brian, for your encouragement through so much more than this novel and for introducing me to the Sassy family, in particular Mo and Traci, who told me to get writing all those years ago; Ian, who encouraged me with his interest year after year; and Selena, who edited the work. To the team at Atria Books—Greer Hendricks, Sarah Cantin, and the whole team, thank you for caring as much about this book as I do and for making the process so much simpler than it could have been!

Finally, to Jacob, for showing me the path and understanding my work better than I could, and to John, for lighting the way, walking by me, and reading every word. This book is as much both of yours as it is mine.

This book would never have been written had I not experienced the beauty of the raag. My sincere thanks to the musicians that dedicate their life to this form of music.

You can find links to some of my favorite musicians, and additional information, on my website: www.manishajolie amin.com. A list of some of my reference texts follows.

Notes About the Music

Pandit Hariprasad Chaurasia (www.hariprasadchaurasia.com) inspired me; his nephew Rakesh Chaurasia plays the music Kalu aspired to. Pandit Ravi Shankar's (www.ravishankar.org) work—in particular his description of raags and of studying music—was invaluable.

For people interested in finding out more about the music mentioned in this novel, you may find these references useful—I know I did!

Bagchee, Sandeep. *NĀD: Understanding Rāga Music*. Mumbai: Eeshwar, 1998.

Batish Institute. "Time of Play." 1997. http://batish.com/archives/rago1/raga/playtime.html.

Bor, Joep, ed. *The Raga Guide: A Survey of 74 Hindustani Ragas*. Wyastone Leys, Monmouth; Charlottesville, Va.: Nimbus Records with Rotterdam Conservatory of Music, 1999.

Bose, Sunil. *Indian Classical Music*. 3rd ed. New Delhi: Vikas Publishing House, 1995.

Courtney, David. "Fundamentals of Rag," Chandra and David's Homepage. Last modified February 4, 2012. Accessed 2004. www.chandrakantha.com/articles/indian_music/raga.html.

Deodhar, B. R. *Pillars of Hindustani Music*. 2nd ed. Translated by Ram Deshmukh. Mumbai: Popular Prakashan, 2001.

Devi, Ragini. "Hindu Conception of Music." Accessed 2012. http://www.mysticalportal.net/1-6music.html.

Holroyde, Peggy. "The Grammar of the Raag," in *Indian Music: A Vast Ocean of Promise*. London: George Allen & Unwin, 1972.

ITC Sangeet Research Academy. "Alankars: A Background." www.itcsra.org/alankar/alankar.html.

Shankar, Ravi. *Raga Mala*. New York: Welcome Rain Publishers, 1999.

———. "On Appreciation of Indian Classical Music," Ravi Shankar Foundation. Accessed 2006. www.ravishankar.org/indian_music.html.

A number of songs have been either mentioned or quoted in this novel. Every effort has been made to contact the copyright holders of nonoriginal material reproduced in this text. In cases where these efforts were unsuccessful, the copyright holders are asked to contact the publisher directly.

"Atma Shatakam" is credited to Adi Sankara.

"Bombay Meri Hai" refers to a song first recorded in 1969 by Uma Pocha and Chorus, with Mina Kava and his Music Makers. Music was by Mina Kava and lyrics by Naju Kava.

"Maari naad tamaaré haath" was written by the poet Keshav Bhatt.

"Mera Joota Hai Japaani" refers to a song from the movie *Shree 420* by Mukesh in 1955. Music by Ravi Shankar and lyrics by Hasrat Jaipuri.

"Naagar nandaji na laal" and "Paani gyaata re beni ame talaavdi" are both traditional Gujarati folk songs.

"Nana mara hath" is a children's nursery song, sung to me by my parents.

"Om Tryambakam yajaamahe," known as the Mahamrityunjaya Mantra, is from the Rigveda.

All translations and mistakes in translation are my own.

Dancing to the Flute

MANISHA JOLIE AMIN

A Readers Club Guide

INTRODUCTION

Kalu, a homeless orphan, survives on odd jobs. In the quiet rural Indian village, Kalu has made a home for himself, and also made friends: Bal, a bonded laborer who herds buffalo, and Malti, a servant, who lives at her mistress Ganga Ba's home. Kalu's life is forever altered when a vaid, a traveling healer, passes through the small town and overhears the boy producing pure, simple notes from a rolled banyan leaf. Impressed by Kalu's talent and passion for music, the vaid proposes an apprenticeship with his brother, Guruji, a famous musician.

Kalu and his young friends grow up apart from one another, yet still connected by bonds of deep affection. When Malti's arranged marriage reaches a crisis point, and Bal's struggle to find freedom and independence leads to tragic consequences, Kalu questions his beliefs regarding life and music. He travels the world playing his flute in search of peace and understanding, and only when he finds the right harmony in his raag will he return home to those he loves.

TOPICS & QUESTIONS FOR DISCUSSION

1. One of Hinduism's popular deities, Krishna, is often pictured as a cheeky young boy playing the flute, much like Kalu. Krishna's role in Hinduism is to restore dharma, or natural balance, to the earth. In what ways does Kalu work to bring balance to his life and those around him?

2. Physical touch plays an important role in Kalu's life. He says, "It was as if he had discovered a secret language communicated by touch rather than words. One Kalu

had never learned." (p. 92) Why is Kalu hesitant to share physical contact? What is his initial reaction to those who try to share a physical bond?

3. Consider the role individual independence plays for each of the characters. How does the desire for independence affect Kalu? Is it the same for Malti or Bal? Discuss your answer.

4. Guruji instructs Kalu to wait before learning to play the flute, and to focus instead on reading and singing. How does this approach shape Kalu?

5. Doubting the accuracy of a book about plants, Kalu digs up a tree in order to measure its roots and proclaims, "At least I know it was true." (p. 105) How do other characters in *Dancing to the Flute* seek truth? What kind of truth is Kalu searching for?

6. The music learned by Kalu in India differs from the classical Western canon as evidenced by the improvised songs, imitation of animal sounds, and emphasis on a free-flowing exploration of mood. When does Kalu use raag to show mood? How does it affect his listeners?

7. Guruji says that "each raag has a particular time and place." (p. 127) Kalu struggles to learn which raags are appropriate for specific circumstances. At what points in *Dancing to the Flute* does he match a feeling to a place, finding the right balance for his raag?

8. In what ways does the narrative mirror the flow of a traditional flute raag? How does the mood change in each

section? How did the emotional highs and lows of the writing affect you as you were reading?

9. Ganga Ba, reluctant to criticize caste, once said, "It didn't pay to mix things around too much. Always more trouble came that way than it was worth." (p. 178) How does Ganga Ba's attitude about social caste change over the course of the novel? What causes her opinion to change for both Kalu and Malti?

10. What are the indications of caste in *Dancing to the Flute*, and how do class distinctions differ from those in the country where you live? How are Malti, Bal, and Kalu constricted by class distinctions?

11. Discuss the process behind Malti's arranged marriage. Both parents want specific criteria in a mate. How do Malti's or Ganga Ba's criteria differ from those of the parents? What are the pros and cons of such a process?

12. While both Kalu and the vaid are comfortable constantly traveling, many of the other characters find it hard to venture from home. Why is Malti resistant to leaving Hastinapore? Why does Ganga Ba stay, even though her daughter leads a comfortable life in the United States? Why does Guruji remain sequestered in his mountain home?

13. Bal muses: "You can never go back, Kalu. Only forward. If people like us focus on the past, we can never move forward." (p. 163) How is this true for Kalu, Bal, and Malti?

ENHANCE YOUR BOOK CLUB

1. At the beginning of the novel, Kalu buys a box of the traditional Indian treat barfi. Try serving this simple delicious cashew fudge at your book club meeting. For a barfi recipe, visit www.epicurious.com/recipes/food/views/Cashew-Nut-Fudge-230905.

2. Pannalal Ghosh is considered the founding father of modern bansuri flute music. To set the tone for your book club discussion, consider playing his music. To learn more about the famous flautist and to listen to "Pannalal Ghosh Radio," visit www.last.fm/music/Pannalal+Ghosh or visit manishajolieamin.com for links to music by a range of musicians.

3. The banyan tree, the national tree of India, needs warm and mild temperatures year-round. While not native to the United States, banyans are commonly grown as houseplants. Provide banyan tree seeds to your guests to help grow a beautiful and unique tree.